Through the Fading Glow

The Stranger

by Vladi V. Lanin

A gust of wind and cold raindrops on his face made him stir. Emptiness and silence enveloped everything around him as if the world had been put on pause.

He opened his eyes slowly, feeling like he had been pulled from a thick, impenetrable darkness. Right before him, he saw the damp planks of a pier, the gray ripples of the water, and the muted glow of distant streetlights. Not a soul in sight. Exhaling deeply, he realized he was lying on a wooden bench, as though this forgotten waterfront had decided it was the only place left for him. How he had ended up here, in this state, he didn't know.

Struggling to his feet, he briefly closed his eyes, trying to gather his thoughts, but was met with a sharp pain in his head. It felt as if someone had left a foreign bullet lodged in his skull. Running his fingers over his temple, he found a fresh abrasion, still bleeding slightly. The blood had dried in places but had managed to stain his shirt in several spots.

Patting his pocket, he felt a heavy, irregularly shaped object. He slipped his hand inside, and a faint chill brushed the tips of his fingers. He found a pistol, a small wad of crumpled cash, and some loose change in his pocket.

He forced his uncooperative body into a sitting position on the wet bench and stared into the gray waters. The waves lazily rolled over each other, lapping against the shore, and for a brief moment, he thought he heard footsteps breaking through the monotonous sound. He turned.

A girl in a white dress, barefoot, moved gracefully along the pier. She walked unhurriedly, immersed in her thoughts, her dress billowing in the wind, with wet strands of hair brushing against her shoulders. As she passed by, she gave him the faintest of smiles, just the corner of her lips curling upward.

"Who are you?" he barely whispered, but the girl simply walked past without breaking her stride and disappeared into the early morning haze.

Time hung motionless. Seconds or minutes—it all suddenly felt irrelevant. A sharp gust of wind and the biting chill snapped him out of his frozen state. Staying here any longer made no sense. His head throbbed, and his memories were fragmented, like a book with its pages torn out.

He stood up, struggling to steady himself, and started by figuring out where he was and what had happened the previous night. He set off along the coastline, and after walking a few blocks, he came across a couple of bars that looked like perfect spots for a wild night out. But they were all closed.

Not losing hope, he looked around and noticed a bar across the street, where a weary-looking man was locking its old wooden doors. Likely a worker at the establishment, the man seemed eager to leave. The stranger awkwardly approached him and asked:

"Excuse me, did you happen to see me here last night? I… I might have had too much to drink and can't remember. And… where exactly are we?"

The man looked at him with a mix of confusion and wariness.

"No, I didn't see you," he replied curtly. "We closed well before midnight, and I don't recall seeing you here at all." The man gave him a once-over as if trying to determine just how dangerous this stranger might be.

Disheartened, the man in the black coat thanked him and, shivering from the biting wind, decided to find somewhere to rest and pull himself together. His gaze caught on a passing taxi—a battered, old-fashioned vehicle that looked like it belonged in a museum.

Raising his hand, the man hailed the taxi, and as it stopped, he quickly approached it.

"Know of a cheap hotel nearby?" he asked as he slid onto the squeaky leather seat behind the driver.

"Sure, there's one a few blocks away—' Northern Pier.' Nothing fancy, but it gets its share of guests," the driver nodded and pulled away from the curb more abruptly than expected. "From out of town, are you?" the driver remarked, glancing briefly at his rumpled appearance.

The driver, an older man in a worn jacket with tired eyes, looked at him curiously. The faint but unmistakable smell of alcohol clung to the stranger, and his disheveled state hinted at a rough night.

"Rough night, huh?"

The stranger smirked, gazing at the deserted streets, the shuttered shops, and the veil of gray rain outside the window.

"You could say that. Your town seems pretty quiet, though—dead silent, really," he quipped, attempting humor, but the driver merely grumbled something inaudible, refusing to engage in conversation.

They drove silently for several blocks, and the stranger reached into his pocket, pulling out a pack of cigarettes.

"Mind if I smoke?" he asked the driver.

"Nah, go ahead," the taxi driver replied indifferently with a shrug.

The stranger clamped a cigarette between his teeth and felt around the door panel, trying to find a button to roll down the window. Instead of a button, he found an old crank handle, which he turned with a grimace. A harsh creak broke the silence inside the car, and he smirked as he finally opened the window slightly.

Searching his pockets again for a lighter, he sighed—it wasn't there. Turning to the driver, he asked,

"Got a lighter by any chance? Or is there a cigarette lighter in the car?

"No lighter, and this car doesn't have a cigarette lighter either," the driver replied without taking his eyes off the road. The stranger frowned. *"In a car like this, a cigarette lighter should be mandatory,"* he thought.

Disappointed, he stuck the cigarette out the window into the rain and flicked it away with a snap of his fingers. Closing the window, he heard the grating sound of the crank again and shivered as icy raindrops that had slipped into the cabin chilled him.

The stranger's gaze lingered on its peeling facade and the cracked sign above the entrance when the taxi slowed down near an old hotel. He quickly scanned the area, contemplating his next move, before glancing back at the driver, who watched him with a weary, slightly mocking smile.

The stranger pulled a few bills from his pocket, leaving them on the seat, and smirked.

"Here's for the 'warm welcome,'" he said, attempting to wink, though the motion was so subtle and tired it was barely noticeable.

The driver nodded briefly, accepting the payment and tip.

"Good luck," he muttered as he watched the man in the black coat open the door and step out into the rain.

The stranger raised his collar against the wind and rain and walked toward the hotel without looking back, feeling the heavy gaze of the driver on his back.

He hopped up the short set of steps at the entrance, hesitating momentarily when he realized the door opened outward. He almost immediately bumped inside the small reception desk, where a tall, lanky young man stood.

"Hi, I need a room—for at least a week," he said.

"Sure, no problem. You can pay for seven days now, and if you need more time, you can extend later," the receptionist explained.

Without hesitation, the stranger handed over a few bills and took the key from the receptionist. As he turned to leave, the receptionist called after him, explaining where the room was located.

He quickly climbed the stairs to the second floor and shut the door to his room behind him. It was small, furnished with plain wooden furniture, and featured an old carpet whose original pattern had long since faded.

The shower was hot and relaxing but did little to help. His head still pounded like hundreds of tiny hammers were at work inside. He grabbed a small bottle of whiskey from the minibar and poured himself a glass but couldn't muster the strength to take a sip. Holding the glass, he sank into the armchair and barely had time to sit back before sleep overtook him, dragging him once more into darkness.

He woke up to the sound of the TV. Apparently, he'd turned it on before sitting in the chair, though he had no memory of doing so. An old program was playing on the screen, the volume low but loud enough to pull him from deep sleep.

The scene with the girl in the flawless white dress amidst the gray dreariness wouldn't leave his mind. That fleeting glance and her faint smile lingered like a persistent echo. He tried convincing himself it was just his imagination playing tricks on him, frayed nerves after a night of drinking and a strange awakening. But the memory refused to let go.

It itched like a freshly scratched wound, a discomfort he couldn't ignore. That fleeting glance from the stranger felt unnervingly alive—familiar, even—despite her being a complete unknown to him. The memory of her presence blended almost eerily with reality, gnawing at his sanity and compelling him to find an explanation. It was as if the haunting call of that brief encounter demanded action, urging him to uncover who this enigmatic woman was and why she now felt like more than just a chance passerby.

At first, the stranger thought he'd simply learn her name to satisfy his curiosity. He figured it would only take a few questions at the bar or with the hotel staff, and the whole matter would disappear. But when he opened the newspaper and saw the headline: *"Missing: Catherine McKenzie,"* his heart seemed to stop. It was her. Not in a white dress with loose strands of hair, but in a formal office outfit, her expression serious and focused. Now, his mysterious stranger had a name.

Shaking off the obsession seemed impossible now. The stranger felt a peculiar excitement—something both mysterious and unsettling. Deciding he had nothing better to do, he took a sip of whiskey, pulled on his coat, and headed for the door. An odd feeling drew him forward, refusing to let him remain a passive observer. He decided to do what he did best: get to the bottom of things, even though he himself had no clear idea where to start.

Wandering the streets, the man in the black coat first stopped by a small pub on the outskirts of town, where a few locals—fishermen, by the look of them—

were gathered. He introduced himself as a journalist from a neighboring city, sent by his editor, and tried to spark a conversation about Catherine. The handful of patrons regarded him with caution, even suspicion, answering tersely and guardedly. Others, however, seemed more open and shared what they knew. Words like "smart" and "unique" came up almost universally from anyone who had crossed paths with her, even briefly.

However, he noticed something peculiar. Almost every time her name was mentioned, his conversation partners cast sideways glances at him. One man smirked and said, "So, you're not here because of the reward, huh? They say her parents put up a nice sum for any information. Easy money, right?"

The stranger deflected with a light, almost meaningless joke, but inside, he understood that the rumor of a reward had made its rounds. This realization put him at ease—it made his arrival seem ordinary, and his interest in the missing journalist appeared perfectly natural.

As he gathered bits and pieces of information, the stranger delved deeper into the story of Catherine's disappearance. He continued visiting bars and small cafés, drinking a glass or two along the way and sinking further into the mystery. Some townsfolk mentioned that Catherine had been conducting an investigation here for quite some time and had even requested access to official documents, which had annoyed local officials. She never stopped at closed doors, and her relentless persistence seemed to have led her through one of them.

Intelligent and determined, with a sharp eye and an even sharper tongue, she often pursued stories that made many uncomfortable. Whether it was corruption schemes, shady deals, or peculiar events on the fringes of town, Catherine was always ready to dig into them. Her dedication reached extremes — spending nights hiding in bushes near her "subject's" house, only to return to the newsroom the next day as if nothing had happened, typing out her articles with unwavering focus.

At one café, the stranger accidentally ran into one of Catherine's colleagues. He decided against presenting himself as a journalist, fearing quick exposure. Instead, he introduced himself as a "truth-seeker," claiming he was playing detective — who could blame him for that? The journalist initially suspected him of being after the reward but ultimately shared some information.

A week before Catherine's disappearance, she had shown particular interest in a laboratory located at the edge of town. As it later became clear, her agitation this time was more significant than usual. The laboratory was the subject of many rumors: no one knew exactly what happened there, but everyone knew that the building was heavily guarded and that outsiders were strictly forbidden entry. Allegedly, experiments were conducted on animals and strange substances, which Catherine had already mentioned in her notes but never published.

The journalist recalled that shortly before her disappearance, Catherine confided in him, expressing concern. Someone from the laboratory asked about her—what she was writing, where she lived, and with whom. Later, they even persistently invited her to visit the lab and meet the local doctors, though the invitations carried an unsettling ambiguity.

In the days leading up to her disappearance, Catherine had begun acting more cautiously. She rarely appeared at the office, preferring to work remotely and avoiding unnecessary conversations. Neighbors noticed her returning home late at night after long walks around the city or leaving on her old bicycle, which was her constant companion. It seemed as though something was weighing heavily on her, refusing to give her peace, yet she stubbornly pressed on, refusing to back down.

On Friday evening, acquaintances noted that Catherine was seen at a bar on the town square. She stayed only a few minutes, glancing at a small list of guests. Then, after finishing her coffee in a hurry, she disappeared around the corner, riding her bicycle toward the waterfront. That was the last time anyone saw her.

The next morning, Catherine's bicycle was found near the pier, abandoned by the roadside as if it had simply been left there. Neither her bag nor the notebook she never parted with were anywhere to be found. The police launched a search involving volunteers and scouring every corner of the area, but the results were fruitless. Only on the fourth day did they officially announce that Catherine McKenzie was missing.

This wasn't as rare as one might expect for a small town of just a few thousand residents. Adults—and even children—disappeared here more often than anyone liked to admit. While the townsfolk speculated about what might have happened to Catherine, the police proposed several theories: from an accident to a deliberate disappearance.

After hours of wandering the town and chatting with locals, the stranger felt like he had stumbled upon a purpose that seemed to come from nowhere. For a drunken drifter, nameless and rootless, nothing stopped him from being the one to uncover the truth about the missing girl.

In the chaos of questions about Catherine and his scattered conversations with the rare townsfolk, the stranger suddenly realized he had completely forgotten his own peculiar circumstances. He didn't remember how he had ended up in this town, and the past few days surfaced in his mind only as vague fragments, like snippets of someone else's dreams. Pale, shaky pieces: a motorcycle, the night, the blinding flash of headlights, and then... nothingness. The thought lingered in his mind, a cold pause, as he, lost in speculation, turned into a narrow alley and instinctively reached for his pack of cigarettes.

Shielding his hands from the drizzling rain with his coat, he pulled out a cigarette. But just as he was about to grab his lighter, a seagull launched itself out of the darkness, swooping down from atop a trash can. With a deft motion of its beak, it snatched the cigarette pack and, flapping noisily, disappeared behind the nearest rooftop.

The stranger clenched his fists involuntarily, glaring after the bird, and growled irritably,

"Well, I'll be healthier than you, you miserable creature." Then, smirking, he added, "Good luck finding a lighter now."

He already understood that neither cigarettes nor answers from fate would come his way that day.

The next morning, despite the headache and the dull aftertaste of the previous day's conversations, the man in the black coat forced himself out of bed, dressed, and headed to the nearest café. He mulled over his aimless wandering through the night's streets, the words of the locals—likely spoken more out of boredom than a genuine desire to help—and the girl's name, which now endlessly looped in his mind. Sitting at a table in the far corner, he discreetly surveyed the room.

There were few patrons—almost none, to be exact. In the corner, two men loudly argued, discussing who had been the last to see the missing girl.

"That's just speculation," he muttered to himself, but then he leaned forward, intrigued.

Waiting for the men to calm down a little, the stranger decided not to let the opportunity slip. Approaching their table, he tilted his head slightly and, with practiced friendliness, asked,

"Good morning. Sorry to interrupt, but I just heard about the missing girl yesterday. I'm a journalist from another town, and I couldn't resist learning more. Perhaps you could tell me something important?"

One of the men squinted suspiciously, giving the stranger a slow once-over. The other, however, merely shrugged and replied, almost dismissively,

"What's there to know? She kept nosing around, especially near the old laboratory," he said, emphasizing the last word. "She was curious—maybe too curious. And now she's gone somewhere. Good riddance, if you ask me."

The stranger nodded, though an unpleasant feeling began creeping into his chest. *"The girl was clearly interested in something others probably thought better left alone. Maybe the locals really do know something—they just don't want to talk. But I won't get a second chance to get anyone to open up,"* he thought and cautiously clarified:

"The laboratory? Sorry, I'm new here. Is it some kind of research facility? Could it really have been a problem for her?"

At his words, the men fell silent and exchanged glances. The stranger, noticing their reaction, sighed, realizing the conversation wouldn't go any further.

He returned to his table and sank into thought. The information about the laboratory could easily be another dead end, but his intuition told him it was the only lead he had.

As the stranger sat there, lost in his thoughts, a voice from the neighboring table interrupted him.

"Are you looking for Catherine too?" said a young man, staring at him with interest.

The man looked to be in his early thirties, with light stubble and dark, slightly messy hair, as if he hadn't put much effort into his appearance. He wore an old brown blazer, worn but clean, and his eyes suggested he understood life in small towns too well.

The stranger studied him carefully, debating whether to continue the conversation. The man nodded toward him, inviting him to sit at his table.

"Well," the stranger sighed as he moved to join him, "you're right. I am looking for her, trying to understand why so many people talk about her—and why she's gone at all."

"Then you're looking in the wrong place," the man said with a faint smirk. "No one here will tell you the truth. They don't know much about her—nothing like what I know."

Intrigued, the stranger leaned in, allowing himself a slight smile, signaling he was ready to listen to a long story.

"My name's Daniel," the man said, extending his hand. The stranger nodded, introducing himself as a journalist from another town.

"So," Daniel began, lowering his voice as if afraid someone might overhear, "Catherine and I met a couple of years ago. We worked together... if you can even call it work. There was always so much to do, too much, really. We grabbed at anything that even slightly resembled a story. From strange objects appearing out of nowhere to disappearances that, even back then, were frighteningly common. And the worst part? No one cared."

Daniel paused as though weighing whether he should continue. The stranger waited silently, not interrupting.

"There were a few stories we managed to crack. Not related to the missing people, but still interesting—fascinating, even."

Daniel hesitated again as if lost in thought.

"The thing is, there were several cases of children disappearing. Boys and girls from different parts of town. No one understood who was behind it or why. But Catherine... she wasn't afraid to dig deeper, to ask the uncomfortable questions, you know? She figured out that all these cases were connected. While the police dismissed it as just a string of unfortunate incidents, one day she came to me, sat down—just like this, across from me—and asked: 'Do you really believe this is all just coincidence?'"

Daniel smirked crookedly, sinking into his memories. He lowered his gaze as if recalling the hardships of those days. The stranger waited, his eyes fixed on the storyteller.

"So," Daniel continued, "I completely believed in her from that point on. I know what she's capable of. And here I am again, back in this little town, because I'm certain that if she disappeared, it wasn't by accident. She probably knew she might be in danger. Sometimes, I think she even expected it."

"Do you mean she got herself caught up in something?" the stranger asked cautiously.

Daniel nodded, his eyes glinting with tension.

"Yes. And I'm here because I know how far she might've gone."

The stranger and Daniel spent several hours at the café. Their conversation ebbed and flowed, but it felt as though they had barely scratched the surface of the mystery surrounding Catherine's disappearance. Eventually, they agreed to meet that evening. Daniel promised to bring some documents that Catherine had kept at the newsroom and had planned to share with him just before she vanished.

The stranger nodded, accepting the business card Daniel handed him, which had a phone number written on it. He studied the card thoughtfully, his fingers trembling slightly from the tension that had built over the past few hours.

At that moment, the loud rumble of a motorcycle passing by on the street outside distracted him. The roar of the powerful engine stirred faint memories—flashes of images long buried in the depths of his mind. Suddenly, he vividly recalled riding down a winding, rain-slicked road on a motorcycle, the night cold and damp. Pain, flashes of wetness from the rain, an old, half-ruined bar glimpsed on a back road and a strange name that left only a hazy impression—all of it felt real again for a few seconds before dissolving into fragments, leaving him with even more questions.

Deciding it might be best to refresh his memory by visiting that bar, he rose from the table, trying to hold on to the blurry image of the old establishment.

He had hours before meeting Daniel that evening—plenty of time for a trip out of town.

He quickly paid his bill and stepped outside.

The stranger felt an acute urge to light a cigarette, hoping it might calm his restless thoughts, but the memory of the seagull snatching his pack earlier made him grit his teeth. Muttering under his breath, he resolved to buy a new pack. Just as he was about to head off to find a shop, his attention was drawn to an old taxi parked across the street. Inside sat the same disheveled driver who had given him a ride earlier.

The car seemed to be waiting for him, and there was something subtly unsettling about this coincidental encounter.

He paused momentarily, then resolutely headed toward the taxi, crossing the street. In doing so, he nearly collided with a passing cyclist.

The cyclist glanced back indignantly, muttering something under his breath, and the stranger offered a brief apology before continuing toward the car.

When he reached the vehicle, he tapped on the window. The driver raised his eyebrows, looking mildly surprised, but without hesitation, he rolled down the window and quipped,

"What, need another ride?"

"This time, I need to go out of town. I'm looking for a bar on a back road. Do you know of one? Old, half-ruined, with a name… something about ghosts, I think."

The driver scratched his stubble, deep in thought.

"Ah, I think I know what you mean. Yeah, I've heard of it. The road there's rough, but I can get you there. Just keep in mind, not many people go out that way."

The taxi pulled out of town, and the narrow road led them farther and farther away, winding between old groves and scattered fields that seemed to slumber under the gray sky. The trees stood dense and unyielding, like soldiers at attention. Their thick, rough trunks had low branches draped with moss. Occasionally, the taxi passed through overgrown thickets where the trees arched so closely over the road that they formed green tunnels, nearly devoid of daylight. The air there was heavy and damp, and the wind occasionally stirred, rustling the dry branches and creating the uneasy sense that something was lurking in the woods, waiting.

The weather changed so quickly that it was almost disorienting. Just moments ago, clear skies were visible through the windshield, but as they rounded a bend, gray clouds rolled out from behind the forest, bringing a light, stinging drizzle. Gusts of wind splattered raindrops against the glass, but the rain suddenly ceased within minutes. Shafts of sunlight pierced through gaps in the trees, illuminating wet trunks and leaves from which a faint steam rose. It was as though nature here lived by its own rhythm, constantly shifting its scenery.

"Feels like we're driving through a labyrinth," the stranger muttered, glancing around.

The driver smirked, keeping his eyes on the road.

"If it were a straight path, it'd only take ten minutes. But in a car, we have to go around the canyon," he replied, not particularly inclined to explain the details of the route.

"A cliff by the sea?" the stranger asked, intrigued by the mention.

"Yeah, and lots of folks go there... you know, to end it all," the old man muttered, leaning closer to the wheel. "Trouble is, it's not as high as they think. The sea's right below, so most survive, no matter how hard they try. But some... well, some disappear for good. The road's rocky, the cliffs are steep, and people are drawn to it for some reason."

The stranger gazed out the window, catching glimpses of the sea between the trees. Mist rose from the water, and the velvet-like surface of the ocean seemed both close and unreachable. Another gust of wind darkened the sky again, and the old man nodded toward the narrow trail running alongside the road, adding,

"See that? The path looks like it's made for them — one wrong step, and you're tumbling down to the sea. Not a road, really, more like a well-worn trail."

In those moments when the trees closed tightly overhead, the light grew dim and soft, like in an old movie. The stranger couldn't help but think that this place felt like it was frozen in time, as if it belonged in some eerie vintage horror film.

The car jolted over yet another pothole, and the old driver winced, glancing at the dashboard as if expecting something to go wrong and resigning himself to the fact that his trusty "workhorse" might soon need another trip to the repair shop.

"Ah, these roads…" he muttered, mentally calculating how much the parts would cost this time.

In the distance, almost parallel to their path, another road appeared—a much better-paved one, with neat curves winding off to the side. The stranger noticed it and instinctively looked at the driver, his expression silently questioning why they were taking this bumpy path instead of the smooth asphalt.

"You see that? Sure, it's nicer over there, no argument," the old man caught his glance and quickly explained. "But that road takes an extra twenty minutes. This one's straight, even if it shakes you like a cart ride."

Indeed, after about five minutes, the parallel road made a sharp turn, almost as if avoiding their route, veering off as though it were afraid of the places they were headed.

They drove for another five or ten minutes, the road hemmed in by dense thickets before it unexpectedly opened onto a small clearing. There, nestled in the open space, stood a building that looked like an old stone barn, seemingly merged with the surrounding nature. The walls were thickly covered with moss and overgrown with ferns, while the branches of shrubs and low-hanging trees nearly brushed against the roof, creating the impression that the building might dissolve into the greenery at any moment.

The bar stood alone in the clearing, and about a hundred meters behind it lay a small cliff, beyond which the distant sound of waves crashing against the shore could be faintly heard. The parking lot was nothing more than a patch of gravel, slightly flattened by the tires of the few cars that dared to make the journey. This place seemed to repel unnecessary visitors.

Nearby, a tiny house was visible, adjacent to a small vineyard. Several hectares of grapevines blended into the wild overgrowth, punctuated by old, rusting remnants of life. Two wheel-less pickup trucks stood abandoned near the house, their metal frames corroding into the earth like forgotten shells, slowly being reclaimed by nature.

They parked right by the bar's entrance, and to the stranger's surprise, the driver didn't wait for payment. He simply opened the door, climbed out of the car with a groan, and headed toward the bar as if he were a regular.

The stranger hesitated briefly before following him.

The bar greeted them with the faintly musty smell of old wood, beer, and damp air.

The driver approached the counter and ordered himself a pint of local beer with a name that the stranger found nearly unpronounceable. Climbing onto a high, battered stool with some effort, the old man tossed a couple of peanuts into his mouth and took a few large gulps. Then he turned toward the stranger, watching him with mild curiosity.

To the stranger's surprise, the bar was pretty lively. Five or seven patrons sat at scattered tables, chatting animatedly and noisily downing their pints.

The stranger called over the bartender and ordered a strong coffee, glancing at his companion and wondering whether the old man could even handle the drive back.

Without waiting for his coffee, the stranger decided to cut to the chase and addressed the bartender:

"Listen, do you remember me? I think I was here a few days ago."

The bartender gave him a once-over, squinting thoughtfully before answering.

"Yeah, I think I do," he finally nodded. "You were on a motorcycle, right? Talkative guy — you said someone nearly ran you off the road. Word was, a car came straight at you, right where those parallel roads split. And then, as you told it, you went flying into a ditch. Lucky you got away with just a scratch on your face."

The stranger frowned, trying to recall the hazy fragments. The fall, the cold wind, the feeling of flying... *"That's right, someone did come straight at me,"* he thought. Meanwhile, the bartender continued:

"After that, you hit the bottle hard. There were three other bikers here at the time. You got into some kind of argument with them — something about motorcycles, I think — and then, after one too many bad jokes, they dragged you out to the parking lot."

The bartender paused, sizing him up before continuing.

"I'm not sure what happened next, but about fifteen minutes later, I heard gunshots. I went outside—I honestly thought you were dead. But there they were, shining flashlights into the bushes—you must've bolted into the woods. I've no idea how you got out of there, though. There's a cliff right there."

The stranger strained his memory. He vaguely remembered snatching a gun from one of the bikers, striking another, and bolting into the bushes. That must've been where he fell off the cliff. Thankfully, it wasn't too high, and he had survived, though battered and bruised, losing both consciousness and, apparently, his memory.

"Must've washed up near the pier," he muttered under his breath, recalling how he'd opened his eyes to the sound of rain and the sea while sitting on that damp bench.

These revelations shed some light on his strange arrival at the pier, his battered state, and the sudden presence of the pistol he'd somehow managed to keep. But why had he ended up in this town in the first place? And even more puzzling—how had he seen Catherine at the pier dressed like that? There were still no answers, and the questions only kept piling up.

He took another small sip of his coffee and turned back to the bartender, who was endlessly wiping a glass with some sort of cloth—either a scrap of a towel or just an enormous handkerchief.

"Hey, you heard anything about this missing girl?" the stranger asked, trying to catch the bartender's eye.

The man shrugged, not giving it much thought.

"Not much. I heard some girl's gone missing, but who was she or why? No idea."

The stranger noticed how the room grew quiet after the bartender's words. The customers, who had been loudly debating at their tables moments ago, now spoke in hushed tones as if trying to eavesdrop on their conversation. Pretending not to notice, the stranger asked another question:

"And what about the laboratory on the outskirts? Ever heard anything strange about it? How do the locals feel about it?"

This time, the bartender didn't even pretend to think. He simply shook his head.

"No, can't say I've heard much about it. You know, I hardly ever go into town. My whole life's here—open the bar in the morning, close it late at night. Almost year-round without a break."

Before the stranger could dwell on the answer, the room filled with noise again. Conversations, chatter, and laughter resumed at the neighboring tables as if no one had paid their exchange the slightest attention.

They sat a little longer, shifting to lighter topics. The bartender, more animated now, began talking about his vineyard, which, despite the harsh climate, somehow managed to yield a decent harvest. Smiling, he recalled how children used to sneak onto his property, carefully picking the rare clusters of grapes and how he'd chase them off—though never too harshly.

"The land here's damp, even clammy, but things still grow," he said with a smirk before adding, "A lot of odd plants thrive around here, like heather—it plays a big role in local folklore. Then there's sea fenugreek and gentian."

The stranger shook his head slightly, watching as the endless rain blurred the gray outlines of the landscape through the window. Wet and heavy fern branches tapped against the glass like sodden wings. He turned to the window, wondering how anything other than moss could grow in a place like this.

Meanwhile, the bartender and the driver had started talking, their voices lively and punctuated with laughter. They seemed to be reminiscing about younger days or swapping old stories. The stranger had stopped listening, retreating into his thoughts. He finished his coffee and glanced at the driver, who had long since drained his pint and looked ready for another.

But rising from his stool, the stranger thanked the bartender, left a generous tip, and dragged the driver out of the bar, giving him no chance for another drink.

"What's the rush?" the driver grumbled as they walked to the car under the light drizzle.

"I have a feeling we've got a long road ahead," the stranger replied with a faint smirk, shutting the door behind him.

On the way back, the stranger asked the driver to take a detour and head toward the laboratory, which was increasingly troubling him with its mysterious connections to recent events. The driver reluctantly agreed, knowing he was earning more than usual today.

They turned off their previous route, and after a few minutes, they were driving down a decent road, leaving behind dense thickets of trees covered in thick gray-green moss. The driver picked up speed, smoothly navigating the curves, and soon they passed through a small settlement—just one street lined with a handful of dilapidated houses.

A little farther on, the road became perfectly smooth, illuminated even during the day. The driver made a gentle left turn, and within less than two hundred meters, they reached a checkpoint.

Two guards stood in the road, armed and dressed in military uniforms with no insignia. Pistols hung at their hips, and rifles were slung over their backs. The stranger noticed the surveillance cameras mounted on nearly every lamppost along the road since they'd turned onto it.

The guards stood silently, smoking, their eyes fixed on the taxi with a mixture of curiosity and indifference, but they made no move to approach or stop them.

Suddenly, the stranger felt an overwhelming urge to smoke. He cursed under his breath, remembering that he hadn't bought any cigarettes after the incident with the brazen seagull. *"These birds are utterly pointless creatures,"* he thought, recalling the recent theft. Suppressing his irritation, he said to the driver:

"All right, let's not make those guys nervous. Turn us around."

The driver nodded silently and carefully began to turn the car around on the narrow road under the watchful eyes of the guards. The checkpoint reminded the stranger of a military zone. Behind it, he could make out another fence and a similar guard post, complete with a parking area for four vehicles in front of automated gates that led into the facility. Between the two fences, a perfectly manicured lawn, reminiscent of a strict exclusion zone, was fully visible from all sides.

Beyond the second checkpoint stood a modern, low-rise building with sparsely tinted windows and large satellite antennas perched on the roof.

As they merged back onto the main road and headed toward town, the driver remained silent, lost in his thoughts. Ten minutes later, he began talking again, casually recounting bits of local history. But the stranger wasn't listening—his mind kept circling back to the peculiar building and its meticulously guarded perimeter.

For a moment, his thoughts drifted to the seagulls again. *"What's the point of these creatures? What use do they have? Sure, sometimes they catch rodents or eat fish, keeping the air a bit cleaner, but most of them have taken to dumpsters, scattering plastic all over town and stealing cigarettes from decent people."*

With these thoughts swirling in his head, they arrived back at the hotel. The stranger stepped out of the car and bid the driver goodbye, this time skipping a tip. His mind was too full of strange and unsettling thoughts, and he suddenly felt an urgent need to find out what was so troubling about this town.

The stranger spent some time in his room, hoping to piece everything together. Upon entering the hotel, he immediately noticed an old woman sitting in a worn rocking chair near a small fireplace in the corner of the lobby. She was wrapped in a knitted blanket, a battered stuffed animal resting on her lap, which she stroked as if it were a living cat.

The stranger froze, watching the scene—it looked like something plucked from another era. After standing there for a few moments, he headed up the stairs to his room, his mind churning with all that needed to be processed.

When he reached his floor, he noticed that the door to his room was slightly ajar, and strange rustling sounds were coming from inside. He didn't feel particularly concerned—he didn't carry anything valuable with him. It was curiosity, more than fear that pushed him to step inside.

In the room, he saw an old man standing by the bed, moving a battered aluminum basin across the floor as if caught up in some invisible game. Looking up, the stranger noticed a wet stain on the ceiling, from which water was slowly dripping onto the floor.

Spotting the guest, the old man launched into an explanation without so much as a greeting. He said that the rain had seeped through the roof because strong winds had ripped off some shingles. A worker was already repairing the damage, and they would use special equipment to dry out the ceiling. The stranger, the old man assured him, would just have to put up with it for a little while—there were no other free rooms in the hotel.

Before he could finish, a loud thud echoed above as if someone had struck the roof. The stranger realized that staying here in peace and quietly reflecting wouldn't happen today. Suppressing his irritation, he waved his hand in acknowledgment, gave the old man a thumbs-up, and left the room without lingering.

As he descended the staircase, a thought struck him—he was sure no other guests were staying at the hotel. Perhaps someone had checked in while he was away, though, for some reason, it felt like the old woman in the rocking chair and the man with the basin were more than just random occupants. Deciding he'd figure it out later, he returned to the café to wait for Daniel—there were still a few hours left.

Passing through the lobby, he glanced briefly at the fireplace—the rocking chair was empty. The blanket was neatly folded on the armrest, and the familiar, worn stuffed animal lay on the seat as though its owner had suddenly vanished. The stranger felt a faint unease but brushed it aside, deciding it was just another peculiar quirk of this hotel.

As soon as he stepped outside, a cold wind mixed with sharp raindrops lashed his face, making him shiver. He tightened his perfectly tailored black coat, pulled up the collar, and strode quickly down the deserted street toward the small square. Though it could hardly be called a town center, it was livelier than the grim, moss-covered streets steeped in mist and shadows.

He briefly considered buying something warmer to wear but immediately remembered his limited funds. His money was already running low, and opportunities to replenish it were dwindling fast. Dismissing the thought, he refocused on the task at hand.

Entering the café, the stranger headed straight for the counter without waiting for a server. The bartender, a young woman, listened attentively, her eyebrows raising slightly as he ordered a cup of strong tea—with additions she clearly hadn't expected: a cinnamon stick, a few slices of ginger root, a pinch of saffron, and a spoonful of ground almonds. She arched a brow but smiled and nodded, asking him to wait.

The stranger settled into a comfortable chair by the window, leaning forward slightly as he rested on the small round table. Beyond the glass stretched a dreary scene: a narrow, seemingly lifeless street bathed in the dim glow of streetlights, their beams barely cutting through the thick fog and cascading rain. Large, heavy raindrops drummed against the windowpane, forming crooked trails of water that merged and trickled downward. The piercing wind chased fallen leaves and scraps of paper along the sidewalk, spinning them in a bleak waltz to its harsh, lashing melody.

His gaze drifted slowly over the gray landscape, but every object he saw felt strangely meaningless, offering no new insight. The peeling facades of old buildings stood like forgotten ghosts, faded to pale gray tones, streaked with rain that looked like tears running down the weathered brick walls. The branches of sparse, long-wild shrubs hung limply along the paths; some half-submerged in puddles formed by the relentless rain.

As he waited for his tea, warmth began to seep back into his body, but his thoughts remained as dark and murky as the scene outside. The past, like a faded photograph, remained incomplete and blurred. Memories slipped away like leaves carried by the wind; every time he tried to grasp a detail, it drifted further out of reach.

When his tea arrived, the small steaming cup seemed tiny in his strong hands. The aroma of cinnamon and ginger filled the air, adding a warm, almost festive note to the cold, dreary surroundings. Leaning over the cup, he felt the steam warm his face and the spicy scent stirred something deep within him — something was forgotten, transporting his thoughts far from here to other places and times.

"Strange, why does this aroma feel so familiar?" he thought, staring at the cup of thick, slightly misty tea. Instinctively, he had chosen this specific mix, asking the barista to add cinnamon, ginger, and saffron — along with something else he couldn't quite remem-

ber, but it seemed like it was meant to be. Now, the faint but surprisingly persistent aroma of spices hung in the air, stirring strange, elusive thoughts. *"But now's not the time to get distracted by trivialities,"* he cut himself off, taking a hot, sharp sip and refocusing on more pressing questions.

"How could I have seen her at the pier? And why didn't anyone else see her, even though this town, to be honest, can hardly be called crowded? More like it's practically dead," he mused, glancing out the window at the empty street shrouded in the familiar gray mist. Suddenly, a memory surfaced—the sign he had noticed in the square: *"The 9,024th resident is born! Congratulations to the proud parents!"* He frowned. *"Where are all these people? In all this time, I've seen at most thirty people, many of them like shadows—silent and mysterious, passing by as if fleeting images in a fogged mirror."*

"If she walked past me that night on the pier, she must have been heading toward the square," he reasoned, recalling her slender silhouette in the moonlight. There should have been witnesses on the square—maybe vendors or even that taxi driver, who seemed to have seen everything. But no one mentioned her. It was strange. *"Maybe I should report it to the police—give them an approximate time when I saw her. Maybe they have cameras… if, of course, this town even has any police at all,"* he thought with a faint smirk, taking another sip of his now-cooled tea.

He was so deep in thought that he didn't realize how quickly time was slipping by. Glancing at his watch, he was surprised that Daniel was already nearly an hour and a half late. A bad sign, especially for a journalist. Being late to a meeting, particularly in a place like this, where even the smallest delay could mean something serious, was reckless. The café was set to close in fifteen minutes, and the staff began glancing at him more frequently and insistently as if urging him to free up the table.

Taking the hint, he called over the waitress, paid his bill, and left a generous tip, noting the slight relief that crossed her face.

Stepping outside, the wind once again lashed his face with heavy, damp drops, pulling him back into his thoughts. Daniel still hadn't shown up—what could have happened? It was too early to file a missing person report, of course, but he needed to find the newsroom where Daniel and Catherine had worked. Perhaps Daniel had been delayed at work or been called out on a sudden assignment. Maybe an article about this incredibly "cheerful" and "life-loving" town.

"All right," he decided, heading toward the newsroom. *"I need to check."*

"But how do I find it? It could be anywhere in this maze of gray buildings and wet, deserted streets," he wondered, strolling past the damp houses. His eyes scanned the faintly lit buildings, illuminated only by dim streetlights until he noticed a faint light in the distance. A flickering sign glowed feebly on one of the facades, its light seeming to struggle against the encroaching darkness. The letters were barely legible, as though dissolving into the shadows, but he managed to make out the name: *"Main Office of the 'Herald' Newspaper."*

"This is getting stranger and stranger," he thought, pressing his lips together. If Daniel was in the office, why hadn't he bothered to come out and at least apologize for being late? Maybe he'd simply forgotten about their meeting or gotten caught up in something urgent, but it still didn't fit the image of someone for whom interviews and schedules were a priority.

He headed toward the newsroom, watching its faint light flickered on and off, barely illuminating the narrow path leading to the heavy wooden door.

He pushed the door, and to his surprise, it gave way easily and opened without resistance. Peering inside, the stranger called out loudly, hoping to find someone, but silence greeted him instead. The corridor ahead was long and dimly lit, leading him deeper into what felt like the quietest place in the world.

At the end of the hallway, he entered a large open room filled with desks—no fewer than twenty—cluttered with piles of papers, computer monitors, and scraps of notes.

At the far end of the room stood several offices with doors, one of which bore the words in bold black letters: *"Editor-in-Chief — Daniel Skye."* He couldn't help but smile, realizing that Daniel might have mentioned his title before, but at the time, it had seemed unimportant and quickly slipped from his memory. Now, every detail seemed significant.

The stranger walked up to the door and knocked, but there was no answer. He tried the handle—it was locked, and no light shone from inside. The entire building was empty. In a town this small and almost lifeless, it struck him as odd to leave a newsroom full of equipment and documents unattended.

Nearby, by a window, stood a large desk. A small plaque read: *"Catherine M."* It was immediately apparent that this had been her workspace. The stranger moved closer, compelled to examine what had been left behind.

Leaning cautiously over the desk, his eyes skimmed its surface. Papers, newspaper clippings, and several open notebooks cluttered the space—it looked as though Catherine had been bottomless into some complicated investigation before her work came to an abrupt halt.

On the topmost sheet, a rough diagram with dates and names crisscrossed with question marks. It was a web connecting various events without explanations as if it were just part of her scattered thoughts jotted down hastily.

Amid the chaos, he spotted a bright red sticky note attached to the edge of one notebook. Catherine's bold handwriting scrawled across it read: *"Don't forget to check the lab."* Below were several illegible annotations, one of which seemed to include the name of an inspector. The mention of the lab and local inspectors sparked even more questions.

A little further on, he found neatly stacked newspaper clippings with headlines about *"mysterious disappearances"* and *"missing residents."* This added even more layers to the strange situation. Among the clippings was an article written by Catherine detailing supposedly successful research conducted at the newly built lab on the outskirts of town. But on the back of the article, Catherine had made a brief but weighty note: *"What can't be trusted?"*

At some point, the stranger realized he had stepped directly into the middle of her personal investigation.

He sank into Catherine's chair, feeling a strange mix of tension and calm, as though something about this place drew him in and refused to let go. Leaning back, he inhaled the scent of old paper and ink, mingled faintly with traces of her perfume—everything that had surrounded her daily. But his thoughts refused to form a coherent picture. Fragments of memories and guesses surfaced, only to slip away again, like trying to catch water with his bare hands.

"Why was she even alone at that pier? Why hasn't anyone seen her since?" he thought, trying to hold onto the thread of his reasoning as his gaze wandered over her desk. Among the papers and notes were torn photographs, pencils with dulled tips—as if she'd been endlessly sketching, searching... or perhaps retreating into these notes to escape something important.

Hesitantly, he reached for her laptop and opened it. The screen came to life instantly, displaying the desktop. There was no password. That didn't seem like Catherine—she always came across as someone cautious and meticulous. Another oddity.

On the desktop was just one folder, its name tantalizingly cryptic: *"Investigations."* The title stood out against the otherwise empty screen as if Catherine had either been in a hurry or had deliberately left it in plain sight. The stranger lingered momentarily, staring at the folder's icon, a strange premonition tugging at him. It felt like he was on the brink of uncovering a layer of her life she had shared with no one—not even those closest to her.

He clicked on the folder and found several files inside—documents, photographs, scanned newspaper clippings, diagrams, and notes—some appearing hastily gathered, others carefully compiled. One file stood out: its label read *"Report—Laboratory."* A peculiar tension gripped him as though this unassuming title concealed something of profound importance.

The unsettling feeling didn't leave him. The room, the desk, and its contents seemed to hold answers to questions he hadn't yet fully formed.

He picked up a black paper bag and carefully placed inside it the materials he'd gathered—a thick folder labeled *"Laboratory?"*; a few newspaper clippings; a notebook with surprisingly elegant embossing on its cover; and an old, faded photograph of a lighthouse, face-down as if deliberately hidden from prying eyes.

Once finished, he pressed the print button on the file labeled *"Report — Laboratory."* Behind him, the printer began slowly spitting out fresh sheets of paper one by one. About ten pages in total—an account of the laboratory, apparently written by Catherine herself. He skimmed the pages: long paragraphs of text, brief annotations in the margins, a few diagrams—all of it so precise and detailed that it felt like he was holding an entire trove of carefully concealed information.

When the last sheets dropped into the printer tray, he gathered them, placed them in the bag, and took one last look around the office to ensure he hadn't left anything out in the open. The silence of the newsroom, its walls seeming to watch him, felt oppressively heavy. But he didn't let it stop him—he confidently made his way out, stepping into the corridor and leaving no trace of his unexpected visit.

He stepped onto the street, where darkness had engulfed entirely the empty square. Almost at the center, a solitary streetlamp flickered faintly, casting a feeble glow over the damp, deserted town. The drizzle continued, prompting him to pull his coat tightly around the paper bag to keep it from getting soaked.

The shops had long since closed, and he realized his hopes of a cigarette before bed would have to wait. Quickening his pace across the rain-slick cobblestones, the stranger returned to the hotel. Reaching the entrance, he swung the door open with a single motion and stepped inside, shaking droplets from his black coat.

The lobby was empty, and as he glanced around, he felt an almost imperceptible shift in the atmosphere—something had subtly changed, though he couldn't quite put his finger on it. He had no desire to linger and find out.

Climbing the stairs quickly, he entered his room and noticed that the basin that had been catching dripping water earlier was gone, leaving only a wide circle of yellowed stains on the ceiling. The floor was clean and dry.

He kicked off his shoes, tossed the bag onto the chair, and headed straight for the shower, shedding his clothes along the way. Standing under the hot water, he stayed there for what felt like hours, trying to warm up, but the inner chill refused to leave. The dampness and biting Scottish weather seemed to seep deeper into him, draining the last remnants of his strength. Even the scalding water couldn't entirely rid him of the feeling.

At last, he turned off the shower, wrapped himself in a towel, and stepped into the cool room, which had lost all its warmth during the day. The black bag full of documents from the newsroom awaited him on the chair, a silent reminder of the tasks he couldn't wash away with a shower. Shadows flickered on the walls, cast by the small lamp, creating the illusion of movement and a vague sense of unease.

He sighed, reached for the bag, and pulled out the folder labeled *"Laboratory?"* The exhaustion weighing on his mind dampened his eagerness to sift through the pages. He glanced briefly at the faded photograph of a lighthouse before setting it aside, scribbled a few thoughts into his notebook, and began flipping through the printed pages—quickly, without pause, searching for any clue about Daniel or Catherine.

But clarity eluded him. The folder of notes and clippings was nothing more than a collection of hints, scattered fragments from newspapers, as though Daniel and Catherine had been trying to piece together something bigger.

He turned off the lamp and lay in the darkness, listening to the soft patter of nighttime rain against the window. In the quiet, his thoughts kept returning to the lighthouse. Was it important? Or was it just another town landmark? Even mundane details seemed too mysterious in this old town with its scarce and shadowy inhabitants. The dark silhouette of the lighthouse, set against the sound of rain, stirred an inexplicable unease.

Determined, he laid out all the papers on the floor, carefully flattening each sheet to ensure nothing was overlooked. On his knees and elbows, he scanned the scattered printouts and handwritten notes, underlining key points and jotting quick annotations in the margins. Time seemed to dissolve as he focused intensely on every detail, every hint scattered across the pages, leaving no thought unexamined.

After nearly an hour of this absorbed study, his eyes caught on a sheet with a headline that made him freeze. It described the laboratory complex, which, oddly enough, also housed a daycare center on its premises. He reread the text twice, scrutinizing every word.

"A strange combination," he thought. A heavily guarded research facility with a daycare center seemed bizarre. The handwritten list on the page mentioned twenty children brought to the facility and stayed there all day. Parents had apparently signed agreements allowing their children to be there, but what did that mean in the context of the laboratory?

"I understand what might've caught Catherine's attention," he thought, astonished by how out of place this detail seemed in his understanding of such institutions. A daycare center felt absurdly inappropriate on a property surrounded by fences—some of which might even be electrified.

He picked up another page that described the daycare center and noticed that the phrase *"waiver of claims"* had been circled several times in bright red ink. The document seemed to scream that something was amiss. What was hidden behind this *"waiver of claims"*? Was it more than just childcare? Were experiments being conducted there?

It struck him that the answer might be closer than he thought, but his mind resisted—it was all too strange and unsettling to fit neatly into any logical picture.

He took a deep breath, trying to steady himself. *"Don't jump to conclusions,"* he reminded himself. *"It might just be bureaucracy or an exaggeration."* And yet, the detail of the barbed wire—thin but still surrounding the property—and the double-layered fencing told him that the place was not secured for the safety of children.

Thoughts of the laboratory wouldn't leave him, pulling at him like a sticky web. Each thread led deeper and deeper still. Why wasn't there a single mention of the lab online? No photos, no articles—as if it didn't exist. On maps, the site was marked as an empty lot. Too many oddities and unanswered questions to keep calm.

"I need to check out that place again," he thought, running through possible ways to approach the lab in his mind. He recalled the old church with tall towers they had passed on the outskirts—it was nearby and could offer a good view of the entire area. But would they let him in, especially with questions like his? Then again, why not?

Then he remembered the old framed photograph he'd found on Catherine's desk. The faded, gray-toned image showed a lighthouse, and according to the hand-drawn map, the lighthouse was close to the laboratory, at the very edge of the town, right by the sea. From there, he might be able to see more than from any church tower. Even the lab's security might be less noticeable from such a distance.

"Getting to the lighthouse might not be easy," he mused. *"But it's definitely worth a try."* He considered his options: take a taxi? The drivers might get suspicious about such a destination, and besides, who knows who controls the lab? Walk for hours across the town? No, that would be too exhausting.

"All right, I'll figure it out tomorrow. It's already too late; I need at least some rest—tomorrow will be a long day."

The morning came far too early. Dim light filtered through the cloudy glass, but the sun couldn't break through the gray veil of the city, blanketed by thick drizzle and frost. The room was unbearably cold; the radiator had stopped working sometime during the night, and with each passing hour, the air grew sharper, biting to the bone. He had to get up before the chill became unbearable.

The stranger stretched, trying to warm himself. Then, with cold, clumsy fingers, he gathered the papers scattered on the floor and carefully placed them in the bag. He hid the bag in the wardrobe, hoping it wouldn't be thrown away if someone decided to clean the room. Satisfied that the papers were safe, he reached for the chair where he had draped his coat the night before.

Suddenly, a sharp thud against the window startled him. He recoiled as a seagull, a bundle of feathers and fury, slammed into the glass. Now, it was tapping insistently with its beak, glaring at him with what seemed like contempt.

"Burned through my pack already and came back for another, huh?" he muttered with a crooked smirk.

The bird tilted its head, continuing to tap as if offended or issuing some kind of warning. Shaking off the odd encounter, he shrugged on his coat, gave the cold room one last glance, and opened the door.

Outside the hotel, he fastened his coat and headed toward the bus stop on the small, deserted square. The only map and schedule, yellowed from age and weather, hung behind cracked glass at the old shelter. He leaned in to study the map, trying to figure out how to reach the lighthouse. The route had at least twenty stops before his destination. It wound along the coastline, doubling the travel time with twists and turns. Walking would take over two hours—hardly an ideal option.

He checked the schedule and noted the time. The following bus wasn't due for over an hour.

"Don't bother waiting," came an unexpected voice behind him. He turned to see an older man with a worn cane standing nearby.

"They haven't kept to that schedule in years," the man continued. "Buses come whenever they feel like it. And today? Martin's driving, so don't expect anything before noon."

"Got it, thanks," the stranger replied, stifling his disappointment. *"Looks like I'll have to find another way."*

Across the street, as if waiting for him, was the same beat-up car with its equally shabby driver. The driver sat absorbed in an unfolded newspaper, oblivious to the world around him. The stranger sighed, glanced back at the map, and noticed an ancient cemetery not far from the lighthouse on the outskirts of an old district. A road from the graveyard ran almost directly to the lighthouse. It was a perfect plan.

Suppressing a smirk, he approached the taxi driver and asked with faint sarcasm:

"Free? Please take me to the old district. The weather's perfect for a stroll through a cemetery, don't you think?"

The driver looked up from his newspaper, peering at him over the rim of his glasses.

"They say it's worth a visit," he muttered. "Oldest cemetery in Scotland, no less. All right, hop in."

The ride was mostly silent. The driver only broke the quiet a few times, reminiscing about local celebrities buried at the cemetery or recounting grim stories tied to its dark history.

When they arrived at the cemetery gates, the stranger handed the driver some cash.

"For the heartfelt conversation," he added. "I'll probably be here till nightfall, 'enjoying' the view. Don't wait up."

With a trembling hand, the driver accepted the money, nodded, and quickly drove off, casting one last wary glance at him before leaving.

The cemetery stretched before him like an ancient, forgotten world, as if from another era where time stood still, and no sound disturbed the silence. The gloomy morning, low gray sky, and persistent drizzle perfectly complemented the scene, filling the air with dampness and the faint scent of wet earth and withering grass.

Ahead, narrow paths twisted between graves covered in lichen, moss, and the shadows of bygone centuries. The old headstones came in various shapes and sizes—some leaning under their own weight, others barely visible beneath layers of moss, sunken and cracked. Rainwater trickled down the stone slabs, leaving dark streaks on the gray, weathered granite. On some of the headstones, faded names and dates could still be deciphered; on others, unfamiliar symbols and Latin phrases were half-erased and almost forgotten.

Wrought-iron fences, twisted and bent by time, encircled certain cemetery sections like sturdy but worn chains. Some areas were closed off by rusted gates, half-consumed by ivy, while others had been so thoroughly destroyed that only broken metal rods protruded from the ground, remnants of a once-intact barrier. Through rare gaps in the dense ivy, reliefs of angels and cherubs could be glimpsed—their marble darkened over the centuries, appearing more like somber guardians than symbols of heavenly protection.

To the left of the path, set slightly apart, rose massive sarcophagi. The carved flowers and intricate patterns on their stone lids seemed almost swallowed by the twilight of the cemetery as if the earth itself was reclaiming them. Towering above were ancient trees, gnarled and bent by the wind, resembling elders standing watch over the serenity of the place. Each tree stood apart from the others, their black branches reaching skyward, shielding the grounds below and creating the impression of a barrier as though to guard this land from the outside world.

Old crypts loomed at the cemetery's edges, their stone surfaces coated in centuries-old mold and surrounded by barely visible footpaths. Their doors were either boarded up or left ajar, revealing dark voids that invited no gaze. Above the entrance to one of the crypts, a weathered inscription could still be made out, its letters partially eroded. At its base lay fragments of stone, covered in green moss and wild grasses, as though the roots of the past had entwined themselves with these ruins, holding them firmly in place.

On one grave, he noticed a recently lit but now extinguished candle. Around it lay withered flowers. The impression that someone had been here not long ago lent the cemetery an uncanny energy, an inexplicable presence that seemed to hum beneath the surface.

He climbed a small hill from which the entire expanse of the cemetery opened before him. The sight took his breath away. It was truly enormous—the far edge disappeared into the mist, stretching endlessly toward the horizon. But what struck him most was the strange behavior of the people scattered throughout the cemetery, as if they were part of the silent landscape themselves.

Some were carrying heavy objects, moving them from one place to another. Others stood in tight groups around graves, slowly circling as if in a trance, occasionally bumping into each other before wordlessly changing direction.

Adding to the surreal atmosphere were the children, laughing and playing tag as they darted between graves and crumbled headstones. Their cheerful laughter echoed in the foggy silence, sharply contrasting with the silent, aimless adults. Crows and other somber birds perched everywhere, watching the scene with sharp, attentive eyes as if judging anyone who dared disturb their domain.

The stranger, trying not to draw attention to himself, quickened his pace. Based on the map, he had thought the route would be much shorter, but the cemetery seemed to stretch endlessly, slowing his progress. He paused a few times, observing the unusual scenes.

In one section of the cemetery, a group of people dressed entirely in black, featureless clothing was setting up equipment near an old crypt. They unloaded heavy black plastic cases from a small van and silently retrieved strange devices, cables, and sensors, which they immediately began attaching to the crypt's doors and windows. On the partially ruined roof of the crypt, a small transmitter could be seen, connected by a tangle of wires.

"I wonder what they're looking for?" he thought but quickly reminded himself of why he had come. Cautiously, staying in the shadows, he slipped past them and finally emerged onto a narrow path leading to a pair of massive gates.

As he approached the gates, he noticed their towering wrought-iron arches adorned with antique floral patterns intertwined with ivy and wild grapevines, hanging like a tattered veil. One of the gates had long since fallen and now rested on the ground, overgrown with moss. Strange symbols, perhaps Latin or Cyrillic letters, were carved into the arch, but time and weather had worn them away, leaving them indecipherable.

Stepping under the gate's arch, he suddenly felt his breath grow heavy. The air around him thickened, sweet and cloying, almost tangible. Strange shadows flickered at the edges of his vision, and for a moment, he felt dizzy. The sensation lasted only a few seconds, and as soon as he stepped fully through the gates, it vanished, leaving behind a peculiar heaviness in his mind. Shaking his head, he dismissed it as fatigue and lack of sleep, pressing onward.

Emerging from the dense forest of old trees and tangled bushes, he finally caught sight of the peculiar lighthouse ahead. Tall and bizarre, it stood out against the gray sky like a black tower against the clouds.

"That's where I need to go," he murmured, steeling himself, and continued toward the lighthouse.

Up close, the lighthouse looked even stranger and more ominous than it had from a distance. It rose like a cylindrical structure, forty or fifty meters tall, giving the impression of a massive black column. The building was divided into three distinct tiers, each appearing to be constructed from entirely different materials as if built in other eras.

The first tier of the lighthouse, rising to about twenty meters, was an impeccably smooth surface without a single window, door, or any hint of an entrance. At its base, the lighthouse was perfectly round, with no visible cracks, despite what seemed like centuries of exposure to the elements. At the twenty-meter mark, as though marking a deliberate boundary, the structure transitioned into an octagonal shape, encircled by a narrow balcony that wrapped around its entire perimeter. This gave the building an almost architectural elegance, reminiscent of a time when form carried profound significance.

Above the second tier, the lighthouse changed shape again, becoming a hexagonal tower that ended with an observation deck where a powerful beacon should have been. However, it was barely visible from the ground, and it was impossible to tell whether it was still operational or simply a relic of a long-forgotten era.

The stranger circled the lighthouse several times, scrutinizing every detail as if hoping to find a hidden door or even a hint of an entrance. Nothing. The smooth, ideally even wall at the base offered no cracks or gaps. The only imperfections on the otherwise pristine black surface were patches of moss and mildew, which clung to the structure like an organic veil. The mold seemed almost like a part of the lighthouse itself, as if it held the ancient plaster together, protecting it from time.

It was now clear why the lighthouse was nearly impossible to spot from afar. It blended seamlessly into the gray landscape, resembling a rocky outcrop or an abandoned watchtower. Perhaps, at one time, its walls had been painted in bright white or red hues, but now the lighthouse appeared more like a natural monolith, as though it had grown from the earth itself.

The lighthouse's unusual design not only intrigued but also captivated his imagination. Yet what puzzled him most was the lack of an entrance. How had the keepers entered? Indeed, they hadn't lived here forever without venturing into town. There had to be an entrance, presumably at the tower's base. With renewed determination, he searched for a hidden passage, running his hands along the moss-covered walls. His efforts, however, proved fruitless. There was no hatch, no secret door to be found.

One last possibility remained—the cliff. About ten meters from the lighthouse, near the edge of the rocks, he noticed what appeared to be steps carved into the stone. They descended sharply toward the sea, disappearing into the waves. Traversing them would be treacherous, even at low tide: the steps were barely half a meter wide, their edges slick with moisture and algae, posing a genuine hazard.

He crouched at the cliff's edge, peering down at the steps, and contemplated whether the risk of descending was worth it. Just as he was mulling over his options, he noticed the water beginning to recede. The tide was gradually pulling back, revealing the jagged rocks below. Soon, at the bottom of the steps, he saw the entrance to a narrow cave slowly coming into view.

"Well, there might not be another chance," he muttered, rising to his feet. The sense of danger lingered, but the urge to unravel the mystery outweighed it. He descended the steep, wave-worn steps and moved closer to the exposed cave. *"What if there's no way out?"* flashed through his mind, but retreating was no longer an option.

Stepping into the cave, he found himself in a narrow, damp passage immediately swallowed by complete darkness. Feeling his way along the walls, he moved forward slowly, trying to stay calm and aware that the low tide wouldn't last much longer. After what felt like an eternity, his hands brushed against something smooth and cold—a door.

Running his fingers over it, he found a metal handle. He pulled on it with strength, and the door finally creaked open. He stepped through and shut it behind him, sealing himself off from the cold, dampness of the cave.

He was in total darkness, but at least it was dry. Pressing his back against the wall, he exhaled deeply, trying to steady himself against the wave of unease that surged over him.

"Next time, I need to think before jumping into something like this," he muttered.

Edging along the wall, he felt the surface with his fingertips until he came across another door. The space seemed narrow, like a passage or an airlock, and he now stood before a second door. Opening it, he was greeted by a faint light spilling from a room beyond.

In the center of the room stood the base of a massive spiral staircase with wooden railings, winding its way upward—likely toward the lighthouse beacon.

Closing the door behind him, he breathed a small sigh of relief and began his ascent.

The steps were coated in a thick layer of dust, and he could clearly see the footprints of someone who had passed through recently. Two distinct sets of tracks stood out: one from a larger foot, where the person had stepped on every other stair as though in a hurry or unused to the spacing, and the other from a smaller foot, which had carefully stepped on each stair.

The footprints led upward and only returned downward once, as if the two people had climbed to a certain point and immediately descended again. The smaller footprints seemed to repeat in some areas, as though their owner had lingered or retraced their steps. However, the exact movements were difficult to determine—the dust blurred the edges of the tracks.

Reaching the first floor, he saw a narrow balcony running in a circle around the room, barely waist-high, with small observation windows facing outward. This area was clearly designed for perimeter surveillance, turning the lighthouse into something resembling a watchtower. But this detail paled in comparison to the astonishing discovery before him: the next tier of the lighthouse was clearly built in an entirely different era. The walls had a completely different geometry and cladding, as though a temporal chasm separated them. The masonry on the second floor was noticeably thicker, which seemed illogical from the standpoint of architectural load distribution on the foundation.

On the outside, the second tier was octagonal, but it remained perfectly round from the inside, mirroring the lower level's design. However, the space between the railings and the walls of the second tier was significantly larger, now spanning over two meters, creating an impression of emptiness and unnecessary massiveness. The staircase, which had previously clung to the walls of the first tier, transitioned to the central axis here, spiraling narrowly upward—barely half a meter wide—with a noticeable gap between it and the surrounding walls, as though intentionally distancing itself from everything around it.

The most striking details, however, were on the walls. They were covered with inscriptions in numerous languages. He could make out fragments in French, German, Russian, one of the Asian scripts, and several others he couldn't even identify. The text seemed nonsensical even in the familiar languages, more like a jumble of words or ritualistic rambling. The words were disjointed, the phrases unfinished, with only occasional sentences hinting at fragments of some mad prophecy:

"Death is conquered… by those who renounced."

"The river of forgotten lives flows beneath this stone."

"Awaken in dreams from which there is no waking."

In addition to the text, the walls were adorned with numerous illustrations, crafted with precision and almost obsessive attention to detail, far beyond what the chaotic text displayed. These were depictions of nature—trees, rivers, mountains, and stormy clouds—but not a single living soul. There were no people, no animals, as though nature existed entirely on its own, in isolation and oblivion.

His gaze lingered on the staircase. It was made of wrought iron, with treads of charred wooden planks fastened atop the metal frame. The planks appeared to have been treated with some resinous substance to prevent rotting, but now their surfaces had dried out, becoming brittle and crumbly. Each step groaned under his weight, amplifying the feeling that this staircase had been deliberately built to last for centuries, guarding the dark secrets of the lighthouse.

Slowly, he ascended to the next tier, passing through a narrow, low door in the ceiling. At the top, he found himself on a small balcony, even narrower than the previous one, lined with numerous tiny windows. From the inside, the walls remained perfectly circular, in contrast to the hexagonal exterior of this level. The walls were entirely coated in black paint, creating an illusion of infinite emptiness.

But on this blackness, tiny white dots formed a starry pattern. As his eyes adjusted to the dim light, he realized these dots were arranged into a celestial map. The constellations were strikingly accurate and familiar; he even spotted Polaris, shining slightly brighter than the others. The map seemed to draw his gaze, demanding to be read not as a simple image but as a key to some hidden truth.

The staircase here was different: it was constructed solely of thick wooden planks with no metal framework. Its shape and radius mirrored the previous level's staircase, but the gap between the stairs and the walls remained the same, indicating that the walls of this tier were thinner. This struck him as peculiar as if the structure grew increasingly fragile as it ascended.

He climbed cautiously, feeling the firm, unyielding wood beneath his feet. Despite its evident age, the wood seemed untouched by time—it didn't creak or splinter as though protected by some ancient secret.

But what truly captivated him were the inscriptions. Each step was covered in words—short phrases, one or two at a time, written in various languages. Occasionally, he recognized familiar words, but they felt disjointed as if they were fragments plucked from some ancient ritual or cryptic message. Along the banister, inscriptions continued, running the length of the staircase like a companion to the words on the steps.

He slowed, leaning down to read one word, then another, hoping to find some meaning. But the words seemed to elude comprehension, forming something nonsensical or hidden behind an alien logic. The sense of mystery grew with every step, amplifying his unease. There was almost no dust on the steps as if someone had recently cleaned them thoroughly, giving the impression that this place wasn't as abandoned as it appeared.

Reaching the final door in the ceiling, he paused, feeling a strange sense of anticipation. The door, similar to the ones below, was much heavier and didn't open on the first try. He pushed harder, but it refused to budge. Frustrated, he swung his hand and struck the wood, the impact reverberating through the tier with a hollow echo. Something heavy was pressing against the door from above.

After several minutes of effort and quiet grumbling, he finally felt something shift. Another forceful push—and the door creaked open. Squeezing through the narrow passage, he emerged onto the topmost balcony.

The room greeted him with an unusual light. In the center stood a lamp, its design strikingly out of place in the ancient structure. It was too modern, almost technological, with black metallic elements and coils of cables running downward. The light it emitted was cold, with a bluish tint, and it seemed both artificial and unnervingly alive as if its source was something far more than mere electricity.

The stranger froze, staring at the lamp. Around it, on the floor, lay strange objects: a few scraps of paper covered in symbols and an old, rusted key, seemingly left behind in haste. The faint hum of wind and the thin, almost weightless air at this height added to the sense of detachment from the real world.

As he moved closer to the lamp, his attention was immediately drawn to a narrow pipe extending vertically downward. It appeared made of copper, brass, or bronze, as it was covered in a thick layer of oxidation, giving it a greenish-brown hue. At first glance, the pipe might have been used to deliver gas or some flammable liquid to the lamp. The assumption seemed logical, but in the context of the lamp's other features, the device raised more questions than answers.

Wires extended outward from the lamp's casing, neatly secured, and split into two bundles. One bundle trailed downward, following the copper pipe in a coiled embrace, while the other terminated a few meters away in a cluster of connectors. These connectors were unmistakably designed for a computer or other modern equipment.

Why was such a device here, in this ancient tower? And even stranger, every wire was in perfect condition, showing no signs of corrosion or wear.

He leaned in closer, studying the center of the lamp. Thick magnifying lenses, stacked one on the other, created a multi-layered construction. Each lens was framed by thin black metal inserts, forming a geometric pattern of hexagons that resembled honeycombs. The entire structure looked like a giant soccer ball but with such intricate craftsmanship that it seemed its creators had attempted to merge ancient aesthetics with advanced technology.

Through the lenses, he could glimpse a strange glow within. A bluish light emanated from a small, almost spherical object at the heart of the lamp. It resembled a black, nearly impenetrable cloud surrounded by a faint, glowing outline. The cloud enveloped a metallic rod shaped like a spear, which appeared to be glowing white-hot. The spear extended downward, disappearing into the depths of the mechanism.

The inky cloud, about ten centimeters in diameter, twitched slightly as if stirred by an invisible wind. It seemed alive, constantly shifting its form while maintaining its spherical core. He thought he saw it pulsate as if reacting to his presence or air movement around it. The sight was mesmerizing yet evoked an unsettling, almost primal sense of unease.

He reached out and touched the metal casing of the lamp but immediately withdrew his hand. The metal was unnervingly cold, far colder than he expected from a device emitting such a light. Yet, there was no sign of frost or any other indication of freezing temperatures. The longer he observed the lamp, the stronger his conviction grew that this was no ordinary light source. There was something fundamentally wrong about it, as though its existence defied the laws of physics he thought he understood.

Straightening up, he tried to process what he had seen. This device seemed ancient and, at the same time, incredibly advanced. Who could have built such a thing? And why was it here? The thought crossed his mind that the lamp was not merely a part of the lighthouse but a key to understanding its purpose and the mystery surrounding this place.

The room was small, no more than five or six meters in diameter, with a floor of triangular glass tiles, perfectly shaped and arranged in a complex pattern reminiscent of a mosaic, though without color—only transparent and semi-transparent elements. The floor and ceiling were covered in a stainless steel-like material with a mirrored finish, designed to evenly and seamlessly reflect the light. However, the effect was now lost under a thick dust and grime coating on nearly every surface. Evidently, the room had long since been abandoned, left without care or maintenance.

Some of the glass panels were damaged—cracks etched jagged lines across their surfaces like lightning bolts, while in some places, entire pieces were missing, allowing the cold, thin air to seep inside. As he had noticed while climbing to the upper tier, this air felt almost artificial—its temperature and pressure were unnervingly low, sending a slight chill through his body.

The wind currents penetrated the room and carried particles of dust that settled on the glass, the floor, and the mirrored ceiling. In several areas, the glass panels had grown over with green moss, which had dried out and regrown multiple times, leaving uneven layers on the surface like the imprints of time itself.

The stranger's gaze was drawn to something modern among all the dust and abandonment. Along one side of the room stood a small suitcase and a tripod, mounted a professional camera with a massive lens pointed downward. Its placement was deliberate: the lens was precisely aimed at a section of the floor where one of the glass panels appeared perfectly clean, clearly polished for filming.

The stranger stepped closer. The suitcase looked worn but in good condition, with scuffed corners and sturdy metal locks. The tripod and camera had several adjustment mechanisms, suggesting its owner had carefully prepared for precise, detailed work. The camera's indicator light blinked faintly green, signaling that the device was still operational or in standby mode.

He carefully examined the pristine glass panel that the camera was focused on. Its surface was so transparent that he could see reflections of light from

61

the lower levels of the tower. It seemed like more than just glass—it felt like a window into another reality, so vividly it reflected even the most minor details of light and shadow. For a moment, he thought there was something more within this pane than just glass. Perhaps a fragment of light trapped here for centuries or something lying in wait to reveal itself.

However, his thoughts returned to the suitcase and the camera. *Who had been here before him? And why had they left this equipment behind?* Had someone already explored this place, or was it abandoned in haste? The more he looked at these items, the stronger the feeling grew that he wasn't the first to try to unravel this place's mystery—and that the answers he sought might be closer than he thought. Could *Catherine* and Daniel have been here, or had they never reached this strange monument?

He studied the immaculately cleaned glass panel. His expectations were not disappointed: before him lay a view of a futuristic complex with troubling elements of isolation and control. The laboratory consisted of one large building and several more miniature replicas, mirroring the shape of the main structure, like reflections in a mirror.

The main building had a strict hexagonal shape. It was so massive that it covered an area equal to several football fields. At the center of the facade was the main entrance, near which stood minibusses and about a dozen passenger cars. The roof of the building was entirely covered with solar panels, which moved slightly, swaying like waves in a constant search for light. These panels appeared almost alive, adding an even greater sense of alienness to the complex.

Roads extended toward more miniature replicas of the laboratory from the four sides of the building. Two-lane pathways connected the main complex with these facilities. A transparent plastic dome completely covered one of the roads, forming a biologically isolated zone. It looked like a protective measure in the event of an epidemiological threat. Along the edges of the roads, thin magnetic rails could be seen, likely used for transporting goods or for the movement of sorting robots—similar to those often found in high-tech warehouses.

Each smaller building had solar panels on the roof and massive antennas resembling sunflowers. These devices were not meant for receiving television signals but served a more complex purpose. All the buildings were connected by single-lane roads, forming a network that resembled a nervous system organized for quick and precise interaction.

A little farther away was a separate complex that stood out with its architecture. It consisted of a round building with an attached semicircular structure that resembled a greenhouse and a square, single-story building with a green roof covered in trees and shrubs and neatly maintained paths. A separate road with a small parking area and security gates led to this complex. A narrow, one-way road connected it to the main building, along which magnetic rails also stretched.

The entire laboratory territory was surrounded by a double row of fences, separated by a ten-meter gap. Each wall had checkpoints leading to the main building and the second-largest square structure. The fences seemed impenetrable: tall, with elements of barbed wire and possibly electric charges. At the corners of the perimeter stood two-tiered watchtowers, from which guards could monitor every movement. Near the fences were small barracks, likely serving as housing for the guards. There were also parking areas for trucks and ATVs.

The helicopter pad stood out among all the infrastructure, located away from the main complex. It was connected to one of the smaller buildings through a quarantine-type airlock chamber, clearly emphasizing strict safety measures.

As he observed the territory, he noticed armed patrols moving chaotically along their routes. However, after twenty minutes of observation, it became clear that their movement was precisely calculated. They never crossed paths, only slightly entering each other's fields of vision, effectively eliminating nearly all blind spots. The security system was organized precisely and worthy of being a military facility.

There were no trees or bushes anywhere on the grounds. The only exception was the neatly trimmed green lawn, which seemed to highlight the place's sterility and artificiality. His attention returned to the roof of the main building with its moving solar panels, and he found himself thinking that this motion, barely noticeable at first glance, was strangely mesmerizing and almost hypnotic.

A strange feeling came over him as though someone was watching him closely. This sensation stirred something in his chest, making his heart race. Quickly, he crouched on the steel floor, turning his back to the windows, and leaned against the low wall, partially hiding behind it. Deep breaths helped calm his heartbeat slightly, but unease didn't leave him.

Shifting his attention to the items left behind, he turned on the camera's screen. A large message appeared: "Insert memory card." Of course, it had been removed. He scoffed quietly and carefully set the camera down, switching his focus to the suitcase. The locks weren't secured, and the briefcase opened quickly, but its contents were disappointing: a few empty notebooks, a flask with some liquid, and a pack of cigarettes.

"Some discovery," he muttered with a smirk.

He grabbed the pack of cigarettes—there was only one left inside. Placing it between his lips, he rummaged around for a lighter or matches but found nothing.

"Unlucky," he sighed, looking at the cigarette with mild regret.

With care, he returned it to the pack and slipped it into the inner pocket of his coat. Then, cautiously peeking over the edge of the wall, he tried to remain as inconspicuous as possible. He caught sight of a large black truck, unmarked and devoid of identifiers, passing through the first checkpoint almost without stopping. However, it lingered much longer at the second—nearly ten minutes.

Three staff members inspected the truck. One, carrying a massive device, circled the vehicle, scanning it as though with a short metal detector attached to a large monitor. The second, equipped with a more extended instrument, checked the vehicle's underside. The third—a man with a stack of documents and a computer-like device mounted on his forearm—compared data, repeatedly tapping on the screen. Finally, the driver hurriedly opened all the doors, including the cargo bay and engine compartment. After a thorough inspection, the documents were returned, and a guard commanded a fourth staff member to open the gates. The truck seemed to be allowed through without any questions, but the meticulousness of the check spoke volumes about the level of security.

However, his attention was drawn elsewhere: he noticed movement on the trail leading towards the tower. The activity was barely discernible about two or three hundred meters away, but his instincts screamed that visitors were already on their way. Not wanting to wait for them, he quickly headed for the staircase.

Descending to the door of the lower tier, he paused for a moment. A troubling thought struck him—he hadn't paid attention to the sea. The tide might already rise, and the room could be completely flooded. But he had no choice. Taking a deep breath, he opened the first door and entered the airlock chamber. The second door was difficult to open, and water spilled inside. The tide had indeed begun, which meant time was almost up.

He hurried through the corridor, swimming in the icy water that had nearly filled it. The temperature was unbearably cold, no more than ten degrees, but he had no alternative. Emerging outside, he swam toward the nearest rocks, seeking cover in their shadows. The cold stiffened his muscles, and each breath grew harder, but he kept going until he was far enough away.

Onshore, he quickly found shelter among thick shrubs, moving cautiously and glancing over his shoulder. Uniformed individuals without insignia had already arrived at the lighthouse. They patiently waited for the tide to recede so they could enter, unaware that he had long since left. Realizing no pursuit, he hurried along the coastline, sticking to the shadows.

After twenty minutes, the cold became unbearable. His wet clothes clung heavily to his body, and the salty wind from the sea tore away the last remnants of warmth. Nearly exhausted, he spotted an old, crumbling house. Unable to go further, he mustered his remaining strength and went to the shelter.

The house was in ruins: the roof had collapsed, the windows were boarded up, and the walls were riddled with cracks through which faint light seeped. He stepped inside and immediately headed for the fireplace. Inside were partially burned logs, and he found a box of matches on the stone mantel.

"That's more like it," he muttered with relief.

Lighting a fire near the lighthouse was risky, but he had a few hours until the tide shifted, and a small flame wouldn't draw attention. He lit the fire, and warmth slowly returned to his body. Remembering the cigarette, he frantically reached into his inner pocket. But when he pulled out the soaked pack, he realized his only cigarette had perished in the icy waters of the sea.

"Perfect, just perfect," he muttered bitterly, tossing the soggy pack into the corner.

He glanced at his watch and mentally gave himself thirty minutes to warm up and dry off. The heat from the fire dulled the cold, but exhaustion and dark thoughts still lingered. He needed to wait for the right moment and plan his next move, but time was running out.

However, thirty minutes by the fireplace turned into something longer. The warmth finally seeped into his weary body, but it came at the cost of his sense of time. He forced himself to get up only when the logs began to burn out and the firelight dimmed—nearly an hour had passed before he fastened his coat up to his neck and slowly stepped out of the dilapidated house. The cold wind immediately reminded him of its presence, cutting through to his bones, but he could no longer afford to linger.

Carefully surveying his surroundings, he ascended the narrow, overgrown path from the shore. The climb was anything but easy: his wet clothes snagged on bushes, and his boots slipped on the damp soil. After forty minutes, he finally emerged onto a road that stretched toward the old cemetery.

The cemetery seemed even more animated if such a word could be applied to a place like this. People moved slowly, almost as if in a trance. They spoke rarely, and their murmurs barely reached his ears. But now, something had changed. The number of people had significantly increased—possibly doubled or even tripled. Among them were many children who ran across graves and crypts, hiding behind monuments as if playing a silent and eerie version of hide-and-seek. Their faint, barely audible laughter struck him as incredibly unsettling and ominous.

He walked along the narrow path, trying not to make eye contact with anyone, but something felt off. People were beginning to turn toward him. They stared at him, almost unblinking, their gazes lingering for several long seconds before they returned to their aimless movements. This growing attention made him uneasy.

One group caught his eye—seven or eight people standing near a fresh grave. They stood motionless, their backs to the grave, and everyone was staring at him. Their faces were expressionless, their eyes glassy and vacant. The collective gaze, both intense and indifferent, made him feel exposed. His breathing quickened, and his heart began to pound.

Fighting the urge to panic, he quickened, trying not to make any unnecessary noise. Still, the overwhelming feeling of being watched wouldn't leave him. It seemed all eyes, even those he couldn't see, were fixed directly on him. A shiver ran down his spine, but he kept moving, knowing that stopping now was not an option.

The rest of the path through the cemetery was no less unsettling. He passed several dozen more people wandering in the same trance-like state as those he had seen earlier. Their movements were slow, almost unnatural, and their lingering gazes made him feel as though each of them knew something he didn't. Fortunately, the cemetery gates were now in sight, and as he passed through them, he felt a wave of long-awaited relief fill his chest.

Beyond the gates, silence reigned. The street was deserted, and the emptiness reminded him how exhausted he was. After walking a few blocks, he spotted the same familiar taxi he'd seen before. Approaching the car this time, he skipped any remarks or jokes. His voice sounded raspy and weary as he asked the driver to take him back to the hotel.

The driver didn't seem surprised by his appearance: soaked clothes, muddy boots, dark circles under his eyes. Without a word, he pressed the gas pedal. The drive was short, but it was enough time for the freezing, drained man to fall asleep instantly. His rest was shallow and uneasy. When the car stopped in front of the hotel, the driver didn't wake him. Instead, he turned off the engine. The sudden silence stirred something within the stranger, a fear that felt strangely profound, as though the quiet was anything but ordinary. His eyes flew open, his body tensed, and his head felt heavy, buzzing faintly.

He reached into his pocket and pulled out a crumpled, water-damaged bill — the only one he'd saved. His hand trembled slightly as he handed it over to the driver with a guilty look, almost apologizing for its state.

"Sorry... it's all I have," he muttered, barely able to hear his own voice.

The driver merely nodded, taking the money without a word. The stranger hurried into the hotel, desperate to escape the cold and find warmth. Yet, as soon as he stepped inside, that same unsettling sensation crept over him — that strange, inexplicable feeling that something had changed. This time, he was sure of it: the carpet was different. Where there used to be a gray carpet with red borders, now lay another one patterned with identical hexagons.

"Hexagons again..." the thought flickered through his mind.

These small details gnawed at him more and more. Irritated, he quickened his pace past the reception desk, catching a glimpse of an older man sitting by the fireplace. The man was playing chess on a small coffee table, but something about him set the stranger on edge. He couldn't pinpoint what—maybe it was his posture or the faint, almost imperceptible expression on his face. But he didn't linger to find out. All he wanted was to get to his room.

Once inside, he headed straight to the bathroom. Without removing his clothes, he turned on the hot water and stepped under the showerhead. The water pounded against his head and shoulders as he stood motionless, letting it cascade over him. Still fully dressed, he didn't care. Slowly, the heat of the water began to bring him back to life. Washing away the dirt, the salt, and the exhaustion, he started peeling off his clothes under the stream. He lost his balance and sank to the tiled floor at one point.

He stayed there, sitting under the hot stream, letting the water pour over him. Drop by drop, the warmth chased away the cold and tension, wrapping him in a fragile sense of safety. He felt calm for the first time in a long while, though the calmness felt deceptive. It was faint, fleeting—like the stillness before a storm.

Several hours under the hot shower became the only way for the stranger to bring himself back to a semblance of normalcy. His body trembled from exhaustion, but the warmth of the water slowly revived him. Finally gathering his strength, he wrapped himself in a robe hanging on a hook in the bathroom and went to the room. He carelessly draped his wet clothes over the drying rack in the bathroom, leaving them to drip and dry. Then he collapsed onto the bed, knocking the air out of his lungs. Within seconds, he was fast asleep.

He slept for nearly an entire day. All the accumulated physical and psychological exhaustion, the cold, and the tension of the past few days hit him at once. When he finally woke, the stranger sat on the edge of the bed, feeling the world around him slowly come into focus. He rubbed his reddened, sore eyes for a long time, then rotated his neck to shake off the ringing in his ears. Struggling to his feet, he went to the bathroom to retrieve his clothes—and was surprised.

His clothes were gone from where he had left them. He found his belongings on the nightstand near the television: neatly folded money, a small notepad with a tiny pen, and a set of keys with a strange charm attached—all that he owned. "Nice of them to leave this, but where are my clothes?" he thought. Before he could take further action, there was a knock at the door.

Opening it, he found no one, only a large bag with the hotel's logo left on the floor. Down the hall, a woman with a cart was slowly making her way, leaving similar bags by other doors.

"Thank you!" he called out, but the woman didn't turn as though she hadn't heard him.

He picked up the bag and shut the door. Inside was his clothing—neatly folded and freshly pressed. Even the shirt, once stained with blood, looked completely clean.

"Very interesting," he muttered, running his fingers over the fabric, then began dressing.

Quickly putting on his clothes, the stranger grabbed the bag containing his documents and headed toward the exit, distributing small items into his pockets along the way. He still felt a faint tiredness, but this time, it seemed more like the grogginess that followed a long sleep.

As he descended to the lobby, his thoughts once again returned to the peculiarities around him. The hallway carpets had changed yet again: this time, they were burgundy with large brown triangles. A chessboard was now on the coffee table by the fireplace, where the older man had sat the previous day. The game had just begun—white's first move, E4. It's a simple pawn aiming for a quick victory. There was no one around. The stranger shrugged and made his way to the exit.

Outside, he was met by the familiar damp and gray weather. The air was heavy with mist, and the city seemed to exhale a deep, quiet melancholy. He made his way to the familiar café, but it was eerily empty inside. Behind the counter stood the lone waiter, multitasking as a barista.

The stranger asked what was available to eat, but the response was disappointing: the kitchen was closed, and only yesterday's desserts remained.

"Then give me everything you have," he said, glancing at the counter.

The waiter offered him a couple of slices of cake, and he agreed without hesitation, ordering a strong double coffee. As he was about to step away from the counter, he added:

"Oh, and some orange juice, zest, and a pinch of cinnamon in the coffee, please."

He picked his usual corner table, the same one where he had sat the day before, lost in thought. When his order arrived, he added a pinch of salt to the coffee, took a sip, and closed his eyes for a moment. A straightforward thought came to him: before untangling the mystery of this strange city, he had to remember who he was.

He quickly ate the two large pieces of cake, almost gulping them down with the hot coffee that scalded his throat but seemed to sharpen his thoughts. Feeling energy return to his body, he gestured to the waiter for another cup. Pushing the empty cup aside, he pulled out the folder and a small notebook.

The printouts—yellowed, as if they had sat in storage for decades—occupied his thoughts. He began leafing through the pages, occasionally jotting notes in the margins. Yet, the longer he read, the more disappointed he became. Nothing he found explained the cascade of oddities that had overtaken this city.

Occasionally, he glanced up from the papers, looking out the window at the empty, rain-drenched streets as though hoping the answer lay elsewhere. Then, he would return to the text, scouring it for the slightest clue. But the answers eluded him, leaving only a more profound sense of unease.

An hour passed before he neatly folded the papers into the folder and tucked them into his coat pocket. He paid his bill, leaving a tip for the barista, and stepped out of the café. The air was fresh but cold, soaked with moisture that clung to his skin. The gray, wet city greeted him with its usual silence, an almost oppressive stillness that seemed to echo his unresolved thoughts.

By habit, he headed across the road to the usual spot where the taxi would usually be parked, but the car was gone this time. He paused, scanning the street, and noticed a vehicle a few blocks away. The driver, as usual, was sitting behind the wheel, buried in an oversized newspaper. The stranger made his way over.

"You're looking better," the driver remarked, glancing up briefly from the paper.

"And feeling different too," the stranger replied, adding with light irony, "Might even start dancing in a moment."

The driver, as always, didn't get the joke. He merely looked at him intently as if waiting for more. That focused attention stirred mild irritation in the stranger.

"Oh, never mind," he waved dismissively. "I've got a new route today. It might seem strange. I don't fully understand what I'm looking for or where I should be. But let's take a ride along the highway. You know, the one parallel to the old pub by the cliff? Or rather, the backroad, where the highway takes that sharper turn than usual."

"Got it. Let's go," the driver responded curtly, starting the engine.

The car pulled away smoothly, slowly gathering speed. They drove unhurriedly, almost cautiously, as the stranger carefully scanned the opposite shoulder of the road. His gaze darted back and forth, searching for something unusual. So far, nothing noteworthy has caught his eye. The scenery outside remained monotonous: wet asphalt, low shrubs, trees blackened by dampness.

The stranger noticed faint, barely discernible skid marks on the pavement and a damaged hedge along the roadside. He pointed out the spot to the driver and asked him to stop.

"It's not safe here; it's dangerous," the driver said firmly. "This stretch isn't visible enough because of the curve. Oncoming cars might not see us."

The driver finally pulled over several dozen meters further ahead, steering well onto the shoulder. He turned on the hazard lights and, glancing back, added:

"Make it quick. It's still dangerous here."

The stranger nodded and briskly walked back along the shoulder, keeping as far from the traffic as possible. He was acutely aware that, in his black coat, he was almost invisible to drivers against the gray, overcast weather—a risk that could lead to serious consequences.

Reaching the damaged hedge, he stopped and crouched down, carefully inspecting the scene. Beyond the visibly trampled bushes, a sharp drop began. Below, among thick shrubs and massive trees, something metallic glinted. The stranger focused, gathering his thoughts, and started cautiously descending. The wet, slippery dirt threatened his footing more than once, but he kept his balance.

As he drew closer, the wreckage of a motorcycle came into view. It was a matte black Ducati Diavel, a simple model with a large leather side case. The front end was destroyed—its radiator and fuel tank pierced by a massive tree branch, as if it had been speared in motion. Nearby, pieces of the suspension fork and the front wheel lay scattered. The ground around the motorcycle was soaked with oil and other fluids leaking from the shattered machine.

The stranger approached and examined the side case. He tried to open it, but the lock wouldn't budge. Then he remembered the set of keys he'd been fingering in his coat pocket. Pulling them out, he quickly identified the right one and unlocked the case. Inside was a small leather backpack. Judging by its weight, it was filled with something substantial, but the case contained nothing else.

His gaze lingered on the handlebars. Only fragments of the attachment remained where a phone mount had once been. The phone itself was missing. He scanned the area, hoping to spot the device, but it was nowhere to be found—it had vanished as if someone had taken it.

For several minutes, he stood staring at the wrecked motorcycle. It was a strange, almost painful contrast—a machine once built for speed and grace, now lying here like the victim of a brutal impact. But there was nothing else of use to be found.

Deciding to head back up, he chose a different route, further away from the steep incline he'd descended. The new path was less treacherous, though the rain and mud made the climb slow and exhausting. When he finally reached the road, he found himself closer to the car, and from this vantage point, he could make out the distant outline of the old bar where his first fragmented memories had surfaced.

His thoughts were interrupted by the sudden blare of the taxi horn—a harsh, guttural sound more like the roar of a beast than an ordinary car horn.

"You can't stand here! It's dangerous!" came the driver's voice from the half-open window.

The stranger nodded toward the driver as he quickly brushed off dirt, leaves, and grass clinging to his clothes. After allowing a passing car to pass, he crossed the road and made his way to the taxi. The biting wind grew fiercer, cutting through him like a knife.

Sliding into the back seat, he glanced at the ever-stoic driver, who remained as impassive as always. Settling into the seat, he placed the mysterious backpack on his lap and carefully unzipped it, revealing its enigmatic contents.

The first item he pulled out was a thick envelope filled with neatly stacked bills bound together with something resembling a bank band. Next, his attention was drawn to a large yellow envelope. Opening it cautiously, he found a photograph of the journalist he'd been searching for and two sheets of detailed information about her. The typewritten dossier outlined her career accomplishments and referenced several of her most notable articles. Beneath the photograph was a set of keys attached to a keychain with an address engraved.

Another notable find was a thick brown folder containing over fifty pages of text. Sections of the document were marked in light green highlighter, indicating key details the previous owner had deemed necessary.

Digging deeper into the bag, he uncovered two rolled-up maps. One was a detailed topographic map, while the other was a dated landscape map from 1900, which struck him as oddly specific. He also found a pair of old wristwatches with a white dial, a leather strap, and an inscription engraved on the back: *"Never waste a single moment. With love, Liv."* The inscription was written in Cyrillic, making it difficult for him to decipher the name immediately.

He slipped the watch onto his wrist and, after a moment of thought, asked the driver for the current time. Adjusting the watch and winding its mechanism with a few deliberate turns, he felt an unexpected calm wash over him, as if this small act carried some weight he couldn't yet comprehend.

A tiny folded note was attached to the watch's strap. Removing it, he unfolded the paper to reveal a handwritten message: *"This is crucial for our mission. Under no circumstances can it be lost."*

He stared at the note, his mind racing. The puzzle pieces multiplied, but the bigger picture remained frustratingly elusive. He clenched the watch on his wrist tightly as if trying to draw meaning from its presence.

The stranger carefully extracted a small black box from the bag. Inside was a rusty iron key and a tiny black pouch. Opening the pouch, he found two old wedding bands strung onto a braided leather cord, adorned with inscriptions on the inner and outer edges.

The final item in the backpack was a notebook encased in a leather cover embossed with the image of Veles — the Slavic god associated with travelers, nature, and fate. This symbol, a triangle resting atop what resembled an altar, struck a chord of familiarity in his mind. He couldn't place its significance yet, but he knew it meant something important.

The notebook was blank, but inside it was a striking silver pen, intricately engraved by hand. The pen clip bore a long numeric sequence—nearly twenty digits. He slid the notebook and pen into the inner pocket of his coat, keeping them close, and carefully repacked the rest of the items back into the backpack, adding the previously discovered documents.

As the taxi approached the square, the driver turned toward him.

"Same restaurant as last time? That's where you're headed, right?"

The stranger absentmindedly reached into the backpack and touched the first envelope containing the journalist's photo. Pulling out the key, he considered the inscription momentarily before realizing it was simply the key to his hotel room. He returned it to the bag.

"No," he finally said, his tone distracted. "I think I'll try something different today. Is there a bar here with a good steak and whiskey?"

"Sure, there's one close to your hotel. That bar—"

"Perfect," the stranger interrupted. "Let's head there."

The car circled the square, drove a few more blocks, and pulled up to what appeared to be a derelict establishment. Dim light from old lamps struggled to shine through the darkened windows, and the smell of a wood-burning fire wafted from an extension at the side of the building.

"Are you sure anyone's actually in there?" the stranger asked, more to himself than the driver. Handing over some cash, he stepped out of the vehicle without waiting for a reply.

Entering the bar, he was immediately enveloped by warmth. The room was unexpectedly spacious, its interior crafted from massive wooden beams, roughly hewn yet imbued with a rustic charm. Behind the bar stood an older bartender leaning casually on a roughly assembled wooden counter. In the center of the room, under a large dome, embers smoldered in a firepit.

Inside, only two patrons were sitting silently at a far table, sipping their beer in near-absolute quiet, interrupted only by the occasional crackle of the embers. The stranger approached the bar, greeted the bartender, and asked what was available to eat. Without a word, the bartender handed him a menu that listed just two items: pork barbecue and fish barbecue. He ordered the pork and a whiskey. The bartender nodded and gestured for him to pick a seat.

The stranger chose a table near a small fireplace in the corner. The heat radiating from the embers made him remove his coat. Outside the window, a courtyard with a massive withered tree planted in a bucket added an eerie charm to the scene. Soon, the bartender brought over a bottle of whiskey without a label and a simple appetizer: a few slices of bread, nuts, and cheese.

Taking the edge off his fatigue with a few sips of whiskey, the stranger felt warmth and tranquility gradually enveloping him. When the bartender brought his meal, he finished his second glass. The whiskey had a surprisingly smooth flavor, with a slight bitterness that left a long, warming aftertaste. At some point, he realized the bottle, which had been full when it arrived, was already half empty.

He attacked his meal with ravenous hunger, barely pausing between bites. The pork was juicy, its crispy crust perfectly complementing the smooth, fiery whiskey. Alternating between bites of bread and sips of the rich amber liquid, he seemed entirely absorbed in the process. From the outside, it might have looked almost feral, animalistic, but he couldn't have cared less about appearances or the thoughts of the bar's sparse patrons.

When the plate was empty, he pushed it aside and took a deep breath, feeling the relief of long-awaited satisfaction. The fullness brought an unfamiliar sense of calm, though the tension in his mind still lingered. He reached into his backpack and pulled out a thick stack of worn pages marked with pale green highlighter streaks.

He placed the papers on the table before him and took another sip of whiskey. His gaze briefly lingered on the dormant fireplace, where the embers glowed faintly before he focused on the text. His fingers instinctively traced the edges of the pages as he read carefully, searching for something crucial that might finally make sense of the chaos and oddities surrounding him.

The stranger read the lines intently, trying to find logic or some explanation for the events unfolding around him. Yet much of the text remained cryptic and detached from reality. The documents contained a myriad of data that, at first glance, seemed like a random assortment of numbers, descriptions, and procedures. But the more he read, the more precise a troubling pattern emerged.

The first pages described experiments on humans, including children. Initially, the tests did not appear to be illegal or sinister. Participants were shown identical images under varying conditions: changes in lighting, different music playing, or at varying times of the day. The primary goal seemed to be studying how participants' reactions to visual stimuli changed depending on their surroundings. It all seemed relatively routine, even mundane.

But as the text progressed, it delved into much stranger experiments. The materials mentioned tests involving unknown substances identified only by numbers: "0734, 0735, 0736." The participants were divided into four groups: men, women, girls, and boys. Each group was administered three different substances. The participants' identities were concealed—referred to only by initials, serial numbers, and birth dates.

After several weeks of taking the substances, the participants were assigned tasks: guessing to whom a particular object in a photograph belonged, predicting names based on images, and describing sensations evoked by music or visuals.

The further he read, the more unnerving the descriptions became. His grip tightened on the pages as he flipped through them, and he felt a creeping unease settle in.

However, the tests didn't stop there. The documents referenced intricate studies involving sensors, scanners, and equipment with names the stranger couldn't even recognize. These devices monitored the subjects during sleep, recording the slightest changes in their bodies and minds.

Particular attention was given to the perception of light and darkness. Subjects consistently gravitated toward darker tones, choosing dimly lit areas of the room as if it brought them relief. On the other hand, sound didn't affect them—loud auditory stimuli elicited barely any reaction. The experiment lasted three months but concluded with the note: "Experiment unsuccessful—no ability to return identified."

The following pages describe a new phase. This time, substances labeled "0737, 0738, 0739" were administered. The procedures grew harsher: subjects were deprived of sleep for extended periods, subjected to tests resembling the earlier ones, and their conditions were closely monitored. Each new group of participants replaced the previous one, but the fate of earlier participants was left uncertain. Only brief notes like "Experiment concluded. Proceeding to next phase" offered any clues.

Researchers focused on the reaction to "special light spectrums," paired with psychological tests and interviews. The descriptions became increasingly bizarre. According to the text, these spectrums uniquely affected perception, triggering inexplicable reactions not observed under ordinary lighting conditions.

The stranger ran his fingers over the highlighted lines, feeling a growing sense of unease. Clearly, something far greater than initially seemed to lie behind these studies. Experiments that started with examining perception gradually drifted into realms that defied conventional science. Darkness, light, substances, alterations in the psyche—all of it suggested an attempt to alter how reality was experienced.

He set the papers aside, took a sip of whiskey, and glanced again at the grill, where embers glowed faintly. His mind struggled to piece together a logical explanation for what he had just read. Each line pulled him further from the familiar. This town, the laboratory, and the people who lived here seemed part of something sinister, something he couldn't yet fully grasp.

The whiskey itself felt strange. It carried the familiar aroma and characteristic taste of classic peaty whiskey, yet there was an elusive note, something unusual that didn't fit the profile. Slowly swirling the glass in his hand, the stranger pondered what about the drink felt off. He had already consumed nearly 300 milliliters but didn't feel the usual effects of intoxication. Oddly enough, his mind was clear, and his body felt faint vitality, as though the whiskey worked in a way he didn't expect.

His thoughts were interrupted by the bartender, who seemed to have read his mind.

"This is an old family recipe," the bartender began, leaning on the counter. "It's regular peaty whiskey, but we add nutmeg, cinnamon, and black pepper. It's aged in charred oak barrels, over a century old. It's not as strong as your classic smoky whiskey, but you won't wake up with a headache, that's for sure. Should I bring you another glass?"

The bartender looked at him expectantly, but the stranger slowly placed the empty glass on the table and shook his head slightly.

"I don't think so," he replied, weighing the offer. "But pack me a bottle to go."

The bartender nodded knowingly and disappeared behind the counter. The stranger's gaze returned to the smoldering grill at the center of the room, the taste of the whiskey lingering on his tongue. There was something ancient and untamed about it, as though the very earth, peat, and wood had imparted their secrets to the drink. It was more than just whiskey—it was a fragment of history distilled into a bottle.

He pulled out the next bundle of papers, held together by large, rusted clips. This set contained about 15 to 20 pages, mainly scans from various books. At first glance, they appeared to be excerpts from religious texts. He recognized fragments related to Christianity, Hinduism, Islam, Buddhism, and even ancient pagan traditions.

The passages delved into the nature of light and darkness—how light is born, and darkness emerges. They explored the transitional moments between the two, how one gives way to the other, and the spaces in between that seem neither light nor dark.

Following these excerpts were interpretative notes, as though someone had attempted to weave all these teachings into a cohesive understanding. The notes suggested that the laboratory's researchers genuinely believed they could sense—or even measure—something supernatural. They referred to it as magic or divinity, something that could be felt at a specific point they called "the death of light and the birth of darkness."

The subsequent pages contained photographs of various artifacts. Some were ancient, encrusted with layers of time, while others appeared more modern. Surrounding the artifacts were numerous symbols, which the accompanying annotations attempted to decipher. The symbols were intricate, seemingly derived from various cultures and periods, each carrying layers of meaning that eluded immediate understanding.

But what struck him as most bizarre were the final pages. They consisted of equations, mathematical sequences, and patterns of numbers that seemed to belong to a scientific paper. Yet they were completely out of context. There were no captions or explanations to accompany the data—just rows of symbols and figures that might as well have been a foreign language to the stranger. It was as though these pages had been misplaced or perhaps intentionally included to confuse or mislead.

He frowned, leaning back in his chair and rubbing his temples. The collision of ancient mysticism and cold mathematics made no sense, but the deliberate way the pages were assembled suggested they were more than random fragments. He just couldn't piece it together yet.

The stranger moved on to the next section of the printouts, and what he saw made him freeze inside. Before him was a list of more than thirty names with surnames. The first column listed the names and the second contained dates of birth. The third column was titled "Days in Program," and the fourth, "Days After Program." But it was the fifth column that sent chills down his spine. Its header was starkly simple: "Outcome."

He ran his finger along the rows of the last column, and a cold shiver went down his back. Nearly every entry ended with the word "suicide." Only five rows stood out, but their contents were no less unsettling: "Death under unusual circumstances."

The stranger lingered on these entries, rereading them several times. The list contained no further details, but the subsequent pages revealed more. They included copies of obituaries describing the deaths of each program participant. There were far more obituaries than names on the initial list. He read one after another, desperately searching for clues. Some he read multiple times, struggling to believe what his eyes told him.

What struck him most was a separate group of ten obituaries. These were children, barely seven or eight years old. They had died in what was described as a mass suicide, though it was more apparent in the reports that their deaths were caused by their parents, who then took their own lives. None of the cases mentioned evidence of satanic practices, religious cults, or any apparent motive. Every account pointed to the same thing: nothing had foreshadowed the tragedy.

The stranger clenched one of the obituaries tightly in his hand. A single, relentless question echoed in his mind: "How could so many suicides be hidden?" He could not comprehend how such a wave of deaths could go unnoticed by the public.

He set the papers aside and stared into the space ahead of him, his thoughts racing as they tried to piece everything together.

"What the hell is going on here?" he asked himself, feeling the weight of the unknown pressing harder with each page he'd read.

On the last page of the printouts was a list titled with one simple word: "Candidates." It contained twelve names, along with their surnames and dates of birth. Most of the names meant nothing to him, but one immediately caught his attention—the surname of the missing journalist.

There was no additional information, no explanations as to why these individuals were on the list, how they were connected to the laboratory, or what tied them to the events unfolding in the town. The stranger stared at the page for a long moment before arriving at one clear conclusion: "This is where I need to start."

He carefully organized the papers, leaving out the page with the "Candidates" list. He placed the rest back into the folder and slid it into his backpack. However, he folded the list neatly in half and tucked it between the first few pages of the leather-bound notebook.

"I need to figure out where these people live and try to visit them. But under what pretense?" he thought, his eyes scanning the names again.

"Unknown if they'll want to talk to a fake journalist. And if they suspect something's wrong, they might even call the police... if such a thing even exists here," he thought, sighing deeply as he shelved the plan for tomorrow. "I'll deal with it in the morning," he concluded, his exhaustion mingling with the slight haze of alcohol.

Gathering his belongings, the stranger approached the bartender and asked him to pack the bottle of whiskey and something to snack on. After a few minutes, the bartender silently nodded and returned with a neatly wrapped package and the whiskey bottle encased in plain gray paper without any identifying marks.

He headed toward the exit after paying the amount and leaving a generous tip. As usual, the street was already shrouded in darkness and completely empty. The now-familiar cold wind, mixed with rain, barely bothered him this time. He hardly felt the chill, though he instinctively raised the collar of his coat and quickened his pace toward the hotel.

His silhouette dissolved into the gray mist of the street, where the dim light of the occasional streetlamp reflected faintly off the wet cobblestones. His mind was racing with hundreds of questions, but one stood out above the rest: "Who are these candidates, and why are their names on that list?"

Entering the hotel, he walked at an unhurried, measured pace over the dull burgundy carpet. His gaze landed on the older woman seated by the chessboard. Only one piece stood on the board—a white pawn on E4. For a moment, he nearly decided to approach her and strike up a conversation, but the woman unexpectedly turned to face him, staring directly at him. Her cold, unblinking gaze seemed to pierce right through him, leaving an unsettling feeling in its wake. A chill ran down his spine, and he suppressed the sudden urge to speak, instead altering his path and heading directly toward the staircase.

On his floor, he retrieved his keys to open the door to his room. But the lock wouldn't budge. He tried again, chalking it up to clumsiness after a drink or two, but after several attempts, he realized something was wrong. Looking closely at the key, he noticed it wasn't for his room. The tag displayed the number of the adjacent room.

Recalling how he had come to possess the key, a sobering wave of unease swept over him.

The stranger quietly approached the door to the adjacent room, inserted the key into the lock, and turned it. The door opened softly, and he quickly stepped inside to avoid drawing attention. Closing the door behind him, he paused momentarily to steady his breathing, which had quickened with nervous anticipation. Then, he began methodically surveying the room.

On the bed lay a neatly folded jacket and trousers. A shirt hung over the back of a chair, and part of the blanket was pulled back, creating the impression that the occupant had recently left. A fresh newspaper sat on the bedside table while scattered blank sheets littered the floor. The stranger crouched to look under the bed, finding only a single old coin rolled far beneath the frame. Ordinarily, he wouldn't have bothered, but the coin glinted with an unusual engraving on its reverse. He had seen something similar before.

He retrieved the coin, brushing off a thin layer of dust that suggested it had been there for quite some time. On closer inspection, the coin bore engravings identical to those on the pen he had found earlier in the rucksack with the leather notebook. Small, precise numbers were etched around the edge of the coin, interspersed with slight gaps.

Rising to his feet, the stranger mulled over the scene. "Someone's been tidying up here. No personal belongings, just a suit, a shirt, blank pages, and an open wardrobe."

He turned his attention to the wardrobe. Inside, a tracksuit hung from a wire hanger, and a pair of sneakers sat on the floor beneath. He checked the tracksuit pockets, finding them empty.

"Too convenient," he murmured under his breath.

His gaze fell on a small stool beside the wardrobe. Stepping onto it, he climbed onto the top of the wardrobe and checked the space above. Pressing his hands against the ceiling, he felt the slight give of old drywall. Carefully, he lifted one of the panels and found a small bundle, roughly the size of a chocolate bar, wrapped tightly in cloth.

He replaced the panel, climbed from the wardrobe, and tucked the bundle into his pocket. Glancing around the room one last time, he approached the door.

The stranger abruptly opened the door and came face-to-face with a small boy, no older than seven or eight. The boy stood just outside as if he had been eavesdropping. The stranger apologized, but the child said nothing, simply turning around and skipping away down the corridor. Choosing not to linger, the stranger returned to his room.

Once inside, he locked the door and slid the latch into place. The flimsy piece of metal was hardly a secure barrier, but it offered a faint sense of comfort. A nagging, inexplicable fear gnawed at him, and he couldn't shake the feeling that it wasn't unfounded.

The stranger retrieved the paper bag of printouts from his wardrobe and spread them across the bed. The sheets looked as before—yellowed, aged as if by time. Yet now they lay perfectly flat, as though they had been carefully pressed with an iron. At first glance, the text and his hasty handwritten annotations appeared unchanged, but something was off. The lines of text had become shorter, leaving more white space on the last page.

"It's as if someone edited the text, removing words and sentences," he thought, a slight tremor passing through him.

His rough, uneven notes, scrawled with a poorly functioning ballpoint pen, confirmed that these were the same pages he had marked earlier. But this did nothing to dispel the chilling realization that the content had somehow diminished.

He placed his rucksack on the armchair, took out the bottle of whiskey, and sat down, pressing the bag firmly against the backrest. In one hand, he held the bottle; with the other, he clutched his coat, where his newest discovery was securely tucked away. In this tense and guarded posture, exhaustion overcame him, and he drifted into sleep, the unopened bottle still gripped tightly in his hand.

He couldn't fully wake up this time. The stranger opened his eyes after about 4–5 hours of sleep, greeted by the dull ache of a hangover. The room was still dark, but faint light from the approaching dawn began to seep through the thick curtains. He took a moment to collect himself before attempting to rise from the armchair. Surprisingly, he managed it on the first try.

Staggering slightly, he made his way to the bathroom. Hot water streamed forcefully onto his back and neck as he leaned against the wall with one hand. His thoughts were chaotic, an unending swirl of questions without answers. Time seemed to dissolve under the shower. The room was filled with dense, almost impenetrable steam—the old exhaust fan had long since given up and could not handle the volume of hot air.

He thought about everything at once and nothing at all: the symbols on the notebook, the numbers on the pen and the coin, the strange printouts. "I need to compare the numbers on the pen and the coin. Maybe there's another puzzle hidden there," flashed through his mind. However, the primary focus of his thoughts was the list from the folder—the participants of the program under the codename "Candidates."

"How do I get them to talk?" That question lingered, refusing to leave his mind. Coming up with a concrete plan seemed impossible. "Well, I'll improvise based on the circumstances," he muttered quietly as he turned off the water.

After steaming himself thoroughly, he dried off slowly and put on his now all-too-familiar clothes. The weighty trench coat sagged heavily over his shoulders once more. He checked his pockets and confirmed that the notebook, pen, coin, and still-sealed bundle were all in place. The folder containing the discovered documents lay on the armchair, while the remaining printouts were strewn haphazardly across the bed.

He stood for a long time, staring at the folder. "I can't leave this in plain sight," he thought. But where can you hide it in a room like this? Taking a deep breath, the stranger returned to the bathroom. Standing on the toilet, he cautiously lifted one of the plastic ceiling tiles. He slid the folder in the gap he created, having first removed the sheet with the list of "Candidates."

"It's far from ideal, but under these circumstances, it's the best I can do," he reasoned.

Returning to the room, he began "hiding" the remaining printouts. One portion he folded neatly into a paper bag and placed in the closet, covering it with a fleece blanket to create the impression of casually stored belongings. Another portion he slid under the mattress. It was a simple and obvious spot, but perhaps obviousness would throw off anyone searching through his things.

The stranger pulled the notebook from his pocket and retrieved the folded paper with the twelve names. Running his eyes over the list, he chose the first name and wrote it on his palm with the pen. Folding the paper again, he carefully returned it to the notebook, which he slipped back into his pocket.

But his hand instinctively returned to his pocket almost immediately. He pulled out the same pen and the silver coin he'd found in the journalist's room. For a few moments, he examined their engravings closely. At first glance, they appeared identical, but it became evident that the designs were subtly different upon closer inspection. They were handcrafted from the same template but bore minor deviations. His eyes caught the numbers on both items. They were arranged differently, yet the recurring digits and faintly noticeable spaces hinted at a cipher.

"A1Z26," he muttered under his breath—a cipher where numbers correspond to letters of the alphabet.

Returning to the bed, he sat down and opened the notebook. On a blank page, he wrote out the alphabet in the center. Below it, he transcribed the numbers from the pen: **"1 16 26 9 15 - 10 3 17 20 21 17 6."** After a few minutes, he converted the numbers into letters: **"apzio - jcqtuqf."**

Next, he repeated the process with the numbers engraved on the coin: **"8 11 16 17 9 - 15 2 26 3 25 18 6."** The result was: **"hkpqi - obzcyrf."**

"Hmm... nothing," he muttered, frowning at the meaningless strings of letters. "Alright, I'll think about it later."

The stranger closed the notebook and slipped it

back into his pocket. Rising from the bed, he headed toward the door to leave his room.

Descending the stairs, he caught the faint sound of music. It was muffled as if coming from an old radio receiver, and something was hauntingly familiar. Judging by its tone, it was unmistakably from another era. The melody seemed to be coming from the reception area below.

On the ground floor, his attention was again drawn to the carpet. The very same carpet that seemed to change every time he came downstairs. Now, the floor was covered in a dark green rug with clear signs of wear and age, looking both antique and unusually heavy. "How do they manage to change it so quickly?" he thought, a twinge of perplexity crossing his mind.

Near the fireplace, the space was devoid of any presence. The chessboard and rocking chair were gone. The music had ceased, replaced by the loud ticking of an old cuckoo clock mounted above the fireplace. With its intricate wooden carvings, the clock looked like it had been crafted decades ago by a skilled artisan and was meticulously polished, perhaps daily. The stranger rolled up his sleeve, checked the watch on his wrist, and adjusted the time with a few deliberate turns of the winding key.

The watch under his sleeve caught his attention once more. On its edges, he noticed engravings he hadn't seen before—or perhaps had simply overlooked. Fine lines were etched with precision, but their meaning still eluded him. He tucked the watch back under the cuff of his coat and cast one last glance at the fireplace before heading for the exit.

Stepping out onto the street, he turned his thoughts to the next step: finding a device with internet access. A computer, tablet, phone—anything that could help him dig deeper into the enigmatic threads he was pulling at.

Several blocks later, he came across a small electronics store. The sign above the entrance was peeling, the windows coated with the grime of years, but the interior looked relatively tidy. The stranger stepped inside without greeting the elderly shopkeeper, who was lazily flipping through a magazine behind the counter. Heading to the back row, he found a small display featuring a few cameras and about a dozen old phones. Most of the models were outdated, with analog interfaces, but one modest smartphone with a small touchscreen stood out as the most modern option.

Next to the phone was an unopened box. The stranger grabbed it and made his way to the counter, curtly adding,

"SIM card and a top-up card, please."

Standing at the counter, he noticed a fridge near the door. Taking a step back, he opened it and pulled out a bottle of still water. The glass was frosted entirely—evidence that the bottle had been sitting there for weeks, if not longer.

The shopkeeper scanned the items and named the total. Without pulling out the entire wad of cash from his pocket, the stranger carefully counted the exact amount, leaving a small tip. The shopkeeper said nothing but slightly nodded as he took the money.

Back on the street, the familiar damp chill greeted him. The drizzle, accompanied by gusts of wind, quickly found its way under his coat. "I need a place where I can sit quietly with some tea and figure this out," he thought.

After wandering through several streets, he only found one other café, apart from the one he'd visited before. Its door was locked, and a "Closed" sign dashed hopes of getting in.

Sighing, he turned back toward the familiar café on the square. Inside, it was just as empty as it had been recently. The same lone waitress—who had served him before—stood behind the counter, sorting something in a small wicker basket.

"Sea buckthorn tea," he requested as he walked toward a table by the window.

Her surprised glance prompted him to correct himself.

"Or just tea with lemon, then."

While she prepared the order, the stranger sat at the table and unpacked the phone. After inserting the SIM card, he powered on the device. The smartphone emitted a faint startup chime as the stranger patiently entered the basic setup details. Once the phone was fully operational, the waitress returned with the tea. There were a few large cookies and a couple of candies on a small saucer.

Before she could turn to leave, the stranger quickly asked,

"What's the Wi-Fi password?"

Her expression turned noticeably more serious. Without saying a word, she reached for a small notepad, scribbled something on a page, and handed him the torn-off slip.

Connecting to the internet, he entered the first name from the list: **Marie Allison.** The results appeared almost instantly. But instead of relief, he was hit with shock. The face staring back at him from the photo of a "Distinguished Citizen of the City" was none other than the waitress who had just served him tea.

The stranger ran a hand over his chin, mulling over his next move. "How do I start this conversation? What do I even say?"

Finishing his tea in one big gulp, he coughed slightly, stood up, and approached the waitress.

"Could I get another cup of tea? It's just so delicious," he said with a slight smile.

The waitress gave him a look of mild surprise but nodded. The stranger pressed on, trying to sound friendly:

"You know, it just occurred to me... I'm practically a regular here, but I don't know your name. Sorry if this seems intrusive, but there's hardly anyone to talk to in this charming little town. It feels so... lonely."

The woman looked at him for a few seconds, her gaze a mix of understanding and sympathy. Then, she raised her hands and gestured, indicating she couldn't speak. She was mute.

The stranger froze, caught off guard by the unexpected revelation.

"You can't imagine how sorry I am," he said, trying to mask his surprise. "Maybe one day, I'll learn sign language... I really hope so."

She smiled slightly and nodded, gesturing for him to sit at the table. The stranger returned to his seat, realizing how much harder it would now be to talk to her. While she prepared the tea, he pondered how to proceed. *"If she really is that Marie Ellison, I'll have to find another way to learn what she knows."*

The stranger took a deep breath, acknowledging that he had absolutely no time to learn sign language. *"That would take at least six months in ideal conditions, and I don't have that kind of time."* He smirked, mentally trying on a new scenario. *"Guess I'll have to play charades. There's no other option. But how do I start without offending or scaring her?"*

He rose from the small old table, which creaked slightly under his hand, and walked to the bar counter. Taking a seat on a tall stool, he felt a strange unease. The counter had long lost its original function and had become an improvised display, cluttered with trays of sweets under glass domes. In the corner stood an ancient cash register, seemingly made a couple of centuries ago. A few small flower pots placed among the trays caught his attention.

The flowers looked peculiar. They were alive, but their stems, leaves, and buds seemed as if they were made of plastic. Intrigued, he reached out to one of them and barely touched a leaf with his fingers. It was real—soft and alive—but it seemed to have lost all its color, turning unnaturally pale.

"Just like everything else in this cursed town," he muttered under his breath.

The waitress interrupted his musings. Hearing his whisper, she turned around and gave him a slightly questioning look.

"That wasn't directed at you," he quickly clarified. "It's just... your flowers are extraordinary. They look like they're made of plastic."

She smiled and, shrugging her thin shoulders, gently shook her head. Apparently, she had heard this comment more than once. Finishing stirring the tea, she carefully moved the flower pots aside to make room on the counter and placed the cup in front of him. Then she stepped back and leaned against the table, her hands tucked into her apron pockets. Her gaze was attentive, studying as if she expected him to speak.

The stranger took a small sip of tea. The drink was hot, scaldingly tart, with a light bitterness from the lemon. He set the cup back on the saucer and reached for the sugar. Breaking a packet in half, he poured its contents into the tea and stirred it slowly with a spoon. In the silence, his movements sounded almost deafening. Every clink of the spoon against the porcelain echoed in his ears, breaking the strange stillness between him and the waitress.

His thoughts raced. He desperately tried to devise a way to start a conversation, but no words came. Finally, he decided to improvise.

"You know, this town feels calm and unsettling to me," he said, lifting his gaze to the waitress as if waiting for her reaction. "Strange things happen here. The streets, this bar, your flowers, even the weather. It's all like something out of another time, another world."

He paused, cautiously observing her face. She listened intently, not taking her eyes off him, but she revealed no emotion beyond mild curiosity.

"I recently visited your lighthouse," he began again after a few moments. "And, well, it's an extraordinary place, in my opinion. In my work, I've often visited various ruined castles, houses, towns, and, of course, lighthouses. But I've never seen such a combination of architecture anywhere. At first glance, it seems to be in one style, but on closer inspection, I noticed it's from three different eras. And honestly, it looks like it was built well before our era. Its height is astonishing, and its location—perched almost on a sheer cliff—with those proportions and architecture... It should've made some kind of wonders-of-the-world list. Yet I'd never even heard of it. Isn't it fascinating?"

She shrugged slightly in confusion, spreading her hands as if to show she didn't understand what he meant. Then, pointing to herself and her eyes and miming something small with her hands, she tried to explain.

The stranger raised an eyebrow in surprise, thought momentarily, and smiled.

"No, I mean the lighthouse behind the large cemetery. That one's not small—it must be at least fifty meters tall."

The waitress's smile widened. Turning around, she started rummaging through some papers on the table behind the counter. Finally, she found a small photograph. In it, a little girl with bright yellow hair posed in front of a four- or perhaps six-meter-high lighthouse painted white with red stripes.

The stranger took the photo and stared at it. The clearing in the picture looked familiar; the trees in the background seemed to have grown taller, but it was unmistakably the same place.

"I don't get it. Is this the only lighthouse you have here?" he asked.

She nodded silently.

"And it's located near the old cemetery that stretches several kilometers?"

Her smile grew even broader as she nodded again.

"So the cemetery isn't as big as I thought either?"

She shook her head enthusiastically, still smiling.

"Perfect... That's it—enough sampling the local booze," he muttered.

She kept smiling. The stranger decided not to

press the issue further and shifted the conversation. He started recounting stories about encounters with seagulls, embellishing the details and occasionally exaggerating for effect. This clearly amused the waitress.

"Do you also think it's a sign that I should quit this bad habit?" he asked, grinning playfully at her.

She nodded enthusiastically, still smiling.

"There you go," he said, wagging a finger at her with mock seriousness. "Fine, I'll believe you. But I still hate those wretched birds—with their enormous, nasty beaks and claws."

She laughed silently, covering her mouth.

During journalistic assignments, the stranger continued sharing made-up tales about places he supposedly visited on his motorcycle. Yet, all the while, his thoughts kept circling back to the lighthouse. It was real—he was sure of it. After all, he had the photograph in his room, the one he had found among the journalist's belongings. This was madness. The cemetery was actual, too; the taxi driver had taken him there. So why did this woman know nothing about the lighthouse or the cemetery?

As for the laboratory, he decided not to bring it up—not yet.

The stranger drained the last sip of his now-cold tea, placed some money on the counter, and thanked the waitress for the conversation. Standing, he made his way to the door.

"So what's the next step? Checking the lighthouse is still too risky. I don't want to run into the guards again. They're probably keeping a closer watch now, expecting the stranger who suddenly vanished." These thoughts occupied him as he stepped out of the café.

He needed to follow the next lead. Pulling out his notebook, he shielded it with his coat from the relentless drizzle. *Sophia Hamilton.* He repeated the name silently, committing it to memory.

Reaching into his pockets, he searched for his phone, but it was nowhere to be found. *It must have fallen out at the café,* he thought. *Maybe I should go back before I get too far.*

Just as he was about to turn around, a loud, raspy car horn blared across the street. The stranger looked up and saw the same old taxi. Waving to the driver in greeting, he crossed the road and headed toward the car. The taxi driver was quickly the most talkative among all the people he'd encountered in this town.

Plus, it was an opportunity to pass by the cemetery again—maybe he'd notice something new.

He had no intention of going near the laboratory. *Nothing I'll see standing by the fence, but they'll definitely see me. A second appearance won't be dismissed as an accidental wrong turn.*

"Good afternoon. How's it going?" he said, a faint smile playing on his lips as he approached the car.

The driver, his lips curling into a slight smile and his eyes betraying a lifetime of experiences, answered confidently:

"Good. Everything's fine. Just thinking about who to take to some unknown place this time."

"Well, I'd like to go there," the stranger quipped as he walked around the front of the car. "I've got a few names for my investigation. Maybe you know someone on this list? I'd be interested in talking to them."

"You never mentioned you were a journalist," the driver remarked, looking at him with mild surprise. "Last time we met, you didn't say anything about yourself. Got your memory back?"

"No," the stranger replied tersely, shrugging. I found some documents in a backpack by the roadside. But that's not important. I travel to interesting places and talk to people the editors suggest. They've sent me a list of names, and I need to interview a few of them—if they're willing to talk, of course."

He pulled a sheet of paper from his notebook and handed it to the driver. The man reached into his shirt pocket, took out an old pair of thick-rimmed glasses, and examined the names closely.

"Well, I know two of them. Sophia—the second name on the list—and this unpleasant fellow, Charles Gunn."

"That's great. Can you take me to Sophia? I'll try to talk to her," the stranger said eagerly.

"I can take you there, sure. But talking to her?

That's unlikely," the driver said, looking up and noticing the confusion on the stranger's face. "She's been in a coma for over two years now. No one knows why or how it happened. Back then, it was all over the papers. They say it happened at the summer fair—she was giving kids little gifts. Then she just collapsed. They rushed her to the hospital, but she never woke up."

The stranger's face darkened.

"I see. And what about Charles?"

"No idea. As far as I know, he's our esteemed policeman. But I've never been interested in his life and can't tell you much about him."

The stranger fell silent, deep in thought. *Sophia is in a coma, and talking to Charles might be a bad idea. Pretending to be a journalist in front of a cop—that's too risky.*

While the stranger mulled over his options, the driver's attention shifted to a page in the notebook, where numbers from the pen and the coin were scribbled.

"Interesting notes you've got there. Reminds me of the World War II era," the driver remarked casually.

"What?" The stranger snapped back to reality. "You mean this?" He gestured toward the notes in his notebook. "Yeah, someone I know left me a message but didn't explain what it means. I thought it was just a simple A1Z26 cipher, translated it... got some nonsense. Must be more complicated than that."

"No, you translated it correctly," the driver replied thoughtfully. "But there's probably a second layer to it. You cracked the numeric part, but now you need to rearrange the letters into the correct order."

"Can you do it?"

"Of course not," the driver chuckled. "If I'm right, this is a cipher generated by something like the Enigma machine or its equivalent. Back in World War II, breaking codes like this took a lot of effort. Polish, British, and French intelligence worked on cracking these. You'd need a cryptanalytic machine like the Bombe to figure it out. Museums might have one."

"Or the internet," the stranger murmured, a small smile forming.

"Yeah. Try finding a simulator or something."

"Can I borrow your phone for a couple of minutes?" the stranger asked.

"Why not?" The driver handed over an old button phone with a dim orange screen.

The stranger grinned and opened the car door.

"No rides today. Or maybe later. Thanks for the idea."

He stepped out of the taxi and quickly headed back toward the café.

Entering the café, the familiar chime of the doorbell made him pause for a second. *How many times have I heard that sound already?*

Marie, as always, was behind the counter, sorting through some items. Hearing the chime, she looked up and greeted him with a soft smile. The stranger nodded in acknowledgment and made his way to his previous table.

But the phone wasn't there. He quickly scanned the area, but there were no signs of it anywhere.

"Excuse me," he called to Marie, trying to get her attention. "I think I left my phone here. Have you seen it?"

Marie frowned slightly, deep in thought, then pointed toward the counter. The stranger approached and spotted his old smartphone nestled among folded newspapers and other odds and ends. He exhaled in relief.

"Thank you," he said, nodding as he picked up the phone.

Marie smiled again, raising her hand in a gesture that could be interpreted as "You're always welcome."

He sat down at the nearest table and powered on his phone. He opened his notebook while waiting for it to boot up and pulled out the damp sheet with the cipher. The ink was starting to blur from the moisture, so he quickly copied the information onto a fresh page to preserve it.

Once the phone was ready, he opened the browser and started searching.

"*Cipher decryption simulator... Enigma machine simulator...*" Thoughts raced as he skimmed through the links. After a few minutes, he stumbled upon some amateur websites offering virtual tools for working with ciphers.

"All right, let's give this a shot," he muttered.

It only took a few minutes to decode two more coherent phrases: *"Sound — Gravity"* and *"Light — Faraday."* But instead of clarifying things, they only added to his confusion.

"Ugh, I shouldn't have even bothered," he grumbled. "Fine, let's move on. The next name's waiting."

He typed the following name into the search bar. The first few attempts yielded nothing, but he found a small article on the fifth try. The name and surname matched and clearly referred to a local resident.

"Now that's a jackpot," he whispered to himself.

The article was on a personal website belonging to a clairvoyant. It described Taleri McKenna as a prophet, a clairvoyant of some generational lineage, and more.

"Well, this is someone I definitely need to talk to. Coming up with a pretext for that won't be hard at all," he said to himself, jotting down notes in his notebook.

The phone suddenly emitted a short, unpleasant beep, warning of a low battery. It only had a few minutes of power left. It seemed the time spent in the café had drained the battery significantly—or maybe the phone needed a new one altogether.

The stranger quickly copied Taleri's address and phone number into his notebook. Rising from his seat, he approached Marie.

"Do you have a charger for this phone?" he asked.

She examined it and nodded approvingly, extending her hand. He handed her the phone.

"I'll stop by this evening or maybe tomorrow for tea," he said with a small smile.

Marie nodded again in agreement.

This time, he left the café without saying goodbye, offering Marie a faint smile before stepping out.

To his astonishment, the taxi he was sure had been following him for days was nowhere to be seen. The stranger smirked to himself. *"Well, let's try to find him… or at least another taxi. There's no way he's the only one in this town."*

However, ten minutes of wandering the streets yielded nothing. The roads were deserted, and the drizzle had turned into a full-blown downpour. The rain lashed against him in thick, heavy drops, forcing him to seek shelter under the awning of a bus stop.

The shelter was a transparent glass structure, long stained with rust and grime. A faded city map hung on one wall, its street names barely legible, peeling, and torn in places.

The stranger pulled out his notebook and checked the address of the clairvoyant. *"Morrison Street,"* he read to himself. Predictably, the street wasn't marked on the decrepit map.

"Now would be a great time to have my phone," he thought irritably. *"But I'll have to improvise."*

The street was empty of pedestrians, though he no longer found that strange. The light drizzle had shifted to heavy, pounding drops, and the gusts of wind that had previously swept through the town had disappeared entirely. Now, the rain poured in steady, vertical sheets, creating the effect of an enormous water curtain. Overhead, the sky was blanketed with thick, dark clouds, further deepening the oppressive atmosphere.

He stood under the shelter for several minutes, watching the empty streets, until he spotted a bus approaching in the distance. It was an old vehicle, its two large round headlights casting a dim yellow glow that seemed on the verge of fading. A sign in the windshield displayed the route number: "27."

The stranger waved, hoping the driver would see him in the darkness. The bus deliberately slowed down, stopping just short of a large puddle near the shelter. The door creaked open with a loud, grating noise, setting his teeth on edge.

Climbing inside, he immediately addressed the driver:

"Do you pass Morrison Street?"

The driver hesitated, clearly running through the route in his mind, then replied with a slight frown:

"You'll have to walk a bit. No bus goes directly there. It's in the old part of town. Once you get off, it'll be about a five-minute walk through a few blocks. You shouldn't get lost from there."

"Perfect," the stranger nodded, tossing a few coins into the fare collection dish.

The door closed with the same unpleasant screech, and the bus rumbled forward, its engine groaning as it resumed its journey.

The stranger tried to observe the fleeting scenery outside the window for the first ten minutes of the ride. But the view was monotonous: gray, lifeless buildings and empty streets. Not a single passer-by. Before long, he grew tired of it, though he kept looking out, hoping to see something unusual. Yet, throughout the journey, he didn't see a single soul.

The bus rumbled for 30 to 40 minutes, though the stranger wasn't keeping track of time. When the driver finally began to slow down, he did so with extreme caution, as if afraid that a sudden brake might cause his aging vehicle to fall apart. Coming to a halt, the driver opened the door and pointed in a direction with his hand.

"That way, straight ahead. You'll come across a sign that says *'Witch Street.'* That's what it used to be called—now it's Morrison Street. Good luck."

"Thanks," the stranger replied curtly as he stepped onto the deserted street.

The drizzle had softened into a melancholic whisper of raindrops tapping against the stone facades of buildings. As he followed the driver's instructions, the rare houses lining the road increasingly caught his attention. Most of them were abandoned, with their windows and doors boarded up with wooden planks and faded, outdated signs clinging stubbornly to crumbling walls.

Further along, newer buildings began to appear—multi-story ones—but they too looked lifeless, as though deserted decades ago.

"Why does this not surprise me in the slightest?" he thought with bitter irony, continuing forward while keeping an eye on the occasional street signs in search of Morrison Street.

He arrived at a perpendicular road after passing a few more two-story houses. *"I need number one,"* he thought. But which way to go—left or right?

"The right side looks gloomier... so it must be that way," he smirked as if trying to make the choice feel less weighty.

He walked for another ten minutes before finally coming upon a small, single-story house with a sign that read: *"Morrison Street, 01."*

The house was far from new. No higher than half a meter, a decorative fence painted in a peeling lavender hue stood before it. The house's once-white facade had turned mostly gray with age and grime, large portions concealed beneath a thick carpet of ivy. The ivy clung to the walls as if embracing the structure, supporting its aging frame.

By the entrance to this green fortress were dark burgundy rose bushes. They grew untamed, sprawling in all directions, seemingly competing with the ivy for sunlight. The bushes looked alive and well cared for, a surprising contrast to the otherwise decrepit appearance of the house.

The small gate had neither a bell nor a sign. Beyond it, a narrow path of cobblestones barely three or four meters long stretched from the gate to the house's porch. On either side of the path lay an overgrown lawn, thick with moss in many places, giving the impression that time had stopped here.

The stranger unlatched the small gate, stepped through, and closed it behind him. He walked down the cobbled path toward the porch. On the porch, his attention was drawn to a bell—a small brass one with a lever attached to the side. A string hung at the end of the lever, clearly meant to be pulled to ring the bell.

"How quaint," he murmured to himself. *"Well, here goes nothing."*

Reaching for the string, he gave it a firm tug, the faint chime of the bell breaking the eerie silence around him.

He pulled the string a few more times. The bell let out a sharp, jarring chime that resonated unpleasantly in his ears, making him wince. He waited a few seconds, listening to the silence. No response. Just as he was about to pull the string again, a voice grumbled from behind the door:

"Who's out there? Coming, coming! If I get up for nothing, I'll curse your bloodline!"

The voice was female, elderly but surprisingly energetic, and tinged with irritation. The stranger stepped back half a pace from the door.

The door creaked open, revealing a woman around sixty-five years old. She was short and wearing a dark purple dress. Her hair was tucked neatly under a kerchief, and she had a thick, patterned shawl draped over her shoulders. The shawl was embroidered with a design that resembled the combination of ivy and roses—just like those he'd seen growing on the house's walls near the porch.

"Hello, I'm looking for—" he began, but before he could finish, the woman cut him off:

"Come in, but take off your shoes at the door."

Not wanting to argue, he stepped inside, quickly removing his shoes, and hurried after her as she disappeared through a doorway.

They passed through a small room where the furniture seemed to be a mismatched collection from different eras. The stranger's gaze lingered momentarily on an old side table and a rickety chair, then he followed her into a cozy living room.

A brown couch sat beside a glass coffee table paired with wooden beams that looked hand-carved, likely centuries ago.

"Sit," she said, gesturing to the couch.

The woman sank into a massive armchair with a high back, throwing a blanket over her lap. The blanket looked soft and warm, seemingly designed for days as cold and damp as this one.

She looked in his direction, but her gaze was strange—distant as if she were staring not at him but through him.

"You have many questions," she said calmly. "But not all questions need answers, and not all answers should be heard. You have little time left in this state, so ask quickly."

Her words were sudden and enigmatic, leaving him momentarily stunned. *"In this state? What does she mean?"* The stranger forced himself to regain composure.

"What's happening in this town?" he asked, trying to buy himself time to process her cryptic remark.

"Past. Present. Life and death," she replied curtly.

"Don't waste the little time allotted to you on empty words," she said sharply.

He frowned, trying to grasp what she meant.

"Why do I have little time?" he asked, his tone more insistent now.

"Your light has long since gone out," she replied, looking directly at him but with that same detached, otherworldly expression. When you return to your body, it depends solely on *them*."

"I need to ask more specific questions, or this will lead nowhere," he thought, forcing himself to stay focused.

Her words hit like a cold blow. The stranger stifled the urge to ask what she meant by "returning to his body" and instead pressed forward, concentrating on the task at hand.

"What do you know about the laboratory? And why are you on the list with other people? Why is the list called 'candidates'?"

"The laboratory seeks answers to many questions," she began slowly. "They're trying to solve a problem that has plagued humanity for centuries—no, millennia. They're searching for the truth on both sides of absolute nothingness: the point where light dies and darkness is born. The candidates are people who don't belong to this world."

Her words sounded entirely disconnected from reality.

"What does that mean?" he asked, leaning forward slightly, unable to hide his growing curiosity and unease.

She was silent for a moment, staring at him as if measuring his ability to comprehend, then spoke:

"The point where light dies and darkness is born is the moment where everything—light, life, warmth—ceases to exist. And at that same point, something new is born. What the laboratory calls 'the awakening.' They believe certain people can sense this point. To see it. To experience it. These special people don't belong to this world and will disappear if they don't leave it."

"Special people?" he echoed. "You mean… people like you?"

The woman smiled faintly, but her eyes remained cold.

"Each of us has a past and a future, a purpose. Some notice it; some pass by. But if you see it and feel the fragility of existence—it changes everything."

"What's happening in the laboratory?" The stranger's voice was tense, barely masking his anxiety.

"Experiments," the woman answered coldly, her face devoid of emotion. "They study everything, testing hundreds of theories and hypotheses. Their main focus is experiments with light and sound. They're trying to understand how these elements affect people under special conditions, how to amplify their effects, and what comes next."

"But... why? Why do they need this?" He leaned forward, hanging on her every word.

"Because they seek what they cannot understand. Their experiments fail. Now, they're combining light and sound with chemicals and other substances, draining the physical and psychological strength of their subjects. This is just a continuation of what happened hundreds of years ago."

"They killed all those people? Forced children and adults into their cult?" His voice trembled, and a shadow of anger appeared in his eyes.

"No one was forced," the woman replied emotionlessly. "And they killed themselves."

"After their experiments?" He struggled to contain

his anger. "Why would parents give their children up for this?"

"We all believed we could change our future. That each of us could awaken again."

"They killed the journalist too?" He leaned forward, almost rising from the couch.

"The scientists don't kill anyone," the woman said, looking straight at him. "She disappeared. But I feel that she's no longer on this side. And she won't remain long on the other."

"Why is the lighthouse important?" he asked, abruptly changing the subject.

"It's an anchor," she answered briefly. "That's something I can't explain. There's not enough time."

"Why are you telling me all this?" He stared at her intently, suspicion in his gaze.

"Because you're important. You can end this."

"What does that mean?" His voice betrayed open unease.

"You'll know very soon," the woman said, tilting her head slightly as if weighing her words. "I'm not allowed to say."

"Does the laboratory forbid you?" He leaned closer.

"No," she replied firmly.

"Do the others on the list of 'candidates' know all this? Can they tell me?"

"No, almost none of them know," the woman squinted slightly. "It's my gift. No one else will tell you, even if they could—they won't have time."

Suddenly, her eyes darkened, and her voice became low, stern, almost a whisper:

"The back door. Through the grove, crouching about fifty meters. There's a shed—behind it is a path through the woods. It will lead you back to town. The hotel is safe. They don't know who you are yet."

He froze, staring at her in shock. At that moment, a loud knock resounded against the front door as if someone were pounding on it with their fists.

"Hurry, they've come for you. Go through the back door," she said quickly, pointing in the direction.

He stood abruptly, his head spinning from the rush of adrenaline. Without looking back, the stranger ran where she had directed, leaving the woman behind as rising commotion echoed from the hallway.

Within seconds, he crouched and pushed through wet grass, brushing thorny branches aside with his hands. He reached the dilapidated, rotting shed and, running around it, found a narrow path barely visible through the overgrown grass and the low-hanging branches of dense trees. The forest surrounded him on all sides—dark, damp, and nearly impenetrable.

Fifteen minutes later, he emerged onto a paved street. Then, he realized he'd been running barefoot the entire time, leaving his shoes in Taleri's house. Looking down at his wet, frozen feet still in socks, he muttered a quiet curse.

He walked a little further down the street, turned into an alley, and saw the old bus with its round, dim headlights slowly pulling away from the stop. It was the same bus he'd arrived on. It had completed its circuit and was now heading back.

The stranger sprinted, shouting and waving his arms to catch the driver's attention.

The driver saw him, stopped the bus, and opened the door.

"To the central square," he said curtly, still catching his breath.

"Of course," the driver replied.

The stranger handed over a banknote, quickly reached an empty seat, and sat down, trying to ignore the water slowly seeping from his soaked socks and forming small puddles on the floor.

There were only a few passengers on the bus. On the back seats, he noticed a scruffy, bearded man asleep across the benches. The bus started moving, and the stranger felt slightly relieved for the first time in hours.

The return trip felt much faster. The stranger sat with his frozen feet drawn closer to the floor heater, which barely emitted warmth and needed repairs. Throughout the journey, not a single coherent thought formed in his mind. There was only a strange, hollow sense of emptiness.

When the bus reached his stop, he stood up and glanced back at the rear seats. The man was no longer there.

"He must have gotten off at one of the earlier stops, although... I don't remember the bus stopping anywhere. Maybe I didn't notice," he thought.

He nodded at the driver in gratitude, stepped off the bus, and walked briskly toward the hotel. The rain had intensified, but he did not notice the puddles he splashed through, almost running.

Entering the hotel lobby, he moved quickly through it, not even glancing toward the fireplace. However, he did look down when he felt polished wood beneath his feet instead of the soft carpet he expected. The carpet was gone. The floor appeared almost new as if it had just been replaced.

The stranger climbed the stairs, turned the key in the lock, and pushed open the door to his room. Without undressing, he headed straight to the bathroom. Once inside, he removed his wet clothes, carefully hung his coat on the hook behind the door, and dropped the rest onto the floor.

The scalding hot water hit the back of his head and shoulders, washing away the cold and exhaustion.

He slid down to the shower stall floor, wrapping his arms around his knees. The water continued to cascade over him, enveloping him in heat, but he no longer paid attention. His thoughts churned like waves crashing against the cliffs of his mind. The sheer volume of information that had come at him in the past few days felt overwhelming. None of it made sense, yet it all carried an unsettling certainty that everything was connected.

Sitting on the cold tiles, he drifted off to sleep unnoticed.

After about two hours of sleep under the monotonous noise of running water, he reluctantly opened his eyes. Realizing where he was came over him slowly, like a dawning sunrise. The stranger turned off the water, flexing his numb fingers. With some effort, he stood up, wrapped himself in a towel, dried off, and put on the hotel's bathrobe. He exited the bathroom, taking the wet coat from the hook.

But after only a few steps, his body succumbed to exhaustion. His legs buckled, and he nearly collapsed onto the floor, correcting his fall at the last moment. He fell onto the bed, breathing heavily like he'd just completed an arduous journey. Struggling to pull himself under the blanket, he dragged the damp coat with him, too drained to get up and hang it. His muscles ached, his consciousness faded, and within minutes, he was in a deep, almost oblivious sleep.

This time, he slept for about eight hours.

The stranger opened his eyes and stared at the texture of the pillowcase just inches from his face. He had fallen asleep clutching the damp coat, never resting his head on the pillow. His gaze lingered on the pillow, searching for answers in its barely discernible pattern.

A sudden gust of wind slammed against the window, which flew open with a loud bang. The window hung precariously on its hinges and trembled under the force of the wind. The unsettling creak of the window persisted for several seconds. The stranger ignored the sound—his thoughts were far away, and his mind felt blank.

Squeezing his eyes shut, he rolled onto his back, spreading his arms to the sides. For a few moments, he stared at the ceiling with his eyes closed as if expecting clarity to come on its own. Then, gathering his strength, he pushed himself up from the bed, tossing aside the heavy, damp blanket.

Sitting on the edge of the bed, he slowly turned his head toward the window, which continued to swing open with each gust of wind. Outside, the same dreary scene awaited—gray skies, rain, and a chilling wind scattering fine droplets across the empty street.

"I'm so tired of this," he muttered to himself quietly, almost resignedly.

Forcing himself to rise, he headed back to the shower. This time, the hot water wasn't for warmth but to fully wake himself up. The shower didn't take long; most of the time was spent trying to clean his clothes. The pant legs were muddy up to the knees and still damp. He washed them in the sink and attempted to dry them with a hairdryer. The effort was only partially successful, but he put on the pants, a shirt, and the hotel's soft slippers before stepping back into the room.

Approaching the bed, he donned his coat, checking the contents of its pockets. Everything was in its place. Suddenly, he remembered the small box he'd found in the journalist's room but had yet to open.

Taking it out of his pocket, he carefully unwrapped it, trying not to tear the paper. Inside was an old box decorated with glitter and butterfly designs. It looked like something that had once been given with great affection.

Opening the box, he found a dozen multicolored crayons, half of which were partially used. They rested atop a folded newspaper clipping. The brittle paper contained a short article about a missing seven-year-old girl, offering no details beyond a photograph.

The photo showed a little girl delicately holding the same box between her fingers, smiling brightly.

The stranger stared at the old photograph for a long time, feeling an inexplicable heaviness in his chest. Finally, after a moment of hesitation, he carefully rewrapped the box and hid it in the secret compartment along with the printouts.

"I don't think this artifact holds much value for my investigation," he muttered to himself. "But it meant something to the journalist. And honestly… it's hard to tell right now what might be important and what isn't."

He closed the compartment and paused momentarily, listening to the sound of the wind howling outside the window.

Yesterday, while searching for a taxi, he noticed a small clothing store sign. Deciding it was time to update his wardrobe, the stranger headed there first. The soft slippers he wore weren't suited for walking through puddles in this weather, and his clothes were starting to look worse.

Descending to the first floor, he was surprised to see a couple—a man and a woman of middle age—standing by the reception desk, discussing their check-in. Beside them were neatly packed leather suitcases. The stranger glanced toward the fireplace, expecting to see the familiar chessboard. This time, only one piece remained—a fallen white king.

He checked the wall clock and then compared it to his wristwatch. After winding his watch slightly, he once again admired the simplicity and beauty of the antique mechanical clock, which a skilled craftsman had clearly restored. Then he made his way to the door.

Beneath his feet was a brown rug, clearly artificially aged to match the hotel's overall decor better.

"Hm, fair enough," he muttered with a smirk, stepping outside.

The drizzle had started again, prompting him to quicken his pace. As he thought of it, the shop—or the tailor's workshop—wasn't huge.

Upon entering, he noticed an elderly tailor with square glasses in thick frames and a measuring tape draped around his neck. The old man's tired gaze carefully examined his visitor.

"Good day. How are you? I need to refresh my wardrobe," said the stranger.

"Good, good. Of course, come over here, and I'll take your measurements," the tailor replied, gesturing toward a small platform.

After a few minutes of measurements and thoughtful murmuring, the tailor suggested he sit on the sofa.

"We don't have any coats, just suits. But I can clean yours for you," the tailor offered.

"That would be wonderful," the stranger agreed.

He emptied his coat pockets, carefully laying their contents on the coffee table. Folding the coat in half, he handed it to the tailor, who disappeared into the adjacent room. When he returned, he brought several pairs of trousers, shirts, ties, and a pair of rounded-toe shoes.

"The fitting room is over there," the tailor said, pointing to a screen in the corner.

The stranger tried on the suggested clothes. Everything fit perfectly. He selected a white shirt and a tie, fiddling with the knot for a few moments. Emerging from the fitting room, he was met with the tailor's approving gaze.

A few minutes later, an older woman, presumably the tailor's wife, appeared. She handed him his cleaned and pressed coat before disappearing again without a word. The stranger didn't even have a chance to thank her.

Putting on his coat and checking the pockets, he asked the tailor about the cost. The amount was surprisingly low, and he left a generous tip, nearly doubling the quoted price.

"Thank you for your work!" he said as he stepped out to the soft chime of the shop's doorbell.

He headed toward the café.

The familiar, almost painfully comforting aroma of freshly baked pastries and coffee beans greeted him as he entered. After the gray and gloomy streets outside, the interior felt bright, almost blinding. He instinctively squinted before making his way to the counter. This time, Marie wasn't there. Instead, a woman in her mid-forties with short dark hair stood behind the counter, muttering something under her breath as she stared at a tablet.

"Good morning. How are you? Would you like a cup of coffee and a few croissants?" he asked politely.

"Good morning. I'm doing great. Of course, you can. Have a seat, and I'll bring it right over," she replied with a light smile.

He settled into his usual table, ordering the most straightforward black coffee this time. A few minutes later, the waitress brought his order: a cup of coffee, a minor milk pitcher, sugar sticks, two croissants, and tiny jelly jars.

"Excuse me, is Marie not in today? I left my phone charging with her yesterday—did she mention anything about it?" he asked.

"Yes, she did," the waitress said, pulling his phone from her apron pocket. "She took the day off for personal reasons. She also asked me to tell you that she's sorry she didn't get to say goodbye. She said she was glad to have met you."

"I see. Thank you," he nodded, taking the phone.

The waitress smiled and returned to the counter. He took a few sips of his coffee before pulling out his worn notebook. As he began to jot down disorganized thoughts, the past few days' events replayed in his mind.

"Taleri, the clairvoyant or whatever she called herself, said a lot but essentially nothing. The laboratory is some sort of crazy cult obsessed with eternal life. Parents voluntarily participate in experiments, subjecting their children to tests. According to the printouts, it all ends in suicides. And no one, except the journalist and her editor friend, seems to care. Judging by what I've found, they disappeared without a trace. Though, if the clairvoyant is to be believed, the journalist is still alive. She said something like, 'She's not yet on this side. But she doesn't have much time left on that one,' or something to that effect."

"Why was Taleri so protective of the scientists? If the facts are to be believed, they're nothing more than mad cultists who've destroyed hundreds of lives. Maybe even

more—those are just the names that made it into the printouts, if those can be trusted. Who put them together, and why did they give them to me? And why me?"

The stranger turned on his phone and searched for information about the remaining names on the "candidates" list. However, no matches came up. Only one name—the last one on the list—matched the name of a bar restaurant on the pier: "Martinos." The description read, *"A small bar with the best shore view."*

"The bar where I woke up," he thought. *"It was closed then... but what if it's open now?"* He decided to check it out.

Before leaving, the stranger requested another cup of coffee to go.

A few minutes later, the waitress brought him another cup of coffee in a disposable cup. She had added a touch of sugar, cinnamon, and lemon, even though he hadn't requested it. The stranger left a few banknotes for payment and a tip.

"Thanks for the coffee," he nodded.

"Good luck. Take care," she replied.

He stood up from the table and headed for the exit. Pulling up the collar of his coat, he stepped out into the familiar grayness of the streets.

The pier wasn't far. As he walked, his mind turned over the clairvoyant's words. Why had she been so adamant about protecting the scientists? When pieced together, the facts painted them as mad fanatics who had caused the deaths of hundreds.

What was this "point of light's death and darkness's birth"? And why had she said he didn't have much time?

When he reached the pier, the weather had started to clear. The rain had stopped, and the waves had calmed. However, the atmosphere remained heavy and gray, as if the world itself was holding its breath.

Then he saw something completely unexpected. A person in a black tracksuit with a hood pulled up was running toward him. The face under the hood was obscured, and an inexplicable sense of unease crept over him.

As the runner drew closer, the stranger froze. The face beneath the hood looked familiar. It was the editor from that very same newspaper. The runner passed within inches of him, and the stranger turned to follow with his eyes. But the person was gone. It was as though they had vanished into thin air.

At that exact moment, a sharp pain pierced his chest. Looking down, he saw the white shirt beneath his coat staining a deep burgundy, the spreading blotch framing his black tie. The cup slipped from his hand and hit the pavement with a dull thud.

He collapsed to his knees, gasping for breath. His uncooperative body continued its descent until he lay sprawled on the damp asphalt. As his vision faded, he saw people rushing toward him—five, maybe seven, coming to help—but their faces blurred into indistinct shapes.

Life left his body.

Angela conducted her evening rounds as usual, giving careful attention to each room despite the emptiness of the floor. Her exhaustion was evident — she spent most of her time at the hospital with almost no rest. Returning to her station, she poured herself another cup of coffee, sat down at her desk, and began sorting through the pile of documents left by the daytime doctors and their inexperienced interns.

The corridor was almost entirely silent, broken only by the soft hum of medical equipment. Over decades of work, Angela had grown so accustomed to this sound that she even missed it at home, where the silence felt unsettling in comparison.

But recently, her life had grown increasingly difficult. There was a shortage of staff, constant overtime shifts, and now an inexplicable sense of unease that followed her even during the rare hours she spent at home.

A sudden scream from one of the rooms made her jump. Her coffee cup tipped over, spilling its contents onto the open documents before her. She sprang to her feet, tossed a paper napkin over the stain, and ran toward the source of the sound.

In the room, sitting upright on the hospital bed, clutching his chest with both hands, was a patient — a man around 35 years old. His face was pale, but his eyes burned with a strange mixture of fear and confusion. His unkempt hair stuck out in all directions, and his hands gripped the center of his chest tightly.

Angela rushed to his side, quickly checking his condition while trying to calm him down.

"Incredible... You decided to come back to us," she said softly, gently easing him back onto the bed. "Do you know where you are? What year is it?"

She gently moved his hands away from his chest. Beneath his palms, there was nothing but a faint 15-millimeter scar near his heart.

"Is your heart hurting? What do you feel?" she asked, slipping a pulse oximeter onto his finger.

The man took a shaky breath, clearly trying to calm his rapid breathing.

"I... I don't know where I am," he said hoarsely. "I guess... a hospital. The year... I don't know that either. And... I don't remember my name."

Angela froze momentarily, then gave him a reassuring pat on the shoulder.

"Don't worry. If you understand that you're in a hospital, it means your brain is working. Your memory will come back; give it some time. For now, let's go step by step. Your friends came by recently and left us some information. You didn't have any ID when you were admitted, so this is all we have."

She picked up the file with the notes and, sitting on the edge of the bed, continued:

"Michael. They said your name is Michael. You've been in a coma for about a month. You were brought in from the city park after a patrol officer saw you collapse suddenly. Our doctors didn't find any injuries. We ran many tests, but you didn't wake up... until tonight."

Michael nodded slowly, still struggling to piece his thoughts together.

"Friends... What friends?" he asked, a hint of doubt in his voice.

Angela raised an eyebrow.

"They were very concerned about you. They asked to be informed the moment you woke up, no matter the time—day or night. They care deeply, though they only showed up a week after you were admitted. A woman, around 30, with long blonde hair, and a man, about 30–35, with a short military haircut."

She handed him a business card with a phone number on the back.

"Who are they? Do you remember them?" she asked, watching his reaction closely.

Michael shook his head, staring at the card.

"No... I don't remember anything," he murmured, his voice tinged with distant but noticeable despair.

"I need to reattach your IV," Angela said, pointing to the broken catheter in his arm. "And you need to lie down and rest. I get it—you've 'rested' enough to last a lifetime—but you just came out of a coma. You need to regain your strength. We'll call your friends tomorrow morning, but only after the doctor checks on you."

She carefully replaced the catheter and affixed a few new sensors to his chest and temple.

"Now rest."

But sleep didn't come. Lying on his side, Michael stared out the window, motionless. The stars were visible beyond the glass, their cold light almost unreal, as if he were in another world. He simply gazed at the celestial expanse for hours until he decided to get up.

The first moments were challenging. His legs, unused for so long, barely obeyed him. He nearly fell but managed to steady himself, gathering his strength. First, he turned off the monitor displaying his pulse and vitals to avoid the loud alarm that would sound when he removed the sensors. Then he carefully peeled them off and headed to the bathroom.

Standing before the mirror in the small room, he paused. He studied his reflection for several minutes—an emaciated, unkempt face with an overgrown beard and slumped shoulders.

"Damn, I don't remember a thing," he muttered.

There was a razor with a trimming attachment on the counter near the sink, its green light indicating a full charge. He picked it up, unplugged it, and set the trimmer to its lowest before trimming his hair. Then, removing the attachment, he shaved off his beard and mustache completely.

The process took about fifteen minutes, and he spent several more cleaning up after himself.

Returning to the room, he began rummaging through the cabinets, searching for clothes. In one, he found a sealed bag with the hospital's label. Opening it, he pulled out a pair of dark, worn jeans, a shirt, a vest, and white sneakers.

In another, smaller sealed bag, he found the contents of his pockets: a bit of loose change, a wallet with no cards but a couple hundred dollars in cash, and a black leather notebook with a silver pen attached.

A little irritated, he tossed the notebook onto the bed and started dressing. After distributing the change and wallet into his jeans pockets, he sat on the edge of the bed and picked up the notebook, flipping through it absentmindedly.

Michael examined the worn leather cover of the notebook; its texture was rough but somehow comforting. The silver pen clipped to it felt disproportionately heavy as if it concealed more than just a writing tool. Carefully opening the notebook, he noticed the yellowed pages, weathered as though time had left its mark. Many of the pages had been torn out.

The first few were blank. On the third, he spotted clear handwriting, precise and almost calligraphic:

"If you're reading this, it means you're no longer where you were."

Michael frowned. The words seemed to be addressed to him personally, yet there was no name or clue as to who had written them. He turned the page and saw an intricate drawing—a circle with intersecting lines that resembled an ancient symbol or diagram. Beside it was a note:

"You don't remember, but you already know."

"What nonsense is this?" he muttered, absent-mindedly tracing the design with his finger.

On the next page was a series of numbers interspersed with letters:

"A1-23, B5-12, C9-47…"

"Why would I have written this?" Michael murmured as he flipped the page. The following pages contained only fragmentary notes—sentences cut off mid-thought as if written in a hurry.

After turning a few more pages, he found an envelope inside the notebook. On it was written:

"Important."

His fingers froze as they brushed against the envelope.

"Alright, let's see," he whispered, carefully opening it.

Inside was an old, faded photograph. The image showed three people: a young woman with short blonde hair, a man in a dark suit, and… himself. He looked younger and clean-shaven in the photo, with a faint smile. In the background stood a lighthouse whose shape felt vaguely familiar.

On the back of the photo was a note:

"The lighthouse—point of origin."

Michael stared at the photo, unblinking. His questions multiplied, but the answers remained elusive.

"Who are these people? Why don't I remember anything?" he murmured, gazing at the younger version of himself in the picture.

Suddenly, soft footsteps echoed from the hallway. Someone was approaching. Michael quickly lay back down, pulling the thick blanket over himself. The door creaked open, and Angela appeared in the doorway.

"Can't sleep?" she asked, studying him attentively.

Michael gave a vague shrug.

"We thought as much. A coma can disrupt the body's internal rhythms. Rest up. If you need anything, call me."

She gently closed the door and walked away. Her exhaustion seemed to catch up with her; she hadn't noticed he was dressed under the blanket or that the monitor had been turned off.

Michael let out a sigh of relief and picked up the notebook again. Retrieving the photograph, he studied its details.

The picture showed a small clearing on a cliff dotted with sparse trees. In the background stood a lighthouse, about ten meters tall, painted white with broad red stripes. There could be hundreds of lighthouses like it around the world, and this brought him no closer to clarity.

"I'll have to look up references to this online," he muttered, setting the photo aside.

Michael slowly got up from the bed, picked up the business card from the table, and slipped it into his pocket. Carefully cracking the door open, he peeked into the hallway. Empty. Moving quietly but quickly, he headed toward the stairs. Passing the nurse's station, he noticed a tablet lying on the desk. Without hesitation, he swiped it, hiding it under his coat.

On the staircase, he stopped, overwhelmed by a wave of dizziness. His body was still weak from the coma, and he realized he needed to be more cautious. After a short rest, he descended to the first floor, where the hospital was bustling with activity. Doctors hurried through the corridors, occasionally glancing at Michael, but to his surprise, no one stopped him.

Once outside, he quickly put as much distance as possible between himself and the hospital. Dawn was breaking, and the city was coming alive. People hurried about their business, cars honked, and frustrated drivers shouted at each other. The cacophony of sounds echoed in his ears.

Turning into a narrow alley, Michael stopped to catch his breath and calm his racing heart.

The alley was quieter, more subdued. Exhausted and dejected, he walked a dozen meters, instinctively keeping low, before stopping by a dumpster. Sitting down and leaning his back against its metal side, he felt the cold, damp asphalt beneath him soaking up the remnants of the rain. Nearby, steam and smoke billowed from the vents and chimneys of numerous restaurants and cafes. The air was thick with the heavy smell of frying meat, rancid oil, and a medley of other sharp, almost suffocating odors. The stench of urine and rotting food mingled with the rest, creating an indescribable, oppressive atmosphere.

And yet, despite it all, Michael felt an odd, almost unnatural sense of calm. This filthy, reeking street corner felt like the safest, cleanest place in the world to him. Sitting there, curled up with his arms around his knees, he tried to gather his thoughts.

After about fifteen minutes of motionlessness, he finally decided—it was time to think about what to do next.

He had almost no money—barely a couple hundred dollars in his pocket. Worse still, he had no identification. He didn't even honestly know who he was. All he had was the name "Michael," given to him at the hospital, unsupported by any memories.

He also had a business card with a phone number, supposedly belonging to his friends. It was his only concrete lead. But some strange feeling prevented him from taking obvious actions and stopped him from dialing the number. It was the same feeling that had driven him to flee the hospital. He didn't understand why, but he was sure it mattered.

He slipped the business card back into his pocket and took out the notebook. Tucked between its pages was the photograph of the lighthouse. Michael stared at it long, trying to understand why this image felt so significant. Logically, it made sense to start with the lighthouse, but where was this place? How could he get there without money or documents?

Pulling out the stolen tablet, he quickly realized it was useless—the screen demanded a password. With a heavy sigh, Michael stowed it in the inner pocket of his coat. After taking a few deep breaths, he stood up from the dirty asphalt, brushed off bits of trash, and headed down the alley toward the bustling street.

As soon as he stepped out, the chaotic noise of the city assaulted him. The roar of engines, the chatter of pedestrians, the hiss of buses, and the screech of brakes all merged into an overwhelming cacophony.

He walked for hours, crossing streets, dodging aggressive drivers who sped through red lights, and enduring their shouted insults. It grated on his nerves, but he pressed on, determined to ignore them.

After some time, his wandering brought him to a pawnshop—a dark, shady establishment with grimy windows and a battered sign. Michael crossed the street quickly, once again drawing curses from impatient drivers, and stepped inside.

A thin man greeted him, wearing a dirty baseball cap from a local sports club and an absurdly gaudy ring on the middle finger of his left hand. With faint amusement, Michael noticed that the man wore a watch on each wrist.

Without saying a word, Michael placed the tablet on the counter.

"No papers, huh?" the man asked with a mocking squint.

"No," Michael replied curtly.

"I'll give you fifty. No more."

"Deal."

Having pocketed the money, Michael quietly exited the pawnshop, which was crammed with trinkets and outright junk. Outside, he paused in thought. He now had a little more cash, but it wasn't enough to solve anything significant. He wandered on, pondering his next step, and soon noticed a small park. Among the trees, a sign on a columned building caught his eye. The sign read: *"City Library."* The building looked old, with peeling paint and slightly uneven steps leading to heavy wooden doors.

"Time to figure out exactly where I need to go," he thought, heading toward the entrance.

Despite their massive and imposing appearance, the library doors opened surprisingly quickly. Michael stepped inside and climbed a short flight of stairs, arriving in a spacious hall. At the entrance, behind a large wooden desk, sat an older woman. She spoke softly to two young women, pointing at printouts before her—likely giving them directions on where to find books or information.

Trying not to draw attention, Michael walked almost on tiptoes toward the far corner of the room, where a row of computers stood. Most of them were unoccupied—only one girl sat close to her screen, staring at it with tired eyes as if she had been searching fruitlessly for hours.

Michael chose the computer furthest from everyone, sat down, powered it on, and opened the search bar. But instead of typing, he paused, pulling his hands back from the keyboard.

Taking the notebook from his pocket, he scanned the cryptic notes within again. Then, he retrieved the photograph and scrutinized it closely, searching for any coordinates, hints, or clues that could help. But as before, the back of the picture offered nothing helpful.

"This won't work," he muttered quietly.

He decided to try reverse image search. Placing the photograph in front of the webcam, he snapped a picture and started the search. Within seconds, the results appeared: 2,324 partial matches.

"Well, no one said this would be easy," he smirked.

After ten more minutes of comparing the results, Michael finally found the lighthouse. The image on the screen was nearly identical to the one in his photograph. His gaze lingered on the monitor—there was something oddly compelling about this place. Below the image were the lighthouse's name and exact coordinates. He quickly jotted them down in his notebook.

The lighthouse was in Scotland, United Kingdom, while he, based on what little he'd gathered, was in the United States.

"A plane's out of the question," he thought. *"So I'll have to look for a way by sea."*

Michael opened a map, zooming out to assess the distance. It was immense but still within the realm of possibility. He zoomed in again to study the nearby streets and the port's layout. It was only a few blocks away, and it happened to be one of the largest ports in the world. Memorizing the route, Michael shut down the computer, closed all applications, and headed for the library exit.

He left quietly, avoiding the gaze of the elderly librarian, and stepped back onto the street. Orienting himself, he set off toward the port.

When he reached the outskirts of the port, he was met with towering fences topped with barbed wire and numerous security checkpoints. Observing from a distance, Michael realized he'd need to find another way inside.

Circling the area, he spotted a small homeless shelter nearby. A group of people loitered outside, their appearance typical for such places.

"Who else would know more about this place than them?" Michael thought, heading toward the shelter's entrance.

The two young women in bright yellow T-shirts over long-sleeved tops greeted Michael with warm smiles and asked how they could help.

Michael briefly explained his situation: he couldn't remember anything, had no money, and no documents. He added that the police could not assist beyond checking their databases and filing a report. Despite the bleak story, the woman remained upbeat and tried to reassure him.

One of the women gestured toward the entrance, still smiling.

"Michael, you can grab a bite to eat if there's anything left," she said, pointing to a table. "And over there, you can rest. I'll bring you a blanket and a sheet."

"That's not necessary; I'm fine," he waved her off.

"Alright. Stay here for a while. Later, our staff will try to figure out how to help you," she replied, her tone as cheerful as ever.

The room was spacious, with rows of beds in the center that reminded Michael of a wartime hospital. Although there weren't many people, the pile of folded mattresses and belongings suggested the shelter had many regular occupants.

Michael walked over to a table by the wall, where boxes of leftover cookies and thermoses of hot beverages were laid out. Pouring a cup of light brown liquid that smelled vaguely like coffee, he grabbed a piece of cookie and began scanning the room.

His attention was drawn to two men playing cards near one of the beds. They appeared to be in their mid-to-late thirties, talking animatedly and laughing.

Trying to seem as natural as possible, Michael approached and greeted them.

The men turned out to be very friendly and open. Before long, they began sharing their stories, explaining that they were undocumented workers employed at the nearby port. They described how they'd found a way to earn money, though the conditions were far from ideal. Half of their wages went to their supervisor, who managed to smooth things over with the HR department.

"Maybe you could help me get a job with you?" Michael asked cautiously. "Just temporarily until I figure out who I am."

"I think we could try," one of the men replied, glancing at his watch. "Our boss is finishing his shift in a couple of hours. He'll be at the bar nearby."

"For now, let's enjoy this… delightful beverage," the other added with a grin, raising his cup of coffee.

After a few hours of playing cards and chatting about unrelated topics, the group decided it was time to go. They packed their cards, cups, and other small items, rolled up their mattresses, and carefully tucked them under the metal beds. Then, after a quick look around, they slung their heavy backpacks over their shoulders and headed out.

Michael silently followed them.

They arrived at a place that lived up to every stereotype about bars. The air was thick with noise, chatter, and the pungent smell of alcohol. It seemed the entire work shift had gathered here—men in grimy overalls and unkempt patrons eager to relax with a cheap drink. The bar's cacophony nearly drowned out the soft tunes from a jukebox in the corner. Glasses cluttered the tables, some empty, others barely touched.

Near the center of the room, a group of men were already drunk in the billiards area, loudly arguing as they monitored the game.

On the right side of the hall, a row of four tables with soft couches stood apart from the chaos. At one of these tables, a man sat in the company of another, who appeared to be his conversation partner. Judging by his demeanor and how the two men waved at him, it was clear this was the boss.

When Michael's new friends entered, they immediately started waving to the man and calling out their greetings. He barely turned his head, nodding slightly before resuming his conversation.

The men made their way to him and, upon approaching, cautiously broached the subject.

"Hey, boss. So, here's the thing… We've got a relative—well, almost a relative," one of them began. "He's got the same kind of problems we do. He could really use some help, like the kind you gave us."

"We vouch for him," added the second man.

The boss smiled and nodded briefly toward his companion, signaling the end of their conversation.

"Bring me a couple of pints. The good stuff," he said dismissively before gesturing for Michael and his companions to sit at a table opposite him.

"So, who are you? Where are you from?" he asked bluntly.

"Michael. I have memory problems—I can't remember much," Michael began, attempting to explain.

"Alright, enough," the boss cut him off, waving a hand. "I'm guessing they already told you about the terms?"

Michael nodded silently.

"I need someone to operate a forklift. Can you handle it?"

"I think I can manage," Michael replied tersely.

"Good. Tomorrow at 8:45, go to the central checkpoint. There'll be an envelope for you. Inside are your pass and papers. Sign them, take the pass, and leave the envelope there. Once you're inside, wait—someone will come to get you and take you to orientation. Clear?"

"Crystal," Michael replied, doing his best to sound confident.

"Good. Now get out of my sight," the boss said, waving them off toward the exit.

Michael felt a slight relief—at least the first step was taken. Tomorrow, he'd have to figure out what came next.

Not wanting to linger in the bar and waste his limited funds, Michael bid his new acquaintances goodbye and returned to the shelter. Looking for another place to stay seemed impractical; a cheap alternative would take time he didn't have.

He grabbed a mattress from the neatly stacked pile at the shelter and headed to the far corner of the dimly lit room. The weak light from ceiling lamps cast long shadows, and the silence was dense, almost absorbing any sound and turning it into a whisper.

Lying on the mattress, Michael tossed and turned, trying to piece together fragments of thoughts.

The notebook he'd found in his possession wouldn't leave his mind. Its pages, filled with cryptic phrases, seemed to call out to him yet remained frustratingly elusive. He tried to recall something about himself—just one moment from his life before waking up in the hospital—but the void inside him was terrifyingly absolute. At the same time, everything that had happened since waking up came to mind with painful clarity—even down to the faint scent of Angela's old perfume. The fragrance felt oddly out of place in a hospital, where such things were, as he believed—or thought he believed—prohibited. Yet it lingered in his memory as though he'd encountered it before.

The hours dragged on. Near dawn, his eyelids began to droop, but sleep eluded him. Gritting his teeth, he got up and stepped outside as the first weak rays of sunlight pierced the thick morning mist. With three hours still to go until his meeting, he decided to look for an open café for coffee and a bite to eat.

To his surprise, the city was already alive: small cafés, bakeries, shops, and even a pawnshop were open. Stopping in one shop, he picked out a few items. A hastily purchased bag proved practical, though its worn appearance hinted at a long history. He noticed a small box behind the counter containing old wristwatches on his way out. For some reason, he felt an immediate urge to buy one. Pointing at a simple Seiko watch with a leather strap; he handed over the money without negotiation.

After putting it on, he checked the time. The watch was ticking, and the steady movement of the hands gave him an odd sense of order and calm.

He made his way toward the port. Across the street from the main entrance was a small café with three or four tables inside and a couple of high-standing tables outside. A group of workers in dirty jackets stood chatting at one of the outdoor tables. Their shift seemed to be starting in a couple of hours.

The port itself buzzed like a massive anthill. Cranes, manipulators, and forklifts moved in a chaotic yet constant rhythm.

Michael ordered a coffee and asked for caramel syrup with a pinch of salt—an unusual request even to him, but the result was satisfying. The drink was hot, strong, and prosperous. However, the croissant he bought to go with it was dry and clearly not fresh. He wrapped it in a napkin and tucked it into his bag for later.

Sitting at a table, sipping his coffee, Michael stared at a single spot, his mind blank. It was the same unnerving emptiness that had haunted him since waking up. But within that void, something was beginning to take shape—like the faint outlines of buildings emerging from the morning fog.

When the time came, Michael shouldered his bag, thanked the barista, and went to the checkpoint, where workers were already gathering. The crowd buzzed with chatter, short exchanges, and the occasional joke. Some stood silently, gazing toward the port as if mentally preparing for the day ahead.

Pushing through the crowd, Michael spotted a table with boxes, folders, and stacks of envelopes. It appeared to be a delivery drop-off point, as couriers weren't allowed into the port itself.

Michael's eyes immediately landed on a bright orange A4 envelope labeled with a sticker that read: "Michael." He grabbed it, opened it, and pulled out its contents without hesitation. Inside were an access badge and several documents. Flipping through the pages quickly, he didn't bother reading the text, instead focusing on the signature lines. Once he had signed everywhere required, he carefully placed everything back into the envelope, slung his backpack over his shoulder, and followed a group of workers to the turnstiles.

Swiping the pass, he saw the light turn green and stepped through.

The port greeted him with its characteristic cacophony: the hum of engines, the beeping of lifts, and the muffled shouts of workers. The flow of people split—some headed for the next set of doors, while about a dozen gathered by a row of chairs along the wall. Michael joined the group near the chairs.

The wait wasn't long. Soon, a short, thin man with a heavy belly emerged from a nearby office. The lanyard holding his badge seemed stretched to its limit, barely holding on.

"Michael. Michael Smith!" the man called confidently, scanning the group.

Suppressing a smirk, Michael raised his hand. *"Such a creative surname,"* he thought, holding back a grin.

"You're with me," the man added, nodding in his direction. "Forklift driver. I hope you have experience."

"I hope so, too," Michael muttered under his breath.

The man called a few more names, assigning them to forklifts as well, before leading the group of recruits inside.

The day began with theory. In a small room with monitors, the group was given safety instructions, shown training videos, and handed numerous documents to sign, including liability waivers. Afterward, each recruit was assigned a forklift and given a brief hands-on tutorial on its controls.

The day ended with driving tests. To Michael's surprise, he performed exceptionally well, even though he was sure it was his first time operating such machinery. *"I guess I was a laborer in a past life,"* he thought wryly.

At the end of the day, Michael was given a key to a locker for storing his belongings and instructions on how to begin and end his shifts. Leaving the port, he reflected on how quickly the first day had passed but realized, with some regret, that he was no closer to his goal. He held onto the hope that things would move faster the next day.

However, one day, it turned into two, then three. Operating forklifts consumed all his time, and it wasn't until two weeks later that he was finally allowed to work with containers and ship-loading operations.

Around that time, he began talking to sailors during short breaks, managing to strike up conversations with deckhands and even captains of smaller vessels. Then, he met the chief engineer of a container ship headed for the United Kingdom.

Michael's story of memory loss and a family supposedly waiting for him in Scotland moved the man. The engineer proposed a risky plan, which Michael accepted with relief.

The plan was simple: during the loading operations, Michael would use a pretext to board the ship and hide in a hold typically used for smuggling contraband. He would remain there until the boat set sail. Once at sea, he could emerge and pretend to be the engineer's assistant.

Getting on board went smoothly, but the wait in the hold dragged on. Departure was delayed due to a damaged container of equipment. The captain insisted on waiting for insurance agents to inspect the damage and oversee the re-sealing of the cargo.

Michael spent nearly 24 hours in the dark, stuffy hold before the ship finally set sail.

Once underway, he emerged from his hiding spot. The engineer handed him a uniform and explained his duties for the next two weeks—the expected duration of the journey to the United Kingdom.

There wasn't much work aboard the ship. Most of Michael's time was spent cleaning, polishing floors, and tidying things. On modern container ships, nearly everything was automated, and manual labor was more of a formality. Still, his "position" allowed him to remain aboard, which was all he needed.

On the third day, luck was on his side. During a cargo inspection, he encountered a damaged container with a box sticking out containing a tablet. Opening it, Michael was thrilled with the find. The device became his constant companion for the remainder of the journey.

Time seemed to fly by. To his surprise, the ship had a reasonably good internet connection. He immediately began researching the destination and the lighthouse that had taken hold of his thoughts.

Days passed in relentless searching. Michael scoured the web for any clues, delving into the lighthouse's history, structural changes, records of its keepers, and sailors' accounts of stopping in the nearby port.

What he found was disappointing: the lighthouse was relatively new and unremarkable. It was a simple structure serving its functional purpose. Michael understood that the answers he sought weren't likely to be found online. He'd have to uncover whatever he was looking for in person.

While continuing his research online, Michael tried scanning the photograph for face recognition and searching for matches. However, he had no luck. The faces in the pictures remained nameless, as though they had never existed. This failure weighed on him, but he forced himself not to dwell on it, convincing himself to focus on his immediate goal.

As days went by, Michael grew closer to the chief engineer. The man was kind and understanding, and his easygoing manner helped ease Michael's tension. Together, they devised a straightforward but risky plan for Michael to disembark without attracting attention.

Official appearance in the port was impossible — his lack of documents would immediately raise suspicions. Exiting "in the open," even on the outskirts of the port, was equally unfeasible due to the high risk of being noticed or stopped by security. Their daring plan involved immediately lowering a lifeboat into the water, allowing Michael to reach the shore undetected.

Timing this operation required meticulous planning. Many factors had to align: minimal security activity, suitable weather, and a lack of prying eyes aboard the ship. Rowing the distance to the shore would be challenging, but it was doable. The engineer assured Michael it was the best and safest option. Michael agreed—there were no alternatives.

Every night before falling asleep, Michael rehearsed the plan in his mind, like preparing for a critical exam.

He stood by the ship's railing, staring into the darkness where the Scottish shore lay hidden beyond the horizon. At night, the sea became particularly menacing: its endless black expanse resembled an abyss, ready to swallow anyone who dared challenge it. The plan he had been refining for days felt plausible and utterly insane.

A lifeboat, a rope, 15 kilometers of frigid Scottish waters, and 300 miles of land… It all seemed simultaneously achievable and completely mad.

The height he would need to descend from was intimidating—50, perhaps 60 meters. Michael imagined the moment the lifeboat touched the water, and he slid down the rope, gaining a speed that would make his heart race uncontrollably. He knew the wind at that height would be unforgiving—strong gusts capable of knocking him off balance and possibly plunging him into the sea if he lost control for even a second.

In his head, he went over the details again and again. *"The key is to choose a spot where the chance of encountering other ships is minimal,"* he thought. The map pointed to a suitable location: Mull of Kintyre Lighthouse—a slight curve in the coastline with a relatively safe distance to shore. The 15-kilometer journey would be grueling, but it was preferable to other directions where currents were more substantial or the likelihood of encountering fishing vessels was higher.

Michael knew the Scottish coast would not greet him with soft sand—these were not tropical latitudes. He would most likely encounter a rocky beach, but at least he had identified a place on the map where he could land without the risk of crashing against cliffs.

And what then? Leaving the sea behind, he would need to cross all of Scotland—over 300 miles—to reach his target on the other side. Walking would take weeks, but time was a luxury he didn't have. Michael decided he needed transportation.

A motorcycle or a car? A bike was more maneuverable and faster, but where would he take shelter if the weather turned against him? Scotland's rains were notorious for their relentlessness, especially in remote areas. A car seemed like the better choice. It would allow him to rest, stay warm, and shield himself from the wind.

The financial issue was pressing. Everything Michael had earned during his three weeks working at the port was barely enough to consider purchasing a vehicle. He had been paid weekly—$200 for each week. He still had $120 left from the beginning. However, unexpectedly, the ship's mechanic seemed to like him and handed him an additional $360 for his efforts without waiting for official calculations. "A nice bonus," Michael thought. He was confident he could collect at least one more week's pay before leaving the ship. Everything was coming together: he was finally getting a chance to buy a car.

In his free time, Michael browsed classified ads. He found several offers for old cars in the area he planned to reach. The cars didn't look great, but they were still running. Michael knew this was his only option.

Now, he needed to prepare provisions. The journey by water and land would require a lot of energy. Could he take something from the deck? It was possible, but he preferred not to steal. He knew that if he were caught, his entire operation would collapse before it even began.

Michael tried not to dwell on everything that could go wrong. Scotland was a harsh land, where a volatile climate, rocky roads, and sudden gusts of wind could become just as dangerous an enemy as any pursuers. But hope was all he had left. Everything seemed calculated. Now, there was only one thing left to do: wait for the proper night.

A day before the operation, Michael began discreetly carrying small amounts of provisions he had managed to take from the ship's kitchen. Mostly non-perishable goods and a few cans. He estimated the journey would take two days at most. The ship's usual bustle worked in his favor; no one noticed his quiet movements.

He also prepared a rope and climbing gear, which were plentiful in the maintenance cabin used by crew members for periodic cleaning of the ship's exterior. Later that evening, the mechanic brought him a packed lifeboat, which could be inflated by pulling a safety pin. Michael gratefully accepted the help, knowing that his plan would have been impossible without these small details.

In his backpack, he packed several liters of water, flashlights, and power banks found in drawers left by previous crew members. Just in case, he redrew a schematic map of the area and the route he would need to follow in his notebook. Alongside the tablet, he carefully packed his few belongings into waterproof bags. Now, everything was in his backpack as if prepared for an exam.

Time dragged on painfully slowly. Michael lay in his cabin, listening to the sounds of the ship—the faint creak of metal and the distant splash of waves against the hull. When he finally got up, the clock showed just past midnight—the moment of truth had arrived.

At the agreed time, he and the mechanic quietly slipped onto the deck, hiding in the shadows of the floodlights and staying out of sight of the scattered cameras. They moved without a word as if silently agreeing not to disturb the fragile stillness of the night. Occasionally, they exchanged glances, ensuring they hadn't lost sight of one another.

Michael quickly tied one end of the rope to the railing and threw the lifeboat, attached to the other end, into the sea. A muffled *pop* sounded as the inflation device activated, and the lifeboat unfolded mid-air before landing neatly on the water, pulling the rope taut. Everything seemed to go smoothly as if nature had aided his escape.

After securing the descent mechanism, he checked the knots, nodded to the mechanic, and swung a leg over the rope to begin his descent. At that moment, adrenaline surged through him so strongly that time seemed to compress: it felt like he had covered the distance in mere seconds.

The darkness concealed the sea, but the whistling wind and the creak of the rope filled his entire consciousness.

Michael managed to stop his slide just a few meters above the lifeboat. By the time he climbed inside, the rope had already slackened and fallen into the water. Without wasting a second, he unhooked the carabiner, released the rope into the black abyss of the sea, and allowed himself a couple of minutes to catch his breath.

Like everything around him, the boat seemed like a mere dot in the infinite darkness. Michael pulled out the folded oars from behind his back, assembled them, and began to row after checking the compass strapped to his backpack. The waves were calm, a rare occurrence for this time of year. Each oar stroke sliced through the water with an almost hypnotic regularity.

He rowed almost nonstop, peering into the darkness and listening carefully to every sound. Border patrols or fishermen could appear on the horizon at any moment, which would be the worst possible scenario. But tonight was on his side.

After four hours of exhausting rowing, he finally saw the shore. Dawn was breaking. Michael had miscalculated slightly, landing several kilometers east of the intended beach. The coast was rocky, and when the boat hit sharp stones, its bottom tore open. Water gushed inside, but Michael was prepared for this.

He leaped into the icy water and swam toward the nearest accessible section of land. The thermal underwear he had put on beforehand saved him from hypothermia, but the cold still pierced his body like a thousand needles. Reaching the shore, he caught his breath and slowly climbed a narrow trail leading upward to a small village.

This part of the route was familiar to him. He knew where to go and where the house was and planned to buy a car. But what awaited him there was anyone's guess.

The night was behind him, but the tension had not left Michael. After a silent descent from the ship, a successful crossing of the cold but calm sea, and an exhausting trek to the first waypoint on his route, he was faced with a new problem: the car he had hoped to buy looked more like a relic of the past than a functioning vehicle.

Rust covered the body, the doors barely hung on their hinges, and the deflated tires made it clear that this heap of metal hadn't been driven in years. Michael surveyed it again, hoping that his first impression had been wrong. But no miracle occurred—the car was beyond repair.

He quietly cursed and decided not to look for the owner. Unnecessary conversations could only draw attention, and he was already short on time. Michael continued down the narrow road to the coastline, where a few cottages stood with their glass facades facing the sea. Despite their isolation, these homes appeared well-maintained, and their inhabitants were likely wealthy. Here, he would have better luck.

Michael noticed a small annex with several cars parked nearby near one such cottage-turned-guesthouse. He cautiously approached one of them—a two-door Mini Cooper from the 1990s. The vehicle looked unremarkable but was in decent condition both outside and inside. He spotted the keys left in the ignition through the slightly fogged windows.

As if trying to push away evil thoughts, Michael muttered to himself:

"There's no need. I should at least try to buy it.

He headed toward the guesthouse's entrance. The moment he stepped inside, he was enveloped by the dense scent of old age emanating from everything around him. Intricate antique rugs, massive wooden furniture with worn polish, and paintings in gilded frames all created the impression of stepping into another era. An enormous fireplace in the center of the lounge complemented the atmosphere. Above the fire hung a heavy wrought-iron chain, and around it stood deep sofas draped with thick, soft blankets.

Through the large panoramic windows, one could see the coastline shrouded in a light mist. A few people strolled along the water—families with children and dogs, their silhouettes blurred against the backdrop of a darkening sky.

Michael approached the reception desk, which was empty. On the desk sat an old-fashioned table bell with chipped paint. Pressing it a couple of times, he heard a muffled ring. About five minutes passed before a man in his forties emerged from an adjacent room. He was smiling far too broadly, almost manically, and spoke with exaggerated politeness:

"Good evening! How are you doing? How is the mood of a lone traveler?"

"Thank you, I'm fine," Michael replied, slightly embarrassed.

"You're wet, though it doesn't seem like it's been raining," the man noted, scrutinizing his coat with curiosity.

"It just hasn't dried yet after washing," Michael replied with a faint smile.

The man continued, clearly hoping for a positive answer:

"Are you looking for a place to rest and enjoy some relaxation?"

"Not today," Michael said calmly. "But I noticed an old Mini Cooper in your yard. Can you tell me who it belongs to? Perhaps I could buy it?"

The man pondered for a moment, then frowned slightly and said:

"The car is mine. I haven't driven it in over two years since I bought an SUV—it's more practical for the hills around here. But it always served me well before, never gave me any trouble."

"If it starts, I could offer you $500 for it," Michael suggested, bracing himself for a negotiation.

"That's more than enough," the man agreed. "Let's see if we can get it running."

He gestured for Michael to follow him outside. At the car, the man gestured again with a flourish:

"Give it a try. If she chooses you, I might even knock off fifty bucks."

Michael got behind the wheel, adjusted the seat slightly, and turned the key. The starter gave a few weak jerks—the battery was clearly low. He turned the key back to its original position and tried again. This time, after a moment of strained buzzing, the engine coughed loudly and started. Michael gave it a bit of gas, revved the engine, and stepped out of the car without turning it off.

"Well, it seems she's chosen you," the owner smirked. "I'll grab the documents."

A few minutes later, the man returned with the paperwork. By then, Michael had already counted out $450 and handed it over.

"As agreed," he said.

The man smiled faintly, nodded, and handed over the documents.

"The nearest gas station isn't close, but there should be enough fuel to get you there. There's also a five-liter canister in the trunk, just in case. Safe travels!"

They shook hands, and Michael got behind the wheel of his new acquisition. Driving onto the dirt road, he kept the speed low, testing the handling: he turned the wheel and pressed the brakes a few times. Everything worked as promised by the previous owner.

The drive to the gas station took about an hour. The station was small, with only two pumps and a tiny building beside them. Inside was a little shop where Michael purchased a thermos and filled it with hot tea. When returning to the car, he paused to check the headlights and turn signals. It dawned on him that he hadn't even thought to inspect the car's condition before setting off, but to his relief, everything worked perfectly.

After rolling the car away from the pump, he parked nearby to enjoy the hot tea. After an hour of driving, the engine had warmed up, and the heater was finally starting to work. However, the tea, consumed in just two cups, truly warmed him up.

Finishing his drink, Michael realized he'd need more tea for the road. He returned to the shop, refilled the thermos, and, now fully warmed up, set off on his journey.

The road ahead spanned about 300 miles of winding, aged pavement, which he would have to traverse in his not-so-powerful car. The drive took nearly ten hours, including a stop for rest and a snack. By the time Michael reached the intended town, the sun was already sinking toward the horizon. Exhausted, he decided not to overthink and immediately sought a place to stay.

After about fifteen to twenty minutes of driving slowly through the town, he admired the architecture, which seemed faintly familiar. He tried to recall where he might have seen it before, but the answer eluded him. Finally, his attention was drawn to a small inn with a sign that read *"Northern Dock."* Behind it was a parking lot for five or six cars, currently empty. Michael parked his Mini Cooper as close to the building as possible, grabbed his backpack, locked the car, and headed toward the entrance.

He pushed open the heavy wooden door and stepped inside. The soft aroma of wood and old textiles hit him immediately. The thick carpet spread across the floor caused him to stumble slightly. The room was small but cozy: a few sofas and an antique fireplace gave it a warm, inviting atmosphere. Behind the reception desk stood a tall, thin young man with dry lips that stretched slightly into a friendly smile. In his hands, he held a key and looked at Michael with genuine curiosity.

"Good evening. Do you have any rooms available?" Michael asked, skipping formalities, his exhaustion evident.

"I believe we do. Are we staying long this time?" the man replied with a hint of mystery.

Michael hesitated.

"I... don't think I've been here before," he said uncertainly.

"Perhaps I've mistaken you for someone else. My apologies," the young man responded evenly, his expression unchanged.

Michael nodded, slightly thrown off, and continued.

"I'll take a room for a week, for now."

"As you wish. That'll be 380 pounds."

"Can I pay in dollars?"

"Of course."

Michael counted out the necessary amount, received the key, and provided brief instructions.

"Head up to the second floor. Your room is immediately to the right. It has a large number on the door—you won't miss it."

He nodded and made his way to the staircase, which was covered in a brown carpet with a small, intricate pattern. The steps creaked slightly under his weight as he climbed. Reaching his room, Michael unlocked the door, stepped inside, and tossed his backpack onto the bed. The room was modest yet cozy: a large bed, an old-fashioned armchair by the window, and a nightstand with a lamp.

Without thinking much, he headed straight to the bathroom for a shower. The warm water washed away the exhaustion of the long journey, leaving him with only a faint desire to collapse into bed.

Emerging from the bathroom, he didn't bother making the bed and simply fell onto it. Barely able to lift his arm, he pulled the blanket over himself and rested his heavy head on the soft pillow. Sleep took him completely, dragging him into a deep, dreamless oblivion.

He couldn't say if he dreamed, but his awakening was sudden and unpleasant. An awful screech, like nails on glass, jolted him from sleep. Irritated, he pulled the pillow off his head and squinted at the bright light rudely streaming through the window.

Once his eyes adjusted, he spotted the culprit of the unpleasant sound. Sitting on the windowsill, wings proudly spread, was a massive gray seagull with a bright white belly and head. Noticing Michael, the bird fixed him with an unblinking, cold stare, its shiny black eyes glinting in the sunlight.

For a moment, time seemed to freeze as they locked gazes. Still, after about twenty seconds, the seagull, apparently deciding it had no further business there, hopped off the windowsill and disappeared into the morning sky.

Michael sank back into the bed with a sigh. Returning to sleep was out of the question—the rude awakening had done its job. He resigned himself to the idea that it was time to get up.

He reluctantly willed his body to rise from the bed or at least attempt it. With difficulty, he got up and shuffled to the bathroom, where his clothes hung neatly on the hooks. Grabbing the wetsuit that had accompanied him throughout this strange journey, he folded it almost tenderly and placed it on the small stool next to the shower. Then, with the slow deliberation of someone not fully awake, he dressed.

His dark, distressed jeans now looked even more worn, with frayed edges and small tears.

"Yeah, I'll need to do something about this," he muttered to himself. "Maybe I can afford something decent with what's left."

But first—coffee. Strong coffee.

Buttoning up his shirt, he grabbed his vest, which had his notebook tucked conspicuously in the pocket. The vest itself was worn out, with the stuffing clumping into dense patches.

"This could use replacing, too," he said with a faint smile.

Before leaving the room, he glanced at the window bathed in bright sunlight. Perhaps, deep down, he hoped to see something unusual—another seagull, perhaps. Or maybe it was simply to gauge the weather outside. The weather, as it turned out, looked pleasant. It seemed sunny with a gentle breeze, and since the open window let in no hint of cool air, it was safe to assume it was warm outside.

Satisfied that the key to the room was safely in his pocket, he closed the door behind him. As he descended the staircase, he took in the details of the inn's decor. Though calling it an "inn" felt like an exaggeration—it was a quaint two-story building with an attic and creaky wooden floors. His floor had only three rooms and a corridor leading in the opposite direction, likely to another five or six rooms. He didn't know how many rooms were on the ground floor, but it was unlikely to be more than upstairs.

The ground floor featured a modest lounge with a large fireplace and a humble reception desk. Two vintage sofas with button-tufted upholstery were positioned by the fireplace, separated by a low coffee table barely reaching knee height. Closer to the hearth stood a large rocking chair next to a tall, narrow side table, upon which rested a chessboard. The glass chess pieces and board reflected the dim light of the dying embers, adding an enigmatic charm to the room. The chessboard was fully set up, with all the pieces in their starting positions, as though untouched for a long time.

On the armrest of the rocking chair lay a neatly folded knitted blanket, light red in color, though worn and pilled. It matched the hue of the carpet on which Michael stood, lending a unique touch to the room's ambiance. A voice from behind startled him as his gaze lingered on the chair.

"Good morning! How was your sleep? Fancy a game of chess?"

Michael turned to see the man behind the reception desk, who was smiling warmly.

"No, I don't think so," Michael replied with a faint smile of his own. "I'm not much of a chess player. But thanks for the offer."

"I slept like a log," he added, stretching slightly. "Your bed is so comfortable—I don't even remember falling asleep."

"Do you know where I can get a good cup of coffee?"

"Plenty of great cafes nearby," the man replied good-naturedly. "Any spot will do if you're looking for a quick coffee and croissant. But personally, I'd recommend the café on the square. The coffee isn't necessarily better there, but the atmosphere is fantastic. And the staff—they're simply delightful. I think it's the perfect way to start your day."

"Thanks, I'll do that," Michael said with a nod.

He waved a brief goodbye and headed for the exit.

The weather was terrific: a gentle breeze, a completely cloudless sky, and a warm, inviting sun. Michael crossed the narrow street, heading toward what he assumed was the square, and glanced back at the inn. His car was neatly parked near the building, glinting slightly under the sunlight. The inn, ancient and built in a classic Gothic style, exuded Scottish traditions. Its walls were almost entirely covered in climbing ivy and other plants, creating a stunning living green wall.

He walked for about five more minutes before arriving at a small but lively square. Eight or nine people were waiting at the bus stop—a mix of men, women, and a few teenagers. Couples strolled along the central path while others walked their dogs. Joggers skillfully weaved their way across the square, narrowly avoiding an elderly couple to prevent any collisions.

Several cars were parked near one of the cafes, distinguished by its bright facade. People were coming and going, so Michael decided to head there.

Stepping inside, he was greeted by the rich, pleasant aroma of freshly brewed coffee and baked goods.

"Just what I need," he muttered quietly.

Approaching the counter, where two women in white aprons embroidered with flowers and their names worked, Michael placed his order:

"Good morning. Could I have a cup of your aromatic coffee with cream, no sugar, and a couple of slices of chocolate cake?"

"Good morning, of course," said the woman closest to him with a kind smile. "But you might have to wait a bit—just about five minutes. Monday mornings are always busy; everyone's trying to wake up after the weekend."

"Of course," Michael replied with a slight nod. "Can I sit at one of the tables in the meantime?"

"Any free one," the waitress confirmed with a smile.

He headed to a free table by the window. Se[ttling] in, Michael placed his vest on the table and ob[served] the view outside. Across the square, his attention was caught by a sign for the city newspaper. Judging by the size of the building, it houses not only the editorial offices but also likely a printing press.

"I'll need to remember that," he muttered to himself. "I might drop by for some information. For some reason, I feel like I'll need to learn a lot soon."

He gazed thoughtfully out the window for another ten minutes until the waitress approached him, apologizing for the wait. She carried a plate with two slices of cake in one hand and a cup of coffee on a saucer in the other.

"No trouble, thank you," Michael said with a faint smile. He moved his vest from the table to the chair beside him and arranged his modest breakfast on the table.

The coffee wasn't particularly hot, yet it struck him as surprisingly flavorful. He took another sip, savoring the aftertaste, and pondered for a moment what precisely this drink had drawn him in. He realized that the coffee was lightly salted only after several small sips, and its rich taste carried hints of orange or some other citrus juice. Perhaps the waitress had accidentally mixed up the orders, but the unusual combination suited him. Deciding not to bother the staff over such a small matter, he took another sip, relishing the unexpected blend.

Opening his notebook, he began flipping through the pages, carefully scanning the entries, hoping to find a familiar phrase or clue that could lift him from the fog of the unknown. The pages carried a faintly spicy scent, perhaps from the paper or the ink, and the tiny, precise notes seemed foreign yet somehow his own. He stopped once again on the photograph of the lighthouse tucked between the pages and instinctively checked the coordinates written on a small scrap of paper.

Only then did he realize he had left his tablet and travel backpack in his room at the inn? The notebook, however, had somehow ended up in his vest pocket as if by some minor miracle. It struck him as strange, as he distinctly remembered placing the notebook and the tablet into a bag, which he had then packed into his backpack. Perhaps, in a state of semi-consciousness brought on by exhaustion, he had moved the notebook into his pocket without realizing it.

"Very odd," he muttered under his breath, frowning slightly. In the end, he decided to let the mystery lie for now.

After taking a few more indulgent sips, he gazed disappointedly at the empty bottom of his cup. Rising from the table, he walked over to the counter, where the waitress was absentmindedly wiping clean glasses.

"I think I'm all set with the treats for now," he started with a slight smile, "but I have a feeling I won't resist stopping by again in a couple of hours. How much do I owe you?"

"Fourteen pounds," the waitress replied, glancing at him with a touch of shyness.

"Can I pay in dollars?"

"Yes, why not," she responded, perking up slightly as if the idea intrigued her.

He pulled a few folded bills from his pocket and carefully handed them to the waitress. Her slender fingers deftly counted the money before she nodded, confirming that everything was in order.

Thanking her again and wishing her a good day, he stepped out of the café. The weather outside was still as beautiful as it had been when he admired it through the window. A gentle breeze played with the edges of his unbuttoned vest, adding a sense of lightness and ease to the moment.

Michael headed back to the hotel. It was already clear to him that it would be difficult to reach the lighthouse without a navigator—or, more likely, a car. Walking briskly, he crossed several quiet streets, enjoying the warmth of the sun and the fresh air that filled his lungs as if inviting him to linger a little longer. Yet, as he approached the hotel, he knew there were tasks he couldn't delay.

At the entrance, he paused briefly, glancing up at the Scottish flag lazily fluttering in the wind above the door. The atmosphere was still inside: no one was at the reception desk, and the small lobby looked like time had come to a halt.

He climbed to his floor, almost skipping steps in his haste. In just a few strides, he reached his room, turned the key in the lock, and stepped inside. His backpack lay on the armchair, exactly where he had left it. The room had been tidied: the bed neatly made, the curtains drawn open, and the windows cracked ajar to let in the fresh air. The warm daytime breeze carried in the scent of street dust mixed with the aroma of the sea and sunlight.

Michael realized that leaving his few belongings unattended might not be the best idea in the future. He threw the backpack over his shoulder and left the room without delay, locking the door behind him.

On the staircase landing, his attention was drawn to a painting hanging on the wall. He slowed his pace and stopped to look at it. The oil painting depicted a small, single-story building standing in an open field. Behind it stretched a body of water, and to the left was a field densely planted with what looked like vineyards. The artist's brushstrokes were rough, the details blurry, yet the overall image was remarkably vivid. The place seemed strangely familiar as if he had been there before.

"That used to be a very popular cliffside pub," came a sudden, sharp voice.

Michael flinched and turned. An older woman was slowly climbing the stairs, holding tightly onto the railing with both hands. Her gray hair was neatly tied into a bun, and her eyes were worn and kind.

"Let me help you," Michael immediately offered, moving toward her. Taking her arm gently, he carefully helped her up the stairs.

"You said it was a pub? What happened to it?" he asked.

"The owner passed away long ago—about thirty years," she replied after a moment of thought. "And there was no one else to take care of it. The old bartender only had that pub: no family, no relatives, just a small pub, a tiny house, and a strange vineyard. But the grapes were incredibly delicious," she added with a smile.

"Did you visit it often?"

"Of course! When I was young, I used to run there with my friends. We'd pick the grapes and eat them right there. This painting is my work—I painted it many years ago."

"It's beautifully done," he said, pausing in thought for a moment.

"Thank you for helping me," she said as they reached her floor.

"Not a problem," he replied, letting go of her arm.

Michael hurried back down the stairs, glancing once more at the painting. A series of questions started forming in his mind, each one more complicated than the last. Without stopping, he headed toward his car.

As he approached the vehicle, he stopped a few meters away, puzzled. Sitting on the roof of his car was a massive white seagull. It spread its wings, and oblivious to his presence, it alternated between cleaning its beak and methodically scratching the roof.

Michael rushed forward, waving his arms and hissing in an attempt to scare off the brazen bird. But it refused to budge. It merely stepped closer to the center of the roof and fixed him with a vacant, piercing stare as if trying to peer into his very soul.

Realizing his efforts were futile, Michael looked around. His eyes landed on a stick about a meter and a half long lying nearby. Grabbing it, he began waving it like a fencer, thrusting it toward the seagull. The bird indignantly dodged, its feathers rustling, but eventually, it reluctantly took flight. Spreading its wings slowly, it lazily glided downward and flew off without so much as a backward glance.

"Yeah, that's right—best not mess with me," Michael muttered, watching it disappear. "Fly away while you still can."

He opened the door, got into the car, and muttered irritably:

"Three other cars in the parking lot just had to be mine."

Inserting the key into the ignition, he turned it and immediately cursed loudly:

"Of course... and now the windshield's decorated too!"

He pulled the wiper lever. The washer pump let out a dry, rasping sound—there was no fluid left. The wipers only smeared dirt and bird droppings across the windshield, making the view even worse.

Michael got out of the car. He noticed a garden hose hidden in the bushes near the house. He turned the rusty faucet, waited a few moments, and aimed a thin stream of water at the windshield, barely managing to rinse off the grime. The hose was too short to reach the entire car, but the window was clean.

Filling an empty bottle he found in the car, he poured the water into the washer reservoir and kept some as a reserve. Returning the hose to the bushes, he climbed back into the driver's seat.

Settling behind the wheel, he pulled out his notebook and tablet, entered the lighthouse's coordinates, and hit "Start Navigation." The quiet old engine roared unexpectedly, and the car slowly rolled forward.

The navigator indicated a 27-minute journey. The old town's narrow streets, cluttered with abandoned cars, forced him to drive cautiously. From time to time, Michael stopped to admire the architecture. Stone facades, arched windows, and whimsical turrets gave the city an air of grandeur, yet it felt abandoned as if suspended somewhere between past and present.

After a while, the route made a sharp turn. The streets gave way to open fields and low clusters of trees and shrubs. The road ran just meters from a cliff edge, offering a view of the restless, gray sea.

A few minutes later, Michael found himself among scattered buildings again, but this area looked much more modern. The houses were spaced far apart, giving the neighborhood an unnatural, almost awkward appearance. However, there were noticeably more people and cars here.

After another five minutes, the navigator chimed, displaying the message: **"You have arrived. Continue on foot."**

Parking the car, Michael momentarily picked up the navigator from the passenger seat and focused on the route. Everything seemed straightforward: a path stretched along the shoreline, leading to an open area where a lighthouse towered among sparse trees.

"Alright," he said quietly. "Guess it's time to walk."

He tossed the tablet into his backpack, pulled the notebook from his vest pocket, and placed it there as well. Michael suddenly decided to leave the vest behind as he exited the car. The weather was dry and sunny, and the sun's warmth pleasantly heated his skin.

Closing the door, he headed down the path. He hadn't been walking long when his thoughts began to snag on a peculiar question: what was the point of all this? What was the meaning behind his journey and the marathon of the past few weeks? Was it all worth it?

"Running from the hospital, where they cared for me, where there might even be friends. All because of some inexplicable feeling... I don't remember anything about myself after the coma, but I'm sure I have to be here at the lighthouse. Nonsense," he thought, continuing to walk.

What puzzled him even more was that these reflections had only now surfaced. Such thoughts did not occur in the hospital or when he climbed wet ropes in the freezing darkness.

"This is all so absurd," he muttered, shaking his head.

After walking another few dozen meters, Michael encountered a thicket of bushes that had wholly overgrown the path. He forced through the prickly branches before emerging onto a flat clearing. Skirting around low but dense trees, he finally saw the destination of his journey.

In front of him stood the stone foundation of the lighthouse, no more than two to two and a half meters high. These old polygonal stones had once been part of a grand tower. Now, they were merely fragments of the past.

Michael started toward the foundation but suddenly stopped. On the opposite side, behind the remnants of the wall, he noticed someone's shoulder.

"I guess I'll have to take the risk. There's no other option," he thought, moving forward again, this time much more slowly and carefully scanning his surroundings.

"Don't be afraid; I'm alone," a woman's voice called out as he approached.

Carefully rounding the wall, Michael saw a stranger. A woman, about thirty-five, was sitting on a stone with her legs tucked under her, leaning her back against the old wall.

"I'm sure you don't remember me. I'm Olivia," she said.

Next to her lay a black motorcycle helmet and a backpack. She was dressed in a motorcycle suit that perfectly fit her figure.

"I was actually expecting you earlier," she added.

"Well, got stuck in traffic, couldn't get out," Michael quipped sarcastically. "Maybe we could start from the beginning if that's okay?"

"Yes, of course. But we can't stay here for long. This place isn't safe," Olivia replied, standing up from the stone.

She grabbed her helmet and backpack and began walking briskly in the opposite direction.

"What the hell is going on here?" Michael muttered under his breath, hurrying after her.

They walked silently, weaving their way through densely overgrown old trees and large bushes hanging over the narrow path. After a few minutes, the trail brought them to a massive stone arch with wrought iron elements and wooden inserts. The entire structure was thickly covered in ivy, giving it a gloomy, almost mystical appearance.

Michael hesitated at the arch, feeling a strange unease. He was abruptly pulled inside before he could make sense of his feelings.

"We're almost there. Just hold on a little longer," Olivia said.

Everything changed inside the arch. Michael felt his legs go weak, his head spun, and a loud ringing filled his ears. Shadows flickered before his eyes—faceless human silhouettes. They moved, paused as if to look at him, then disappeared.

Moments later, his body gave out. He vomited and, after taking a few unsteady steps, collapsed to the ground.

"Great, now I have to drag you?" were the last words he heard before losing consciousness.

A biting cold stung his face, cutting straight to the bone. He tried to open his eyes, but his eyelids felt like they were weighed down with lead. Only on the third attempt did he glimpse the world around him. Everything was shrouded in a dense white haze like he had been draped in a thick fog. Michael blinked a few times, trying to adjust his vision. Gradually, shapes began to emerge through the pale veil.

The ice he felt on his skin came from the black marble slab he was lying on. The stone felt alien, its smooth surface so cold that each breath seemed to draw in that chilling sensation. With effort, Michael lifted his sluggish body and sat up, leaning on his hands. He blinked again, trying to acclimate to his surroundings.

In front of him, sitting at a small iron table, was the woman in the motorcycle suit. Her legs were casually propped up on an identical metal bench.

"Awake now," she smirked, tilting her head slightly. "You really picked the worst time to play dead. Dragging you was no picnic."

"Who are you? Where am I?" Michael's voice was hoarse and unsure. After a moment, he added, "And... who am I?"

The woman snorted, but her gaze softened for a brief second.

"Now, *that* is a better question," she said slowly, narrowing her eyes. "Looks like your mind's starting to come back. As I said before, I'm Olivia. And no, we don't know each other. That photo you saw? I'm not in it. But funny enough, I have the same photo—except in mine, it's me with some guy. Funny paradox, huh? A doctor tried to explain it to me once, but I didn't really get it. Over there, they're all too smart, always throwing around complicated terms."

Michael stared at her silently, his expression blank as though his mind was still waking up.

"Oh, right," Olivia said, noticing his vacant look. "There's a lot to unpack. I'm not even sure where to start... Maybe I don't fully understand how this works for me. You could call it astral projection or something like traveling to parallel worlds. But no, it's not a parallel world—it's the same one, just... almost everything is different. Except for some buildings, I guess. And it's not a projection. You're really there, but... in a different body. Or maybe not even a body. It's all tangled up. But hey, the memory comes back eventually. Though, yeah, at first, it's always a mess."

"What the hell are you even talking about?" Michael interrupted, his voice suddenly louder, almost a shout. "Let's start from the beginning. Who am I?"

Olivia rolled her eyes and shook her head with a hint of mockery.

"How would I know?" she retorted. "You're just another poor soul with a problem like mine."

"What kind of problem?" Michael asked cautiously.

"Well, it's complicated. Even the doctors—or, as they call themselves, 'scientists'—don't fully understand what it is. Honestly, going to them was the worst decision I've ever made," she added, lost in thought. "The worst decision in all my life."

"You mentioned memory…" Michael straightened, clinging to this opportunity. "How do I get it back?"

"I was trying to drag you to a place," Olivia replied. "But you're too heavy, so I had to stop." She pulled an apple from her backpack, unfolded a knife, and began slicing it into pieces, eating them one by one.

"It's a cemetery," she continued between bites. "A unique place. Almost everything here follows different physical laws. And what's fascinating—it doesn't change, not here, not on the other side. Well, it mostly doesn't. For example, the arch is a bit bigger there and more ruined, but the overall design stays the same. The cemetery exists simultaneously. And it has a kind of center, a point that never changes. It has its own unique, fundamental physical constants.

"We were heading to one of those points. There, you might remember everything."

"Where is it?" Michael asked, struggling to his feet and leaning on a gravestone for support.

"This way," she smiled, gesturing ahead as if this endeavor was just another routine.

Michael's first steps were laborious. His legs felt like they were submerged in water, each movement sending a dull ache through his body. He focused on every step to avoid collapsing again. After a few minutes, he dared to speak when his body finally began to obey him.

They walked near the center of the cemetery, yet they didn't encounter a single living soul. The place felt deserted despite the sunlight flooding everything with an unusual brightness. Old crypts and graves were arranged in a chaotic pattern, some surrounded by rusty iron fences. In some areas, tall trees broke through stone mausoleums, their roots tearing apart marble and granite.

Still, the cemetery appeared surprisingly well-kept: the grass was neatly trimmed, and the paths had been cleared of debris. At moments, the place resembled a park more than a burial ground. Michael squinted into the distance, trying to discern where this seemingly endless expanse ended, but countless headstones and trees obscured the horizon.

"How long were you waiting for me there? And how did you even know I'd come?" he asked, putting the supernatural questions on hold for now. "I didn't even know myself when I'd get there. A few times, I thought about giving up entirely."

"You wouldn't have been able to," Olivia said without turning around. "And I don't think you seriously considered it."

She slowed her pace to walk alongside him.

"Personally, I think we're robots," she smirked. "Programmed to march toward a specific goal. But seriously, the lighthouse—it's the only thing that draws us. The only clue we get after waking up. Something familiar yet incomprehensible. We see it, and we *know* we have to get there. The only question is *when* you'll make it."

"And how did you know when to wait for me?" Michael asked cautiously.

"Each of us has a gift. For example, I can sense when someone like you is nearby. It's hard to explain, but there's this itch in my mind, like my subconscious is signaling to me. And I just *know* I'll meet someone like you in a specific place. But this time, I waited for about ten hours. My phone died, and I probably would've left if I'd waited another half hour."

"Have you met many people like me?" Michael continued his tone probing.

"Not many. But the others I've met said they've found people like us, too. I'll be able to explain more once you remember anything about your past. Or your present... whatever you want to call it." She waved her hand dismissively and gave a dry laugh. "It's all tangled."

"The lighthouse in the photo wasn't ruined," he reminded her.

"Yeah, it's different for everyone," Olivia confirmed. "It was whole until it was destroyed. About ten years ago, I think. Mercenaries working with the scientists did it. They believe the lighthouse is an anchor that stabilizes the fabric of time. Though I think it's the town itself, that's anomalous. But Roy's better at explaining all that."

"Who's Roy?" Michael narrowed his eyes.

"One of us. A brainiac. He tries to explain everything scientifically. Meanwhile, Sophie and I lean toward the theory that this is all a gift from the Almighty, something predestined."

"With *who*?" Michael raised an eyebrow.

"Don't get hung up on the names," she smirked. "And here we are."

In front of them stood a small crypt, about two and a half meters high and no more than five meters wide. The wooden door, reinforced with heavy iron hinges, was adorned with geometric patterns that almost blended into the gray stone walls. Climbing roses and ivy wrapped around the crypt while wisteria branches sprouted from the stone's cracks as if reinforcing its foundation.

Olivia approached the door and gave it a light push. It creaked but yielded quickly.

"Doesn't exactly scream 'strategic location,'" Michael muttered thoughtfully.

Inside, the air was heavy, carrying the scent of dust and dampness. In the center of the space stood an intricately carved wooden coffin. Michael couldn't help but reach out to touch a symbol engraved on its lid.

"The symbol of Veles," Olivia said quietly. "One of the most powerful gods in the Slavic pantheon. Protector of animals, travelers, and... guardian of the border between worlds. Sounds grand, doesn't it?

They took this as the emblem of our little group."

"Who's 'they'?" Michael asked, keeping his hand on the symbol.

"Who knows? It was a long time ago. I don't really care much about it—there's already enough mysticism in my life," she replied with a shrug.

"What now?" Michael asked, pulling his hand away.

"We wait."

She pointed to a corner where a sack lay. Michael walked over and pulled out two large sleeping bags.

"The red one's mine," Olivia declared, quickly grabbing it and unrolling it against the wall. Without further explanation, she slipped inside and closed her eyes.

Michael did the same. He barely had time to lie down before his consciousness was deep asleep.

Michael awoke to a sudden, piercing noise, sharp and invasive, like a siren warning of an air raid from World War II. The sound resembled the hum of aircraft engines, followed by distant, muffled explosions. He shot up, trying to make sense of what was happening, but within seconds, the sounds faded, leaving only silence.

"Don't mind it. That sort of thing happens around here," Olivia said nonchalantly, still lying in her sleeping bag.

Michael sat up, rubbing his temples. The headache was subsiding, but it left behind an unsettling sensation, as though something was trying to claw its way out from the depths of his mind.

"I remembered something... but it's strange," he began hesitantly. "Of everything I can recall before the hospital... I was killed. At the pier." He paused as if testing the plausibility of his own words. "Then I woke up in a hospital after a coma. But the hospital was hundreds of miles from here. And yet, everything that happened—happened in this city. I'm sure of it."

"That's a good start," Olivia remarked approvingly. "It means your memory's starting to come back."

"Yes, but this city... " Michael continued, piecing together fragments of his memory. "It was completely different. The people, the atmosphere. Constant rain, gloomy weather, almost empty streets. The few around behaved strangely, as if devoid of joy or life. On the other hand, the cemetery was crowded. More people were there than on the streets, but they also acted... oddly. I remember a lot, but I don't remember you. Or the other details you mentioned.

"We haven't met before, " Olivia shrugged. " Well, maybe a long time ago, but I don't remember that. You see, we're mortal, and at some point, death on that side becomes final for us. Oh, and yes, you kind of transitioned to the other side of this world. Over there, you'll find people who have died or are stuck between life and death. And then there are a few still alive but exist solely on that side—they're a rare exception. There are also people like us—wanderers who live in both realms. Some simply observe without interfering, and some can change the course of events. I think you're one of the latter.

"What do you mean by that?" Michael frowned.

"People like you have a physical body," Olivia explained. "Most likely, it's always the same one. But Roy believes it's more like inhabiting a copy of the body. Essentially, while you're on this side, it's as if you're asleep or in a coma on the other. After waking up on that side, you're hit with many questions, but I'm not there with a friendly smile to explain everything to you. Instead, trackers find you. And they either drag you into the lab or just kill you. Though they rarely kill—you're too valuable as specimens—maximum-level anomalies. "

"What do you know about the lab?" Michael asked, studying her closely.

"Enough," Olivia replied, her face briefly turning serious. "I spent quite a bit of "interesting" time there. Until Roy freed me. Ironic, you know. He was the one who killed me the first time. And himself, too"

Michael raised an eyebrow in question.

"It's a strange story," Olivia continued. "I woke up like you—lost and not knowing who I was or where I was. I wandered the streets for several days until I came across a map with a lighthouse. I immediately knew I had to get there. So, I set off through a cemetery filled with people who weren't particularly chatty. Some of them looked like their shadows had lives of their own. I couldn't find an entrance for a long time when I reached the lighthouse. So I decided to climb the wall. And, of course, I fell from five meters up. Woke up in a hospital, but it turned out to be the lab."

She paused, momentarily lost in thought.

"They brought me there unconscious. I took care of my wounds for a while, constantly asking about my well-being. Then, the experiments began. At first, they were simple tests like those for monkeys—blocks and silly puzzles. Lots of conversations with psychologists always ask the same questions. Mostly about my childhood or past, though I remembered nothing. Then came experiments with sound and light. Endless medications. After that, they started grouping us together—children, adults, everyone. That's how I met Roy. "

"Roy, unlike me, had already been in this "wonderful" place," Olivia began, smirking, though a shadow of unpleasant memories flickered in her eyes. "And he came there voluntarily, though they didn't know that. He had his goal—to get inside, find out what the scientists knew, and see how close they were to uncovering the truth. He was always obsessed with finding answers."

She fell silent as if collecting her thoughts.

"But you know what's most interesting? The only way to leave that place was to die. And Roy knew that from the beginning. Of course, I wasn't thrilled with that prospect. But for some reason, I trusted him. Although to be honest, I didn't believe he was capable of just killing someone. Especially me."

She gave Michael a strange look, a mix of sarcasm and bitterness.

"And if I'd known about the risk of the "final death" back then, there's no way he would've convinced me. "

"Final death?" Michael clarified, frowning.

"Yes. It's when you cross over completely, and that's it. Game over." She paused as if recalling something unpleasant, then continued: "So, we searched the entire lab. Memorized a bunch of symbols, codes, and blueprints. And just when we were done, Roy simply shot me."

"What?!" Michael stared at her, wide-eyed in shock.

"Yep, right in the forehead," Olivia nodded, smiling mockingly. "And then, right before my fading eyes, he shot himself, too. Probably immediately afterward. There wasn't much time to take note of things. I can say one thing: the experience wasn't great. Wouldn't recommend it." She sighed, shrugged, and continued in a calmer tone: "Then I woke up without my memory. In a hospital. In Paris."

"Paris?" Michael repeated, stunned.

"Yeah. That's where Roy found me," she explained. "He came up with some story about being a relative, about me losing my memory in an accident, and all that. Eventually, he brought me here, and in this crypt, I remembered everything. The whole mess."

Michael was silent for a moment, processing what he'd just heard. Then, his eyes narrowed as if a new detail had surfaced in his memory.

"Did he visit me in the hospital too?" he asked, furrowing his brow.

"I don't know," Olivia replied honestly. "But it's likely. Roy loves pulling those kinds of stunts. To be honest, I haven't spoken to him in months. He said he had some leads to follow and then vanished. He hasn't been in touch since. I think he crossed to the other side. But I'm not sure."

She paused, then added with a hint of irritation:

"Roy's a weird guy. Secretive, full of mysteries. You never know what's going on in his head."

"So, what now?" Michael finally asked, waiting a moment to digest everything he'd heard.

"What do we do? I remember conducting some kind of investigation and even finding leads. But, as far as I understand it, they can't be brought here."

Olivia thought for a moment before answering.

"Not necessarily," she said thoughtfully. "Some drifters can transfer things. Or rather, it's possible through so-called anchors or lighthouses that exist on both sides. If you leave or place something in the lighthouse, that item will exist in both worlds.

But here's the catch: a person can't be in both places simultaneously. However, I think that, over time, some of us might be able to move freely between the worlds."

She raised her eyebrows as if to emphasize the significance of her words.

"And that's precisely why the scientists in the lab are so interested. They want to merge or absorb both sides. But the problem is, they can't physically exist on this side. They can only observe through their mercenaries and various devices they've developed through experiments on people like us."

"Why do they even care about this side?" Michael interrupted, his voice tense.

"This world, what are they trying to find here?"

"Who knows," Olivia sighed.

"We think their world is just tiny. Maybe the size of this island. Perhaps the city you saw is their entire world. It's inhabited by a few accidentally trapped living people, mainly by the dead or those in comas. It's like limbo if you can call it that. Fundamental laws of physics don't work there—or they work differently."

"For us, it's a wealth of information that could solve all of humanity's problems on this side," a gruff male voice suddenly interrupted, startling both of them.

Michael spun around toward the sound, instinctively tensing. Standing in the crypt's doorway was a tall man with sharp facial features. His gaze was cold and piercing.

"Damn you, Roy!" Olivia exclaimed, rolling her eyes.

"You scared us! Well, there he is. Let him explain everything in detail now." She nodded toward the man and sat down, crossing her legs.

"Michael, right?" Roy's eyes swept over him in an evaluating glance.

"I see you've started to remember things. Good. That means it's time to talk seriously."

His voice was firm, and his tone carried the authority of someone used to giving orders.

For a few seconds, the crypt was filled with an almost suffocating silence, but Roy's next words quickly broke it.

"I understand you have many questions, and I'm confident I can answer them, but let's go step by step. You don't know me, and you didn't know me before. But I spoke with someone who knew you. Or rather, knew another you. Let me start from the beginning." He paused briefly.

"A group of scientists is living on the other side of our reality. It's like the reverse side of existence. That world is inhabited by humans, ghosts, and those who are neither fully human nor fully ghost. They live, make plans, and set goals, just like we do. They're less ambitious than we are, but they still exist. And shadows and ghosts? We have plenty of those on our side, too; it's just that not everyone can see them. But more on that later.

In their world, everything operates according to some kind of plan. At some point, a group of not-quite humans emerged, suggesting that their world was incomplete and something greater existed. They started to evolve, creating a large, well-funded organization with many followers and mercenaries. They began studying everything that mentioned the supernatural, the higher realms, and similar phenomena.

In their world, there are scientists, too—very capable ones. At some point, their research led them to develop a theory about the existence of another side. Based on this theory, they started collecting references—and, of course, people—who talked about it.

And then, at some point, they accidentally invented a device capable of moving objects into another reality. It's not exactly a device but rather a combination of various factors that allow an ordinary cube—or a crypt like this one—to exist in both realities. With living beings, things were far more complicated. The laws tore them apart. Their physical laws are similar to ours, but there are opposites—ideal in their way. This lack of understanding of these constants and their effects prevents them from crossing the barrier between worlds and coming to our side.

Our worlds exist like two sides of a coin. We can't exist without them, and they can't exist without us. And we're never supposed to intersect, now or in the future. But, as you've likely noticed by now, the two worlds have many similarities—and sometimes identical elements—. This is especially true of architecture. Why this happens, I don't yet know. But I'll figure it out soon."

"Was it you in the hospital, insisting they call you when I woke up?" Michael asked, his eyes fixed intently on Roy.

"Yeah, that was me," Roy admitted, hesitating as if choosing his words carefully.

"I came to see you, thinking you'd wake up any moment. I wanted to be there when it happened. But I had other potential people on my list, so I had to leave." His voice wavered slightly, but for Michael, it was enough.

"You could've left more detailed instructions—or insisted I meet you somehow. It would've made this journey here a lot easier," Michael said, shaking his head reproachfully.

"Oh, sure, and I should've written, "By the way, there's another world, and you've been there but temporarily lost your memory"?" Olivia cut in with heavy sarcasm.

"A note wouldn't have conveyed it properly. Besides, I promised myself I'd never lie again," Roy added, tilting his head slightly to emphasize the seriousness of his words.

"That makes sense," Michael admitted, though his expression remained thoughtful.

"But why was I killed? Was that an actual death? I remember Olivia saying it's the only way, but what happens to the body on that side? Is there even a body over there?"

Roy furrowed his brow, clearly deep in thought.

"Yes, over there, your body is practically the same as it is here. We live there quite tangibly. But how exactly we end up there is still a mystery. The body is always identical, almost as if it's cloned. We appear in different places under various conditions. However, the number of these "appearances" seems limited. For some, it might be ten; for others, just one. If you were killed, it was likely because you got too close to something—or it might've just been a mugging or random violence. There's plenty of that on the other side, too."

"So what happens to the body here?" Michael asked, his brow creasing further.

"Here, it goes into a coma. If you die on this side, you probably die there too. Maybe not immediately, but eventually. Though..." Roy paused, considering his following words.

"It's possible that some of those who remain in comas end up there permanently. But that's just a theory—I have no concrete proof. And, if you die there, you don't always miraculously wake up here. There's a chance you'll die on both sides."

Michael fell into a deep silence, digesting this, before shaking himself out of it.

"Can we move somewhere else? It's a bit gloomy here. I feel like I've remembered everything I can—or at least most of it. "

"That's normal," Roy replied.

"In places like this, memory tends to return fully. I think you've reached your limit. It's just how your brain works. Let's grab something to eat. There's a quiet spot nearby with excellent local food."

All three headed toward the exit. Michael was the last to step out, carefully closing the door behind him.

They walked along a narrow gravel path through the cemetery, the tiny stones compressed over the years into a compacted surface. Michael once again noted how well-maintained the place looked—cleanliness, neatly trimmed bushes, and ancient crypts and monuments, many of which had clearly been restored. The atmosphere was both awe-inspiring and inexplicably unsettling.

His unease grew as he noticed Roy constantly glancing over his shoulder as if searching for someone. Roy's tension was almost palpable. Michael wanted to ask about it but decided against it—there was already too much information to process.

They exited the cemetery onto a large asphalt square, where buses turned around. Nearby, two older women stood at a bus stop, quietly chatting. Roy simply nodded toward a road branching off from the square.

"It's not far," he added, noticing Michael's slightly puzzled look.

A few minutes later, they turned onto another street, which soon opened up to reveal tiny two- and three-story houses. The road led toward the coast, where there were children's playgrounds and two old-fashioned-looking cafés.

"This one," Roy said, pointing to one of them.

Entering the café, Roy confidently headed to the farthest corner, where a cozy seating area with soft couches and a six-person table was set up. Massive panoramic windows provide a view of the sea, its gray waves restless under the weight of heavy clouds.

"Nice place," Michael said as he looked around.

The waiter appeared mere seconds after they sat down, presenting menus with the polished precision of a seasoned professional before disappearing as abruptly as he had arrived, seemingly dissolving into the crowd of other patrons. His absence was brief, though, as Roy gestured lightly to summon him back once everyone had decided on their orders.

Olivia's choice was modest: a seafood salad and three cups of coffee, a detail that mildly puzzled Michael. By now, her eccentricities were just another piece of the enigmatic puzzle surrounding this group, so he refrained from asking questions. On the other hand, Roy ordered only a cup of green tea.

Feeling the effects of prolonged periods without a proper meal, Michael decided not to hold back. He ordered chicken with potatoes, a burger, and some kind of salad he had pointed to on the menu without paying attention. He finished the order with a request for the strongest coffee they had. Later, he would realize the burger had been overkill—his appetite had betrayed him.

They began eating in complete silence, the atmosphere broken only by the faint clinking of cutlery and the occasional murmurs from other guests. Unaccustomed to such quiet, Michael quickly worked through most of his meal. Leaning back against the couch, he took a large gulp of coffee and, peering into his empty cup, gestured for the waiter again.

"Another coffee," he said curtly, "and a croissant."

When the waiter had left, Michael shifted his gaze toward his companions. Breaking the lingering silence, he asked the question that had been gnawing at him:

"So, am I working with you? In your... group? Why don't I remember anything from before I woke up? No childhood, no other memories."

Roy looked up at Michael, the corner of his mouth twitching slightly in what seemed like faint irony.

"We're not exactly a company," he replied after a brief pause. "And I wouldn't call it work. It's more of... a way of life."

"...Or death," Olivia added with a sly smile, her eyes hidden behind thick lashes.

"We're trying to stop the scientists, "Roy continued, "and sometimes we rely on the help of people like you. After the first awakening, they always learn about a new anomaly and likely won't leave you alone. It's something like a survival instinct: we band together and try to resist them. But as for your memories, "Roy shrugged, "that seems to be something unique. Most of us have no problems with memory, nearly everyone. But I'm sure you couldn't even be found through facial recognition, could you? You've tried, haven't you?

"I've tried, "Michael confirmed. "But it was something primitive, just publicly available algorithms. I wasn't expecting results. I just decided to check in case I turned out to be someone famous…

"I see. I can ask an acquaintance to run you through some restricted databases, "Roy said thoughtfully. "Maybe something will come up if that's important to you right now…

"Yes, "Michael nodded, absentmindedly turning his cup. "Thanks. I think that's really important. "

The waiter returned with the order: a cup of aromatic coffee and a perfectly baked croissant took their places on the table. Michael thanked him with a brief nod and took a sip. The warm aroma was invigorating, but his thoughts still circled what Roy and Olivia had said. Perhaps he was part of something larger, though he wasn't sure how ready he was to accept that truth.

"Well, how can I help?" Michael asked confidently, looking at Roy.

"Let's start by reviewing your memories," Roy suggested, leaning closer. "You said you were trying to conduct your investigation. What did you manage to find out? Did you talk to anyone or discover any leads?"

"Not really," Michael replied, rubbing his temples thoughtfully. "I had this vision of a girl, and most of the time, I followed her trail. But I don't think she's as important as the whole lab story."

"Everything is important on that side," Roy said seriously. "Time works differently there—in every sense. An hour spent there doesn't equal an hour here. It can be longer or shorter. So, let's go step by step."

"When I woke up, I saw a girl in a white dress. Barefoot, with loose hair. Her gaze—it pierced me, left an imprint somewhere inside. I didn't see her again, but somehow, I could still picture her. She was like a guide... Later, I found out she wasn't actually there, but somehow my subconscious created her."

Michael paused for a moment, lacing his fingers together.

"I actually woke up with the worst hangover," he continued, "after being in an ice bath. I found myself on a bench on a wet, gloomy waterfront. That's where a runner later killed me. And I'm almost sure that guy was the same journalist's colleague I crossed paths with later—the one who suddenly disappeared."

209

Olivia frowned as she listened but stayed silent while Michael went on:

"The girl turned out to be a journalist. She was investigating this laboratory, and her notes became my search's starting point. At some point, I found her notes and printouts. There were articles about the lab and various thoughts. I think I was being watched after I visited the lighthouse. From what I understand, I was spotted by the lab's mercenaries."

"You were at the lighthouse?" Roy asked sharply, his tone suddenly tense. "At those ruins?"

"No, it's a fully intact lighthouse. Three levels. The interior is covered with symbols and quotes in different languages. It has an excellent view of the laboratory. The journalist was definitely there—I think with her editor."

"Do you know anything about the lighthouse?" Roy shot a questioning look at Olivia.

"As far as I remember, it's just ruins, like here," Olivia shrugged.

"Well, I definitely climbed it," Michael said confidently. "I even got exhausted going up the stairs, and finding the entrance took me a while."

He paused as if replaying the scene in his mind.

"There were a few things in my backpack: money, odds and ends, like wedding rings, an old rusty key, and keys to a hotel room. And also an old watch with an engraving: 'This is crucial to our goal. It must not be lost under any circumstances.'"

Roy leaned in closer, his eyes alight with curiosity.

"There was also a notebook with the same symbol as on the tomb in the crypt. Inside was a silver pen with numbers engraved on it. I thought it was a cipher and even decrypted it, but it was meaningless."

"What numbers? And what did you get?" Roy asked, leaning forward.

Michael opened his backpack, pulled out a leather-bound notebook, and flipped to a page with rows of numbers.

"Here, these were on the pen. I also found a coin in the journalist's hotel room — the one I had a key for. The coin had a second set of numbers."

Roy squinted slightly.

"It's an A1Z26 cipher," he muttered.

"Yeah, that's what I thought," Michael nodded. "But it came out as nonsense. Another cipher."

"What exactly?" Roy could barely contain his impatience.

"There were phrases: 'sound — gravity,' 'light — Faraday.'"

Roy straightened up, clasping his hands in thought.

"Excellent. But there must be a third element. Were there more numbers?"

"Maybe," Michael shrugged. "There's also an engraving on the watch, but I didn't think it was important. At the time, it seemed meaningless to me."

"Where are the watches now? Where did you leave them?" Roy asked, his tone suddenly urgent as he leaned forward.

Roy's intense interest struck Michael as suspicious, and he decided not to reveal everything to his newfound "friends" just yet.

"Well... I left them on the nightstand in the hotel room where I was staying. It's the same one I'm in now. And, I think, even in the same room."

"I need to leave," Roy said abruptly, almost in one breath, rising quickly from the table.

"What do those words mean? What's their significance?" Michael tried to stop him, watching Roy's back as he stood up.

"Not now. I'll explain everything later," Roy threw over his shoulder, pulling a wad of cash from his pocket. He placed it on the table in front of Michael. "Here, pay for lunch and buy yourself some decent clothes."

Roy practically ran out of the café without saying goodbye, leaving Michael and Olivia alone.

Deep in thought, Michael remained silent momentarily, but he decided not to waste time and pressed on with his questions.

"You were there only once?" he asked Olivia.

"Once was more than enough," she shrugged. "Although Roy wanted me to go back. Maybe he thought I'd meet someone there, maybe even you. It is to help you remember or figure things out. But we didn't make it. He got some new leads and disappeared. Then, a few months later, he told me about a girl who was supposed to come out of a coma. Supposedly, she was one of us. There was also a guy."

She hesitated briefly, then continued:

"I spent a few weeks at the hospital waiting for them to wake up. But the girl... her heart gave out; she never regained consciousness. And the guy... he woke up, but his mind couldn't handle it. They transferred him from one hospital straight to another. He was pumped full of meds, and by the time I reached him, he couldn't say anything anymore. Then it was you. Only this time, Roy told me to wait in the city. So, I've been waiting here until I felt you were about to show up."

"Do you remember your life before all this?" Michael asked cautiously.

"Not entirely. Or rather, I don't really remember a 'life,'" Olivia looked away. "I was an orphan. After bouncing from one foster family to another and running away each time, I finally ended up on the streets. It wasn't much of a life—living however I could, not exactly taking care of myself."

She smirked, but a flicker of memory passed through her eyes.

"At some point, I latched onto this mediocre rock band. Traveled with them on a European tour—like their personal stray pet. And then, in Paris... I overdosed and slipped into a coma. Well, you know the rest."

"Roy showed up at just the right moment?" Michael clarified.

"Yeah. Now, I believe I have a purpose. Some kind of destiny. Even though I still don't fully understand it. And honestly? I'm not trying too hard to figure it out."

"Well, all of this seems too strange to me," Michael admitted, frowning slightly. "My brain keeps rejecting everything happening, trying to find a logical explanation. However, I do remember people and fragments of conversations. These memories are vivid, even though the weather wasn't sunny then. Just a miserable, drizzling rain with a wind cut straight to the bone."

Olivia lifted her gaze to him as if recalling something of her own:

"Strange. When I was there, the weather was warm and sunny. Only one day stands out as rainy. During another round of experiments, I remember looking through a window near the ceiling. Raindrops were streaming down the glass, and I was almost certain I could hear the rain tapping on the roof. I don't think I saw a single cloud the rest of the time."

She fell silent as though trying to catch fleeting memories, and Michael listened intently, hanging on to every word she said.

"To get there... Do you have to fall into a coma? Is that the only way?" Michael asked, frowning slightly.

"I don't think so," Olivia replied calmly, tilting her head slightly as though pondering the question. "If I understood Roy correctly, there are people... or maybe anomalies... For them, traveling there is like going to sleep. In reality, you're sleeping but fully alive over there. Six hours of sleep here could mean two days or more over there. Roy believes it's possible for everyone; it's just that some people can do it faster and more easily, while others need more time."

She paused, then added with a faint smile:

"'Time is the most valuable thing a man can spend,' as Theophrastus once said."

Michael reflected, thinking back on his strange sensations.

"When we went through the arch... Were those souls? I didn't imagine it, did I?" he asked cautiously, trying to hide the tension in his voice.

Olivia looked at him intently as if weighing his intentions.

"Yes and no," she began cryptically. "Souls are everywhere, but we can only see them under certain circumstances—at least on this side."

She paused briefly, her gaze drifting to the window as if searching for the right words.

"The arch is a very ancient structure. It's supposed to be older than life itself, or so Roy says. No one knows what kind of power it holds. But I think it may draw souls. Maybe it's something like a gate for them."

Olivia shivered slightly as if recalling something unsettling and continued:

"The first few times I went through the arch, I lost consciousness too. In that half-conscious state, I saw strange things and heard voices. It was frightening and bizarre. But over time, that went away. Now, when I pass through it, I only feel a sharp smell and the taste of charged air—like after a thunderstorm."

She fell silent, momentarily lost in thought, then looked up at Michael:

"That's all I feel now. And see. But I'm certain that souls exist."

Michael tensed slightly. Although her words were calm, an unsettling truth beneath them sent a chill down his spine.

He picked up his coffee cup as if trying to cool it, blew over the long-cold drink, and glanced at the dark gray sea beyond the panoramic window. The waves quietly lapped at the shore as though whispering secrets to each other.

What now? There is so much information; just as many mysteries need to be unraveled quickly. I need to go back there. If it's possible to do so through sleep, I must try. But that won't happen without Roy. And yet, Michael thought, *I don't trust him for some reason.*

There's something about Roy that's both unsettling and alarming. And he definitely lied about the hospital. That much was obvious. It's not a great start to any friendship—lying.

Michael frowned, rubbing his temples.

What else is he hiding? And why does he really need those ciphers? Maybe I'm being too suspicious. Hopefully, he's just a man with a difficult personality but good intentions. For now, I need to keep an eye on him.

His thoughts returned to the other side.

I need to get there. And I need to find the watch. They might be the leverage I need for a more honest conversation with Roy. Plus, it'll give me a chance to explore the other side better—assuming my memory doesn't fail me again.

"Can you arrange for me to fall into a coma?" Michael asked, smiling faintly.

Olivia raised her eyebrows in surprise, her gaze a mixture of playful curiosity and slight apprehension.

Michael called over the waiter and asked for the check. After paying and leaving a generous tip, they left the café and headed toward the cemetery. Not far from there, Olivia had parked her motorcycle. They decided to use it to return to the city more quickly.

In the city, Olivia had a contact—a familiar anesthesiologist who had been introduced to her a long time ago for cases like this, in case medical assistance was ever needed. He had been prepared for the possibility that she might reach out to him one day, but he certainly didn't expect this kind of request. Olivia insisted that both of them be put into a coma at the same time. She was convinced that if at least one of them retained their memory, it would make survival easier on the other side.

"Do you understand the risks?" the doctor asked firmly, removing his glasses and cleaning them—not because they were dirty, but as a nervous gesture. "And you're asking me not to be present during this? How will I bring you back? Barbiturates can kill you or cause irreversible brain damage. If you survive, cognitive impairments might follow you even after waking."

"Fine, then do it under your supervision," Olivia said, trying to remain calm.

"This is still a crazy idea!" the doctor exclaimed, sinking wearily into a chair. "I beg you to reconsider."

The doctor's arguments no longer had any effect. Olivia and Michael were unyielding. Resigned, the young physician asked for ten minutes to prepare and then suggested heading to a private clinic to gather the necessary equipment.

Michael proposed conducting the procedure in the crypt. The idea frightened the doctor even more, but he decided not to argue further. They agreed to meet at the cemetery entrance.

The doctor arrived half an hour late, burdened with a bag full of equipment and medications. Without saying much, he followed Michael and Olivia deep into the cemetery.

The crypt was cold and damp, but they did their best to make the surroundings a bit more comfortable. Sleeping bags and blankets were spread out on the floor, creating makeshift beds. By that time, the doctor had prepared the IV drips and checked the syringes with solutions.

"I won't keep you in a coma for more than an hour," he warned, glancing over the equipment. "As soon as 59 minutes pass, I'll start bringing you out of it. Not a second longer."

"That'll be enough," Michael said confidently, nodding.

The doctor sighed, giving them one last look as if making a final attempt to dissuade them, but the words caught in his throat.

They lay on the cold floor, head to head, like a strange mirror reflecting one another. The doctor, moving deliberately, checked the clamps on the IVs. His motions were precise, like those of a watchmaker. The stands behind them cast long, angular shadows on the walls, quivering with every movement he made. The muffled clink of glass ampoules echoed through the room, a reminder of the situation's fragility. The doctor prepared syringes with solutions for reviving the patients.

The IV drips began to tick off the seconds as the liquid flowed into their veins. The steady dripping mingled with the faint hum of the monitor, where their pulse and blood pressure pulsed as green lines as if reassuring that life still lingered within them. The doctor watched the screens closely while their breathing became more profound and measured.

Two neatly arranged resuscitation kits lay on the floor under the muted light of a desk lamp. The gleaming metal instruments and preloaded syringes reflected the trembling glimmers of light. They looked like tools of a surgical illusionist, ready to reclaim fleeting life at the last moment.

The timer on his watch was set precisely to fifty-nine minutes. Its steady ticking was the only time marker in this space suspended in limbo. The doctor sat nearby, hands folded on his lap, his gaze fixed on the monitors. Shadows cast by the lamp stretched along the walls, turning the room into a wavering sea of silhouettes, where everything seemed frozen and alive all at once.

Time dragged on, thick and heavy, saturating the air with an oppressive silence. Somewhere far off, the faint sound of dripping water echoed—possibly condensation trickling from the roof. That incidental noise felt unnaturally loud, disturbing the near-ritualistic quiet.

He tried to open his eyes, but his eyelids wouldn't budge, as if glued shut. He strained with all his might, pushing through a strange, piercing pain. It wasn't just fatigue—his eyes ached as if from a bruise. Every part of his face responded with sharp or dull stabs of pain. Finally, he opened his eyes, revealing an unexpected sight.

He lay face down among tangled branches and grass, lightly dusted with a thin layer of snow. Soft flakes continued to fall, gently covering the trees and shrubs around him. He tried to tense his arms to push himself up, but his muscles refused to cooperate. The only thing he could manage was to roll onto his back. Lying there, he hungrily caught snowflakes on his eyelashes and lips as they swirled in the air.

Summoning his strength, he sat up. The scene became more apparent from this angle: a car had veered into a ditch about fifteen meters away. It had slammed into a tree, its side crushed. The front and side doors were shattered, evidence of a collision with at least one other vehicle.

He examined himself. His neck throbbed with sharp pain at the slightest movement, but it seemed he had avoided a fracture. However, his left arm was in far worse condition: swollen and limp, as if it belonged to someone else. Through the torn sleeve of his shirt, he could see that the arm was broken, though the fracture appeared to be closed. His right arm was covered in scratches, already crusted over with dried blood — a sign that he had been lying here for some time. His face had also taken a beating — every attempt to move sent waves of dull pain through him. Judging by the severity of the injuries, he must have been thrown through the windshield during the crash.

"That's what you get for not buckling up..." Michael muttered hoarsely, only to break into a fit of coughing that sent stabbing pain through his chest. Instinctively, he pressed his good hand against his side. The pain confirmed his worst fears — a fractured rib, maybe more.

"Great, what a nice wake-up call," he muttered with a tinge of sarcasm. "Last time was a bit less painful... Though..." He paused, reflecting. "At least this time, I remember everything. But once again, I have no idea how I got here. Fine, that can wait. Right now, I need to check if there's anyone else around. Someone might need help."

With considerable effort, he tried to stand. His gaze drifted down, and he noticed that one pant leg was torn, the skin beneath scraped raw and bleeding. Although there wasn't significant bleeding, his foot was twisted at an unnatural angle.

"Let's hope it's just a dislocation," he muttered under his breath.

Using a small tree stump for support, he somehow managed to stand. The sudden movement made him dizzy, and for a moment, his vision darkened. Taking a deep breath, he started toward the car, cradling his broken arm with his good one. Every step sent sharp flashes of pain through his body, but he stubbornly pressed on.

Peering into the car, he exhaled in relief—no one was inside.

"At least I didn't kill anyone. That's something," he rasped, his voice rough, before breathing another painful cough.

He made his way onto the road, leaning heavily against the car for support. Snow blanketed everything, erasing any traces of skid marks or signs of a collision. There was no other car, no witnesses in sight.

He stood still for a few minutes, breathing heavily as he tried to gather his strength. The dizziness grew worse, but he knew he couldn't afford to stop for long. Pulling himself together, he stepped forward, not aiming for a specific direction, following wherever his instincts—or perhaps his body—led him. Every step was an ordeal: his twisted ankle throbbed more intensely, the swelling worsening, pulsating with each movement.

Time passed, though Michael couldn't tell how much. One thing was clear: it wasn't on his side. Gradually, the sky darkened, and he still hadn't encountered a single car. The situation was becoming more dangerous—staying on the road after nightfall was clearly not a good idea. Just as despair began to creep in, a faint glimmer of headlights appeared in the distance. As the vehicle approached, its outline became clearer—an old, familiar yellow taxi.

Summoning every ounce of remaining strength, he raised his hand, trying to flag down the driver. The car pulled over, and a middle-aged man stepped out. Turning on the hazard lights, he approached Michael, giving him a slightly crooked smile.

"Rough day?" the driver asked.

"Yeah... skiing's not my thing," Michael managed to rasp, immediately breaking into a painful cough. "Can you... take me to a hospital?"

"No problem."

The driver gently helped Michael into the car, opening the back door. Michael collapsed onto the seat, forgetting momentarily about his broken arm. He let out a short groan of pain but said nothing.

The ride to the hospital took only ten minutes, during which Michael remained slumped awkwardly, the weight of his body pressing into his broken arm. The driver remarked that Michael had been walking in the wrong direction and, at his current pace, wouldn't have reached the nearest hospital for three days—if he made it at all.

When they arrived at the small hospital, the driver helped Michael out of the car. He was clearly trying to be careful, but every movement made Michael wince in pain. Together, they reached the entrance, where the automatic doors slid open to reveal a warm, spacious lobby. At the center was a reception desk, where two nurses in their forties were engrossed in paperwork. One of them glanced up, spotted Michael, and wordlessly nodded toward a wheelchair by the wall.

With relief, Michael sank into the chair.

"Well, I guess this is as far as I go," the driver said. "The weather's turning, and my old girl won't handle the trip back easily."

"I'll... pay you... later," Michael began, but the driver cut him off.

"Don't worry about it. Just get better."

About twenty minutes later, a doctor and a male nurse arrived. Without a word, they approached Michael, and the nurse began wheeling him down a corridor, following the briskly walking doctor. The doctor asked Michael to move to the examination table in the examination room. It took great effort, but once he was lying down, Michael felt a wave of relief wash over him.

The doctor began his work without asking a single question. His jacket was removed, and his shirt and pant leg sleeves were cut open to expose the injuries. Injections were administered to his neck, ribs, and arm, the last thing Michael felt before losing consciousness.

When he awoke eight hours later, he was met by a nurse with a curt, unfriendly smile.

"Good morning. It's time to get up—you've overstayed your welcome. There's nothing more we can do for you."

Sitting on the edge of the examination table, Michael noticed that the pain had become manageable. One leg was bandaged up to the knee, his chest was wrapped in bandages, and his injured arm was in a sling. A neatly folded jacket lay at the edge of the table.

"Here are some painkillers," the nurse said curtly, handing him a small bottle. "Don't overdo it. No alcohol. And don't strain yourself."

Her gaze was so cold and empty that Michael felt like he was in some game where the NPC awaited the following command.

"Thanks... I didn't get to thank the doctors—" he began.

"No need. Just don't come back here," she cut him off.

Michael shrugged on his jacket, pocketed the pills, and walked out into the hall. The two nurses were still standing at the desk as he crossed the empty space and stepped outside.

The snow was still falling, gently covering the city in a soft, pristine layer. It was quiet, almost surreal. It wasn't particularly cold—or maybe he didn't feel it, possibly thanks to the antibiotics and painkillers coursing through his system.

"I should probably bundle up anyway," he muttered to himself. "The last thing I need is frostbite or pneumonia—if that's even possible in this world."

Adjusting his jacket with his one good hand, he slipped the pills into a pocket. His hand brushed against something hard inside the coat. He pulled out a notebook and a wallet.

"Of course. What would I do without you," he smirked, inspecting the notebook.

He found cash, cards, and a press pass inside the wallet.

"Michael Stroller... interesting. Maybe that is my name."

He sighed, put everything back, and looked around.

"Right, back to the plan. First, Olivia. But before that, I need some proper clothes. I think there was a tailor nearby…"

The tailor shop wasn't far—just two blocks from the hospital. A small window display revealed an old sign that looked like it belonged to another era. Michael pushed open the door, and an old bell jingled softly. Inside, a familiar tailor was flipping through a catalog of fabrics.

"Good day. How can I assist you?"

"I need something decent to wear," Michael rasped.

The tailor nodded and gestured toward a mannequin by the wall.

"This way, please."

Michael stood on the designated spot as the tailor quickly took his measurements without asking a single question. Then, the man disappeared behind a curtain in the adjoining room. Fifteen minutes later, he returned with several hangers: a dark coat, a shirt, trousers, and round-toed shoes.

"Try these," the tailor said, handing him the clothes.

Michael stepped into the fitting room and changed quickly. He threw his old clothes into a bag, carefully transferring his notebook and wallet. The new outfit fit perfectly: the coat accentuated his frame, the shirt felt comfortable, and the trousers seemed tailored to him. The only downside was the shoes—his injured foot made them excruciatingly uncomfortable. Still, he wore them out of politeness to the tailor.

He emerged from the fitting room, paid for his purchase, leaving a generous tip, and stepped outside. Around the corner on a nearby street, he found a bench, sat down, and quickly switched back to his old sneakers. He carefully placed the shoes into the bag, then, after a moment's thought, tossed the bag into a nearby trash bin.

"Alright, where do I find Olivia now?" he murmured to himself.

Looking up, Michael suddenly spotted a familiar figure through the large window of a nearby café. A young woman in a light sundress and apron was taking an order from a young couple. It was her. Olivia. The breezy sundress starkly contrasted with the motorcycle jacket he remembered, but it suited her perfectly.

"Very interesting," Michael muttered with a smirk.

He strode toward the café entrance, trying to appear as casual as possible. As he passed by Olivia, he spotted an open table by the window and sat down, grabbing a menu to feign interest. His mind, however, was racing with questions.

Olivia approached a couple of minutes later. Her name tag read, "You can call me Olivia," which made Michael smile slightly.

"Good afternoon. Are you ready to order?" she asked in a soft voice.

"Hi. Could I get a coffee? And what's good here? What's popular?"

"Well, I'm pretty new here," she said, glancing thoughtfully at her notepad, "but I can tell you the cakes are amazing."

"Then, two slices of cake and a coffee, please."

"Of course, I'll have that ready in a few minutes."

Olivia walked away, leaving Michael alone with his thoughts.

"Now what?" he wondered, glancing at her as she moved across the café. "I can't exactly drag her to the crypt. Inviting her to a cemetery date is not ideal. I need a better plan."

Michael sighed, searching for a subtle way to converse with her.

"Maybe I could say I'm a journalist working on an article about cemeteries and need a guide to show me the old graveyard?" he muttered under his breath. "No, that's ridiculous. She'd think I'm some kind of creep and call the cops. That's all I need…"

Olivia returned with his order, setting the coffee and cake on the table with a light smile before heading to another table.

Michael pinched the bridge of his nose, sighed in frustration, and resumed his internal debate. While his thoughts swirled in his head, he failed to notice when he finished his coffee. Glancing down at the empty cup, he grunted in mild annoyance, then shifted his gaze to the untouched slice of cake. He motioned to Olivia for another cup of coffee.

She nodded silently and disappeared into the depths of the café. A few minutes later, the fresh cup was ready. Michael expected her to approach from the same side as before, but she suddenly appeared behind him as she busied herself delivering orders.

"Your coffee," she said, her voice unexpectedly loud.

Startled, Michael turned sharply, accidentally bumping her hand with his shoulder. The cup and saucer slipped from her fingers. He tried to catch them but only managed to graze her hand. For a brief moment, it felt like time slowed to a crawl. He could swear he saw the cup suspended in midair, separated from the saucer, with dark brown drops of coffee scattering through the air around it.

The sharp clatter of breaking crockery shattered the silence. Olivia, suddenly losing consciousness, began to collapse. Michael barely managed to catch her, wincing in pain as his broken arm protested fiercely. Fighting through the agony, he gently lowered her to the ground.

Another waitress hurried over, grabbing a towel from a nearby table and rolling it up to place under Olivia's head. A man from a neighboring table stepped forward, said something quickly to the waitress, and she returned moments later with a first aid kit.

The man knelt, unbuttoning the top button of Olivia's shirt to ease her breathing. Leaning his ear close to her face, he assessed her condition before expertly snapping an ampoule and moistening a cotton swab.

Holding it under her nose, he waited until she coughed and weakly pushed his hand away. Olivia opened her eyes, her gaze unfocused, lingering on the faces of those gathered around her. After a few seconds, she seemed to regain her bearings. Strangely, the café patrons who had crowded around quickly returned to their tables, resuming their conversations as if nothing had happened.

"Well, that's not how I imagined waking up," Olivia muttered, her eyes locking onto Michael.

"Then again, it doesn't look like *you* woke up in a warm bed either," she added, her gaze scanning his battered face and bandaged arm.

Olivier adjusted her apron and, sighing heavily, said:

"My clothes should be here. I don't think I came here like this. Wait for me at the back exit."

Michael nodded. She headed to the bar, and he, grabbing his coat, bent down at the last moment and took a bite of the cake.

"Hmm... delicious cake, didn't lie," he mumbled, quickly chewing.

He left a few bills under the empty cup and headed for the exit.

Outside, he paused, thinking about where to go, and decided to walk around the building from the other side. He was right: around the corner was an alley leading to the back door, where Olevia was already waiting for him in a bright red coat.

"Don't even think about saying anything," she warned, raising her hand. "First, the store."

She pointed ahead.

They walked for several blocks and reached a square. Most of the stores on this side of the city were closed, except for one — a sporting goods store.

"Just what we need," Olevia said, entering.

While Michael examined the shelf with backpacks, Olevia picked out some clothes and disappeared into the fitting room. She returned a few minutes later, handing him the tags.

"Pay... please," she said, pointing to the cashier.

He complied, buying a bag for her items.

"This is better," she said as she walked outside. "Now what? This was your idea."

"We need to find the watch," he replied.

"I think they're definitely not in the hotel room?" Olevia asked sarcastically.

"Correct," Michael confirmed.

"Why don't you trust Roy so much? Why lie?"

"It's not that I don't trust him; I just don't know him at all. I feel like he's hiding something. My gut tells me it's better to keep some cards close to my chest."

"I hope you're wrong, and you'll have to apologize. Well, where to next?"

"I think I know where to look. The watch was on my wrist when I was killed. Now I need to figure out what happened to the body."

Olivier looked at him in confusion.

"There won't be a body; there never was," she objected. "Roy says so. We are no more than spirits here."

"Do you really believe that?" he scooped up some snow from the ground and placed it in her hand. "We feel cold, pain, heat. I don't believe it's only spirited around here. There is life—maybe not how we're used to feeling it, but I'm sure they're alive."

He looked around and, spreading his arms, said, "There's something more here. This isn't just random. We need to figure out what's happening and how it works."

"What do you suggest?" Olivia said calmly.

"Find those who might know about the murders on the waterfront. I think I should visit my colleagues—they should have the news."

He pulled a card labeled "Press" and a journalist's ID from his pocket.

"Well, let's start with that."

They walked for quite a while, carefully examining the surrounding architecture. Occasionally, Olivia would stop to look more closely at something: an unusual stained-glass window or a carved doorframe lightly coated with time. Their conversation drifted to trivial topics as though they were trying to create an illusion of normalcy. It was vital for them to at least regain some composure and sense of calm, even if illusory. Yet, the discussion inevitably returned to more pressing matters.

"I've only just realized how fortunate it was to choose the crypt as the place to shut down," Michael said thoughtfully, gazing into the distance. "After we wake up, we're not supposed to lose our memory… if your understanding of this world is correct."

"Now you're doubting that too?" Olivia said indignantly, quickening her pace to keep up with him.

"Nah, I'm just sure you don't even begin to grasp why this place has such an effect."

Olivia remained silent, but her face revealed everything. In truth, she really didn't understand any of it—neither what was happening nor how these worlds were set up. She was trying to make sense of it all, asking the right questions but unable to grasp what had suddenly befallen her. Her mind flitted between two worlds, which seemed either parallel or two sides of one reality. Yet in neither had she found any firm footing.

Roy, whom she once viewed as a keeper of answers, was far from fully honest. He only answered the questions he felt like answering, skirting all the rest. Olivia had only recently started to see this, and the thought wouldn't leave her alone. This time, she followed Michael more out of curiosity than trust. She wanted to understand what was really happening on this side and who all these people were. But she was sure of one thing: the laboratory was a dark place with a lousy reputation.

"Everything here is extraordinary," Michael continued, summarizing his thoughts. "But it's only strange from our perspective. Maybe, for the locals, our world looks just as unfathomable. We need someone who can at least tell us something about this side. There's a woman who tried explaining some things to me... She spoke in a roundabout way but seemed friendly. Unfortunately, we were interrupted just when it was getting important. If we get the chance, we should visit her. For now, let's look for the watch. By the way, we're here."

They stepped onto a small square lightly dusted with snow, lying in an even layer like a flawless canvas. No footprint marred the pristine white surface as if no one dared disturb it. The trees stood bare, but the snow didn't settle on their branches. Only the shrubs around the square's perimeter stubbornly clung to their orange and brown leaves, partially covered in the new snow.

The snowfall was mesmerizing. Soft flakes drifted slowly through the air, settling almost straight down as though billions of tiny mechanisms were moving in a single rhythm toward a snowy future. For a moment, Michael wondered how many of these tiny snowflakes would melt on the ground, how many would vanish beneath the rare passersby's feet.

On the other side of the square stood the old building of a local newspaper's editorial office. They climbed its snow-covered steps, and the wooden door opened with a drawn-out creak. Inside, all was quiet. The lobby greeted them with emptiness, as though the building had long abandoned its purpose.

Walking down a long corridor lit by dull yellowish lights, they arrived at a large hall. Over twenty desks were scattered here, with documents, printouts, and old office equipment. A single older man sat at one of them—entirely gray-haired, wearing large glasses that made his eyes look unnaturally big. His desk was far behind all the others. Slowly, he typed something on a small black computer.

"Hello!" Olivia called out loudly when she spotted him, but the man merely glanced at her before returning to work.

Olivia looked at Michael in confusion. They walked toward the desk of the uncommunicative employee. Approaching his desk, Michael tried to start a conversation: "We're sorry to distract you from your important work," he said but trailed off when he noticed the computer screen was off, yet the man's fingers kept tapping on the keyboard. It was a strange, slightly unsettling sight. Michael swallowed and continued, "I'm a journalist from a small paper," he quickly took out and raised his press card, but the man didn't glance at it, still typing. "We really need information on a certain incident. Maybe you can help us find an article, an obituary... or something else."

The man did not react. Michael added only after a few seconds, trying not to look at the odd motion of his hands, "It was a man around thirty to thirty-five, wearing a coat. He was killed on the waterfront recently, something sharp straight to the heart."

The man stopped typing. His gaze, magnified by large lenses, rose to meet Michael's. It was as if someone were peering at him through a telescope. The bulky glasses and the utter stillness of his face made the moment unsettling.

"So you're a journalist," the man finally said in a dry voice that echoed in the empty hall.

"Yes, that's right. I realize this question may sound strange, but could you..." Michael began but didn't manage to finish.

Suddenly, the man pushed himself away from the desk, and his chair rolled noiselessly backward. He stopped beside a low cabinet against the wall and, without standing, opened one of its doors. His motions were polished as though he had done this dozens of times. He pulled out a large folder from the cabinet, placed it on his lap, and just as silently rolled back to the desk before standing up. Spreading the folder open on the tabletop, he quickly flipped through it with mechanical precision.

Within a few seconds, he removed a sheet containing a newspaper article. Michael immediately noticed the photo at the top. The victim's face was not visible: the body lay on its side, face down, both hands pressed against the chest. A thin strip of yellow tape surrounded it, and a lone police officer stood nearby. No reporters, no passersby — nothing but emptiness.

"It was an ordinary day," the man began without looking up at Michael as though continuing to type an invisible article. It was most likely a Monday."

His voice was even indifferent, as if he were discussing the weather or yesterday's dinner.

"Male, around thirty to thirty-five years old, stabbed in the heart with a sharp object. No witnesses. No relatives were found. No identification on his person."

He paused briefly as if giving them time to absorb what he'd said, then continued, "The autopsy was conducted at the central morgue. No other injuries were found. The body was cremated. Case closed due to lack of evidence."

Michael listened intently, staring at the article. Each fact felt like a hammer blow on thin ice, cracking the already fragile sense of reality.

"And what about his personal belongings? Where'd they end up?" he asked, not bothering to choose his words carefully.

"In such cases, personal belongings go to the police station," the man answered dispassionately, "as possible evidence for further examination and safekeeping."

"I see. Thank you; you've been a great help," Michael replied succinctly, trying to keep the tension out of his voice.

The man nodded silently, sat back in his chair, and — gathering the papers back into the folder — rolled noiselessly to the cabinet again. After returning the folder to its place, he returned to his desk and resumed typing on the dark computer screen.

Olivia and Michael exchanged glances. The silence felt even more oppressive, and the man's cryptic behavior only heightened the sense that things here were far from normal.

As they were leaving, Michael caught sight of a small office door in the back. Golden letters spelled out, "Editor-in-Chief — Thomas Scoll." His eyebrows rose almost imperceptibly; he clearly remembered that there had been a different name on that door the last time he was here. So, his predecessor was also not found. That thought remained in his head for only a moment, but its echoes lingered in his mind for a while.

They walked out of the editorial office building and came to a halt. The street was buried in a heavy snowfall. Big snowflakes fell almost vertically, forming a solid white curtain. There was no wind or any sound at all — only the gentle whisper of snowflakes, as though the world around them had fallen silent, watching their steps.

Michael gestured toward a café across the square, and they crossed over quickly, trying not to get soaked. Snow instantly covered their clothing in a white layer. Once inside, they brushed off the snow, greeted the waitress, and made their way to a table by the window. Michael recognized this table well, and a flicker of relief—almost joy—passed across his face.

He removed his coat and hung it on the old rack by the wall, then stepped toward Olivia to help her with hers. However, she had already managed on her own and merely smiled kindly upon seeing Michael's attempt to be gallant. He briefly nodded, returning her smile, and headed to the counter.

A young waitress stood there, methodically wiping cups.

"Good afternoon. Could we have coffee, please?" Michael began. "Two cups each, with honey and a bit of caramel syrup. And four slices of cake—one of each kind. If possible, could you add some orange zest to the coffee?"

The waitress narrowed her eyes slightly, smiling more out of habit.

"Is that everything?"

"Yes, thank you," Michael replied with a slight nod. After hesitating momentarily, he added, "By the way… does Mari no longer work here?"

The girl thought for a moment but quickly shook her head.

"I don't recall anyone by that name. I've been here for quite some time, but I don't think we've ever had a Mari."

"Sorry, I might've made a mistake," Michael answered sheepishly, stepping back.

"Your order will be ready in about ten minutes," the waitress concluded, returning to wiping the dishes.

Michael returned to the table and sat on a surprisingly comfortable old chair. Olivia sat there, gazing thoughtfully out the window. Beyond the glass, the snowfall continued to cloak the world in a white curtain, creating an illusion of solitude and peace.

"How peaceful and calming this view is," Olivia began quietly, without looking away from the window. "In this place, it's as if everything has stopped. Even nature seems to be holding its breath. The snowfall is so dense that it feels almost motionless."

She smiled, watching the chaotic yet orderly dance of the snowflakes.

"In my childhood, I loved to watch the snow falling. There was an old attic in one of the houses where I lived. It had a tiny window, really small. It was a proper attic—thick layers of dust, cobwebs, and antique items nearly rotted away by time. Next to that little round window stood a suitcase, old and battered. I felt like it was older than the house itself, as though everything had been built around it."

She smiled again, though there was a faint sadness in her eyes.

"A small rug was nailed to its lid, soft and cozy... You know, I think it was the softest, most pleasant thing in the world. I loved sitting on it for hours, watching through that window. I'd count passersby, imagining what they might be talking about and where they were going... It was my place of power. Only there did I ever feel completely safe."

For a moment, Olivia fell silent as though transported back to that attic.

"Too bad it didn't last long," she added, almost in a whisper. Then she sighed and turned to Michael as if shaking off the memories. "So what are we going to do next? Stage an armed robbery at the police station? Or devise a clever plan to lure all the cops out, sneak into the evidence room, and grab the goods?"

Michael smirked but answered thoughtfully, "I think that's unnecessary. Besides, there are unlikely more cops in there than the number of journalists we found at the editorial office."

He paused, glancing at his reflection in the window, then added, "Plus, there's someone at the station we should talk to. Last time, I didn't dare start with him. But now I think that's the right move."

Olivia narrowed her eyes as if weighing his words but didn't comment, merely giving a slight nod as though accepting his plan.

"What kind of police officer?" she asked, her voice restrained but a hint of interest shining in her eyes.

Michael stirred the spoon in his hand thoughtfully. "In the investigation I was working on before,

I came across a couple of lists," he began. "And in the second list—the list of living test subjects, which they called *'candidates'*—there was one of the city's chief police officers. If I remember correctly, that very policeman is in the photo where my corpse is lying. Kind of a thin clue, don't you think?"

Olivia frowned slightly, her fingers nervously tracing the rim of her cup. "Well... I don't think pretending to be a journalist is a good idea. They can easily check. We need something else."

"Something tells me my press pass is real," Michael remarked pensively, looking at her. "I can't really explain why I think so, but it makes sense."

He fell silent momentarily, then went on: "But you're right. We shouldn't mention any journalistic investigation or anything like that. I think it's better to try telling the truth... well, part of it, anyway. We'll see where that leads."

Olivia remained quiet for a while, gazing off to the side. "We'll see," she finally said softly, sounding less than confident in his plan.

After that, they lapsed into silence. Outside, the snow continued draping the world in white. It was cozy inside the café, but the quiet at their table felt heavy. They only sipped their cups of now-cooled coffee occasionally—despite losing its heat, it still tasted surprisingly good.

However, they couldn't linger much longer. Both knew they had little time left and needed to move on. Exchanging a look of regret, they began putting on their coats. The snowfall beyond the window had started to subside, and the café's light seemed gentler, as though bidding them farewell.

Michael stepped over to the waitress, thanked her for the hospitality, and left enough money to cover their bill plus a bit extra. "Is the police station far from here?" he asked before leaving.

"No, it's really close," the waitress replied. "It's about seven or eight minutes on foot—just head straight ahead without turning."

He paused momentarily as if he had something else to say but changed his mind. He only gave a brief nod in acknowledgment.

They stepped outside, instinctively raising the collars of their coats to shield themselves from the still-damp snow. Both noticed the synchronicity of their movements and burst into simultaneous laughter, unexpectedly sincere, like a sudden flash in the dark.

Though the snow was no longer so thick, its heavy flakes still clung to their coats, slowing them down. Approaching the police station, the snowfall grew lighter until it stopped entirely.

In front of them rose a two-story building—old, made of red brick or perhaps just painted that way—now showing mold patches in places that looked nearly black. Standing out from the time-worn facade was the new and bright roof with no sign of corrosion. Clearly replaced not long ago, it seemed out of place against the weathered walls.

On both sides of the station were police cars,

many so old that their tires had gone flat, as though they hadn't moved in years.

The tall steps leading up to the massive doors with a long metal handle were lightly coated with snow. They ascended quickly, and Michael pulled on the handle. The door opened quickly, and they went inside.

A small reception area greeted them. An older officer stood at the desk, waiting intently for a printer to finish. Spotting the visitors, he squinted, then offered a brief greeting:

"How can I help you?"

"We're here to see Charles Gunn. Could you show us the way?" Michael asked politely.

The officer picked up the phone receiver and asked succinctly, "Captain, you have two visitors. Should I let them through? Yes, I see."

He returned his gaze to Michael and Olivia. "Down the hall, the last door."

Michael and Olivia nodded and walked on. The hallway was narrow and empty, making their footsteps echo ominously, heightening the tension.

Captain... that's a bit worse for us, Michael thought as they neared the door. *But there's no point in changing the plan now.*

He stopped before the door, knocked briefly, and, hearing permission to enter, went in with Olivia.

Behind a desk sat a tall man with a short haircut. His clean-shaven face was set like stone, and his eyes studied the visitors closely.

"I thought you'd show up sooner," the Captain said before Michael could speak. He shifted his gaze to Olivia. "As for you, I'd rather not talk. You won't like what I have to say."

Michael tensed, but the Captain continued without giving him a chance to respond:

"Well, since you came together, I'll hear you out."

Michael exhaled and carefully asked his first question: "Do you know us?" he began.

The Captain smirked coldly, then responded, "And do you know yourselves? You're not in a position to understand who you are or why you're here. Or even who you were."

His words lingered in the air, making the atmosphere feel significantly heavier.

"You know why we've come?" Michael spoke calmly, but a subtle tension laced his voice.

The Captain leaned forward slightly, his gaze remaining just as cold and probing. "I can only guess. But you obviously have a lot of questions, so don't waste what little time you've been given."

"Why do we have little time?" Michael asked with a frown.

The Captain paused and replied with particular emphasis, "You have little time."

Those words hung in the air like a blow that left them uneasy. Michael and Olivia froze, wondering what to ask next.

"How do you know us?" Olivia ventured first.

The Captain nodded slowly as though he'd been expecting that question. "I don't know much—only the general information. The rest is just a feeling. We all sense something similar; not everyone can explain exactly what, but they feel it."

"Why do I have so little time? And what about her?" Michael jerked his head in Olivia's direction.

Glancing at the young woman, the Captain's eyes softened slightly, yet still seemed weighed down by an inevitable tiredness.

"She now has all the time granted on this side."

The Captain's words sounded like a sentence. Michael felt a cold wave of fear wash over him. He shifted his gaze from Olivia to the Captain, waiting for an explanation.

"She won't be coming back," the Captain went on, as though slicing the air with his words. "Her time on your side came to an end."

Michael felt as if the ground beneath his feet was giving way.

"She was killed?" he asked, his voice quivering. The question rang out like a desperate cry, filled with bitterness.

The Captain gave a slight shake of his head, though his words still sounded ominous:

"I can only sense the connection, as many of us do. Nothing ties her to that side anymore. Her light will burn out here, on this side."

Silence followed, deafening in its weight. Michael tried to meet Olivia's gaze, but her face seemed frozen, like a mask. Something critical had changed — and it couldn't be ignored.

"What does 'burn out here' mean?" he asked, though he understood perfectly well; it was as if he needed to voice it out loud.

"It means she stays with us."

"Who are you? Who are all these people in this town?" Michael asked in desperation.

"That's not a simple question. You'll have to come to terms with many things before you can grasp the answer," came the cryptic reply.

Olivia, her expression resigned and her arms hanging in defeat, sank into the chair by the window. She tried to look outside, but a large tree stood right before the glass, blocking the view completely.

"I understand how you feel, which is why I didn't want you hearing this," the Captain said calmly, almost paternally. "But this information is important for Michael and his purpose. We'll take care of you."

"Are you souls?" Michael asked, sounding almost certain.

"Not exactly. And not all of us," the Captain replied. We watch over each other and help one another exist as long as there's light, and we offer support when darkness comes. Sometimes, we can help someone wake up, and sometimes, we manage to help."

"The lab isn't the villain of this story. We're the villains," Michael said philosophically.

"How do I wake up?"

"You need to feel the strength inside you and want to wake up. It's like when you fall in a dream: you jerk and suddenly wake up. You must believe, remember, and picture where you are right now. Then open your eyes."

"Can I take the watch?"

"Yes, of course. If you need it."

The captain opened the top drawer of his desk and took out a small box, handing it to Michael. Inside was the notebook with that same silver pen, some money, and the watch. Michael picked up the watch, slipped it onto his wrist, then closed the box and returned it to the captain.

"I'll come back for the rest later. To wake up, I need a particular place?" he asked.

"Yes. A place that exists on both sides. The point where light dies, and darkness is born. A spot where you're as close as possible to your own light—your body on the other side."

"I see. Olivia, are you coming with me?" Michael asked, uncertain.

"She has a lot to discuss with me," the captain replied in her stead.

Michael simply nodded in dismay and almost ran out of the room. He dashed out of the police station, descended the steps, and looked around.

"You have to be somewhere close by," he muttered anxiously.

The next moment, he spotted an old, partially rusted taxi across the street. He rushed toward it.

Michael opened the taxi's passenger door without a word and got in.

"I need to go to the cemetery."

"You're too young for that," the driver quipped, but Michael's stern look stopped him halfway through the joke. "Well, if that's what you want. About a fifteen- or twenty-minute drive if this old thing doesn't let us down."

"She'd better not," Michael replied curtly.

The driver started the engine, and the taxi pulled away at the maximum possible speed for an old, well-worn car. Throughout the ride, the driver remained silent as if sensing that his passenger wasn't in the mood for conversation.

Michael seemed entirely lost in thought. His face looked impassive, but occasionally, a wave of hopelessness would pass over it—so profound that it appeared he might burst into tears at any moment. Yet he held himself together, staring off into the distance with an empty, desperate gaze.

The car occasionally slid on the turns; the lack of modern stabilization systems was evident. But the driver had a firm grip on the wheel and handled each drift skillfully. The snowfall had stopped; the air was eerily still. Thick black clouds hung over the city, poised to unleash more snow—or perhaps something even more menacing. The atmosphere was as grim as possible, but Michael seemed indifferent to it. He was focused, clear-minded, and finally understood who his enemy was. He could only hope it wasn't too late.

The taxi stopped at the cemetery's main gate. Michael had already opened the door mid-stop, stepped out, and tossed a small wad of bills onto the seat.

"Keep the change. I hope we'll meet again," he said as he turned his back on the driver.

Michael ran along the narrow path that cut almost through the center of the sprawling cemetery. As before, it was oddly "crowded" here—if that word even made sense for such a place. The same children ran and played around the graves, and the same adults moved in near-silent circles around the crypts, gliding across the snow without a word.

There was less snow here than in other parts of the city, yet enough had fallen to almost bury one of the crypts beneath a white shroud. Michael ran up to it and tried to open the door, but it wouldn't budge. He took a few steps back, then rammed it with his shoulder. The wooden surface cracked but held. On his second attempt, the heavy steel hinges gave way; the door hung crookedly, clinging to just one hinge.

Michael pulled on the door's edge, creating a gap to squeeze through. He slipped inside.

The crypt's interior surprised him. It looked noticeably different from its "other side" counterpart. Along the perimeter, coffins were half-embedded in the walls or stuck in them, and small vases on tidy stands stood in neat rows between them. In the center of the space rested an open coffin—completely empty.

Small windows near the ceiling, hardly more than twenty or thirty centimeters tall, were decorated with ancient stained glass. Light passing through the colorful panes refracted into intricate patterns on the walls and floor, like living paintings.

Michael stood still for a few seconds, caught off guard by the unexpected beauty, but quickly pulled himself together. After looking around, he lay down on the floor near the crypt's center. Stretching out on his back, he placed his arms at his sides and shut his eyes.

Dark emptiness swallowed everything. He tried to clear his mind, holding his breath. The sensation of torn silhouettes and snatches of foreign words slowly melted into the ink-black void of consciousness, disappearing completely. Suddenly, a burst of light slashed through the darkness, blinding his thoughts momentarily. Then, it vanished, leaving only silence.

But no sooner had he felt a sense of calm than the light flared up again, this time twice in quick succession. After a short pause, his consciousness seemed to erupt with a searing light from within, forcing him to open his eyes.

Hovering above him with a scalpel in hand stood Roy. In the faint light, the blade gleamed as Roy held it over Michael's throat. Michael managed to grab Roy's wrist, halting the fatal strike. Jerking the scalpel from Michael's grip, Roy slashed deeply into Michael's arm.

"This can't be happening!" Roy whispered, his voice trembling with fear. He dropped the scalpel and, without a second thought, darted out of the room.

Michael tried to stand, but his feet slipped into something sticky and viscous. He collapsed onto his knees, barely keeping his balance.

"O God..." he whispered upon seeing Olivia's body. She looked as pale as marble, lying in a maroon pool that filled the small indentations beneath her. In the corner of the room, the doctor sat motionless, his body slumped, and head tilted onto his shoulder. A dark, viscous fluid oozed from the wound on his neck, soaking into his clothing.

Michael froze. Horror and helplessness gripped him like an icy shell. He knew there was nothing he could do. Olivia and the doctor were gone. But what frightened him most was the brutal precision with which Roy had acted. The doctor had likely not even realized what had happened.

He had no idea how much time had passed—five minutes, ten—but a dull ache in his arm finally pulled him back to reality. Looking down, he noticed the deep slash Roy's scalpel had left. Blood was streaming heavily, staining his fingers and sleeve.

Slowly, Michael got to his feet, clutching his wounded arm. He noticed a medical kit lying near the doctor's body, where Roy must have grabbed the scalpel. Michael moved closer, took out antiseptic, doused his arm with it, sealed the wound with a medical stapler, and bandaged it tightly.

His gaze settled on the coffins propped against the walls at the room's far end. He hadn't paid them any attention before. Walking over to Olivia, he carefully detached the wires and IV lines, then lifted her into his arms. As though afraid of disturbing her peace, he gently laid her body in the central coffin. Casting one last look at her, he closed the lid.

He dragged another empty coffin from against the wall and placed the doctor's body inside. Michael closed the lid and murmured, "I didn't want this."

Surveying the scene, he realized he had no reason to stay. All that remained was to go back and try to find answers on the other side. He now knew exactly where he needed to go. And he knew Roy wouldn't be there.

"But why?" Michael whispered, his voice shaking as though with cold. "They believed in you, you sick bastard…"

These words slipped from his lips in a half-muted whisper, laden with pain and rage. He looked at the closed coffins as if trying to find an answer in the silence surrounding him. There were no sounds other than his own breathing echoing dully in the crypt.

He felt a crushing emptiness filling his chest. Olivia, who had been ready to follow Roy to the end, trusted his plans more than anyone else, and the doctor, who likely knew a great deal but stayed loyal to the one he trusted. Now they were gone. For what purpose?

Michael exited the crypt, pushing the door shut behind him as though trying to lock that nightmare away forever. For a while, he stood there, leaning his hands and forehead against the cold metal, until his legs gave out. Turning around, he slid against the door and sank to the rain-soaked ground. Wrapping his arms around his knees, he finally allowed himself to weep. The salty tears he had held back for so long came pouring out in streams.

He had barely known those who now lay behind that closed door. It was his first time seeing the doctor, and with Olivia, he'd only had a brief acquaintance. Yet the weight of what had happened — its cruelty and senselessness — broke something within him. He felt that it was partly his fault. That thought gnawed at him from the inside. Michael sat for a long time, crying quietly, making almost no sound. Time seemed to stand still.

The rain started to intensify, soon turning into a full downpour. The droplets pelted him mercilessly, running down his face and shoulders and soaking his clothes. Cold water mixed with mud, leaving strange patterns on the graveyard's paths. It was as though even the sky was trying to wash away the burden of what had happened.

He wanted to remain there—lie down by the crypt door and let his body merge with the rain, the earth, and that endless emptiness. But he knew he couldn't let himself. Roy had to answer for what he had done.

The downpour didn't let up, now falling in torrents that streamed across the cemetery's paths, flooding everything around. Michael forced himself to his feet, feeling the cold gripping his body. Glancing up, he noticed a small window in the crypt wall, near which two padlocks hung. A rusty key stuck out of one of them. He recognized that key—it was just like the one he'd found in his backpack on the wrecked motorcycle.

"So I've been here before," Michael whispered, clutching the old rusty key in his hand. *Why did I carry one of the keys to the other side? And how?*

With no answers in sight, Michael felt new questions swirling through his mind. Why couldn't he remember anything? Why did all of this feel both familiar and alien simultaneously? That key was proof—a piece of the puzzle he must have once tried to solve.

"Why do I remember nothing at all?" he asked, his voice filled with exhaustion and bitterness. "I need to stop this parade of strangeness in my memory."

He sensed a dull rage at himself rising from within. Lacking his memories had become an unbearable torment. Each new discovery only added more fog, as if someone were deliberately confusing him, leading him through an endless maze.

Rain pounded his face, turning the cemetery into a shapeless, muddy mess. He lifted his eyes to the sky, letting the drops roll down his cheeks. The cold water helped him stay focused, if only briefly.

"Enough," he said firmly, putting the key in his pocket. "I have to end this. I need to figure out where it all started and why."

He removed the padlocks, then hooked them through the hasps again to be sure the crypt was locked tight. He had to keep moving. Now, he knew one thing for sure—Roy wouldn't escape retribution.

Slowly, he walked along the narrow path, nearly wading through the torrents of rainwater flooding the cemetery. Streams merged into grimy rivulets, creating a loud, rushing, hissing sound. Michael headed for the ancient stone archway at the far end of the graveyard—beyond it lay the path to the lighthouse.

Upon reaching the arch, he stopped just a few meters short of its stone base. He no longer feared passing out or being helpless; something else drove him now. His eyes examined the arch intently. Every crack, every jutting stone, every trace of time—any of it could be hiding a clue.

He searched, determined not to miss the smallest detail, scanning the surface as though hoping to find something familiar or a sign that might answer his gnawing questions. For now, all it was to him was just stone, washed by the rain and shrouded by jagged shadows reflecting in the water.

Summoning his resolve, Michael stepped forward. The moment his foot touched the ground beneath the arch, he stood still, concentrating on his senses. Each step felt more momentous than the last. On his second step under the ancient arch, something changed.

Time froze. Everything slowed to an almost complete standstill, and raindrops—falling in a mad torrent just a moment ago—suddenly hung suspended in the air. They drifted around him in delicate, watery patterns, each one unique. Michael remained rooted to the spot, transfixed by the bizarre spectacle. He watched the slow, mesmerizing motion of the droplets, noticing how every single one differed from the rest.

The air grew thick and heavy as he suddenly climbed to a high mountain peak. Breathing became difficult, and a faint dizziness warned him he couldn't linger. He couldn't stay here.

Taking a few resolute steps, Michael crossed through the archway, passing out of its influence. The world around him sprang back to life. Torrential rain crashed down once more, restoring reality with its clamor and chill. He caught his breath, tried to steady himself, and pressed toward the lighthouse.

A familiar path led uphill through trees and bushes. Michael quickened, determined to reach the lighthouse, which now felt safest. For some reason, he also felt calm at the old hotel, but Roy would indeed send someone there first if he planned to finish what he'd started. Besides, if Michael understood correctly, the lighthouse was also a sort of anchor between worlds, even if it looked entirely different here.

Drenched and muddy, he exited the clearing where the lighthouse ruins stood. A cold wind howled sharply, cutting through his soaked clothes and making him shiver. The weathered stones of the lighthouse were covered in moss and mold, their gray color blending into the overcast sky. His wounded arm ached, but the bandaging with the medical staples seemed to hold. Though the sodden dressing clung unpleasantly to his skin, bringing cold and discomfort, he refused to dwell on it.

All his thoughts revolved around the imminent encounter with Roy and what he would do to him. Yet first, he needed to understand what he was dealing with. The only person he trusted was on the other side, and she had no idea what was happening. *Ah, how I pity her after all,* Michael thought with deep remorse. The damp air in the clearing, heavy with the smell of seaweed and salt, burned his lungs, mingling with the bitterness of regret.

He reflected that he needed to find a place to hide in these rocks, surveying the lighthouse ruins. If he recalled correctly, a tunnel in the lighthouse's foundation led through the rock—another level below ground. If its layout resembled the lighthouse on the other side, the one he'd been to before, it would at least have one more large room directly beneath it. Continuing these thoughts, Michael carefully circled the ruins, careful not to miss any detail.

He approached the cliff and noted that the sea had receded considerably—the ebb tide had recently started. That meant he'd have enough time to get through the tunnel before the tide came in. If he were caught there when it rose, it could be a deadly trap—the retreating waves left behind strips of wet stones and seaweed glistening in the gray light. Carefully, Michael descended the slope, relying on his memory to locate the hidden cave entrance. The rocks, slick with wet algae and mold, were extremely slippery, so each step required the utmost caution. Around him was quiet, broken only by the slow, measured rhythm of the waves.

After several minutes of climbing down, he noticed a small opening. Once he reached it, he realized the passage was much smaller than he remembered. He bent forward to enter, barely fitting his shoulders through the narrow space. A cold, damp draft came from the cave's depths, and darkness swallowed him whole.

Michael thought wryly, perfect for someone with claustrophobia, but there was no other way. After another ten meters, any hint of light vanished, failing to reflect off the walls, so he moved purely by feeling. The cave seemed to shrink even more, and he wondered if he had chosen the wrong one entirely—the diameter and overall look just didn't match his memory, and he might have very little chance of returning to that half-hunched posture. And swimming against the current in a narrow passage... A flicker of panic began to rise in him, but it dissipated the moment his hand bumped into a wooden barrier. This had to be a door, and he started frantically searching for it, feeling around with both hands for a lock or handle.

He didn't find it immediately; even after he did, it took a moment to realize it was what he was looking for. The handle-lock was a solid lump of rust with a small side pin. That pin was made of wood, so it was still in tolerable shape—unlike the rest of the lock. Michael pressed the handle carefully but firmly. It gave a crunching sound a few times as if about to snap, but he got lucky: the rusted mechanism broke loose, and surprisingly, it still worked. After a few more minutes of light rocking and pushing, the handle finally turned. Eagerly, he pulled open the door and stumbled into the room.

Closing it behind him immediately, he slumped against it, exhausted. The dark space greeted him with cool air and almost total silence. A faint sliver of light came in—a thin beam falling from a damaged partition between floors, disappearing into the corners without really dispersing the thick darkness.

In the gloom, Michael made out a small torch attached to the wall. He stood, moved closer, and felt around for something like matches or a lighter, but with no success. Close to giving up, he took a step back and felt his foot nudge something small and solid. Bending down, he found a leather bag coated in dust and damp. Carefully checking it by touch, he pulled an old lighter out of one of its pockets.

Michael tried it right away. It had no fuel left, but the sparks were enough to ignite the torch. The oily cloth caught fire, driving the darkness back with warm light and a bit of smoke. Glancing around, he noticed a few more torches scattered around the perimeter. He gathered them all in one spot, placing them in a corner.

He approached several steps near the center of the room, leading to a blocked passage that once went to the next floor. The blockage seemed dense, likely from a collapse long ago. Moving away from what was once a staircase, he looked at the small openings in the walls that served as vents. The flame flickered, bringing the torch closer to one of them, confirming that air still circulated.

That's. He thought, "That's good, so at least I probably won't suffocate," kicking aside smaller stones with his feet. Michael dragged a few large rocks before the door, reinforcing the barrier. The old rusty lock didn't inspire confidence, and he wasn't about to leave it as it was.

He settled down in a corner by the torches, leaning against the wall. *"It's not perfect, but in my situation, I can't think of anything better,"* Michael said with a philosophical calm. Remembering the bag, he picked it up and opened the remaining pocket. There was practically nothing inside: just a few rolled-up banknotes and a pack of cigarettes.

He felt a surge of relief for a moment, hastily opening the pack—but it was empty. Annoyed, Michael crushed it in his hand and flung it forcefully into the opposite corner, where it struck the wall with a dull thud. The torch flame flickered, illuminating his face with both fatigue and resolve.

He tried to make himself as comfortable as possible, simultaneously leaning against two cold, rough walls. His body tensed at the unnatural position, but he relaxed—he wasn't about to topple face-first onto the dusty concrete. For some reason, he felt absolutely sure the *transition* would work.

Closing his eyes, he slowly exhaled, striving to banish all unwanted thoughts. At first, he succeeded; it was as if the deep silence heightened every sensation within him. His slow inhalations grew more profound, and each exhalation became more drawn out. The air felt thick and heavy, as though steeped in some invisible weight.

Time passed—thirty minutes, maybe forty. Michael opened his eyes a few times, only to see the same impenetrable dimness, then shut them again, determined to empty his mind. Yet nothing happened. Any flicker of thought he felt shattered the fragile balance, stopping him from slipping into a trance. Anger began to build inside him.

Despair gradually took hold. This endless stillness, the waiting, all the failed attempts—he couldn't endure it anymore. Brimming with frustration and disappointment, he leaned forward to stand. But the moment he shifted, placing his hand on the dusty floor, everything abruptly ended.

In an instant, as though a switch were flipped, his body gave out, and his mind plunged into an unfathomable void. He fell face-forward onto the grimy concrete floor, though he felt no pain. The deep, empty darkness swallowed everything.

A sudden, brilliant white light burst forth, like the flash of an old camera, and Michael's consciousness snapped back into awareness. He jerked his head up, squinting at the shock of brightness. Before him was a faint image: a vacant old restaurant or small bar. The ceiling was stained with age, and faded, peeling signs adorned the walls. The tables stood in haphazard disorder, many littered with empty bottles and dirty plates.

Michael noticed movement behind the bar. An older bartender was slowly wiping beer glasses, methodically circling them with a damp rag. There wasn't a single other person in the bar—only the faint smell of stale alcohol and the slightly bitter scent of old wood, creating a strange air of neglect.

He realized he was at one of the tables, his face pressed into a plate with leftover snacks. There was a dry crunching sound as he sat up, peeling bits of peanuts from his cheek.

"Well, at least I'm not broken and lying in the bushes like last time," he muttered, wiping his cheeks with his fingers.

He rose slowly, testing all his senses. There was no unusual pain, just a slight dizziness, but overall, he felt fine. Unsteadily, Michael headed to the counter, where the bartender still stood.

"Make me some coffee," he said curtly, leaning on the polished surface.

The bartender looked a bit surprised—he probably didn't get many coffee orders in a place like this—but he nodded agreeably and got to work. A few minutes later, a steaming cup was already in front of Michael. The hot aroma filled the air, briefly pushing away the persistent sense of absurdity.

Meanwhile, Michael discreetly checked his pockets. He needed transport to return to the city—walking was out of the question unless he wanted to jump off a cliff and swim to the pier. Exhaling deeply, he discovered a small roll of bills in his pocket—enough to pay for the night and travel.

"Can you call a taxi here? Do you have a phone?" he asked, looking up at the bartender.

He shook his head. "No phone. And there's no signal around here," he said slowly as if it were obvious. "There's something in the soil—minerals or whatever—scrambles everything. If you need to go to the city, I can drive you. I was planning to head out anyway—just waiting for my last customer to wake up."

"Great," Michael replied with relief. "I'll go with you then. How much do I owe you for the snacks and the night?"

He pulled out his money, counted the sum, and handed it over. The bartender nodded in approval, placed the bills into an old tin can, and added, "Wait outside for five minutes. I'll close the bar, and then we'll go."

Michael strolled to the exit. Weak morning sunlight filtered through the dirty windows, tinting the dusty floor in shades of golden amber. He pushed open the heavy wooden door and stepped into the fresh air, which carried the smell of sea salt and the slight tang of withering grass. Outside, it was dry and warm, seemingly late spring or early summer—odd, considering there'd been quite a bit of snow just a few days ago.

A loud rumble sounded somewhere to the side, accompanied by an unpleasant metallic screech. It seemed like old, time-worn machinery was rebelling against continuing to work. A few seconds later, a pickup truck appeared from around the corner—so rusted it looked as though it held together only by chance.

The pickup halted at the roadside, and Michael, not wasting time, opened the squeaking door. The seat inside was worn; you could feel its sagging springs with every move. He sat down carefully, pulling the door shut harder than necessary. Metal groaned in protest but didn't break.

Trying to find a seatbelt, Michael discovered there wasn't one at all. *Well, we'll be going without a belt,* he thought, shrugging inwardly.

The bartender, now behind the wheel, pressed the gas pedal, and the truck lurched forward. Surprisingly, it quickly picked up speed, even though the engine rumbled like a disgruntled cat.

"Sorry about the slow driving," the bartender said suddenly, looking somewhat apologetically at Michael. "I haven't driven in twenty years, maybe more. Honestly, I wouldn't be driving now if my supplier wasn't sick. I'm running low on stock, so I had to come myself."

"No problem, it's all good," Michael tried to smile, though his thoughts were far from polite.

The pickup moved steadily along a winding road bordered by low hills and stunted trees. Gradually, the scenery changed to signs of civilization: the cracked asphalt gave way to smoother patches, streetlamps appeared, and buildings became sporadically visible.

Michael realized they had arrived on the opposite side as they entered the city. *Well, that's even better*, he thought.

"Stop here, please," Michael said, pointing to a bus stop just before the intersection.

The bartender obediently braked. Michael got out and closed the door carefully, as if any careless movement might cause the truck to fall apart.

"Thanks for your help," he added before heading toward the crossroads.

Turning left, he was on a level road illuminated by bright streetlamps. Surveillance cameras tracked his every move with neutral vigilance. Up ahead, large metal gates came into view—the first checkpoint.

Michael reached the guard post and noticed security personnel watching him silently from behind armored windows. They quickly opened the gates without a word, and he passed through. At the second line of control, he had to stop and wait.

After a few minutes, two guards carrying rifles approached him. With a gesture, they signaled him to follow past the gates and halt. The wait wasn't long—soon, a man in a black uniform with no insignia appeared. Unlike the others, his face was uncovered.

He held a small folder. Approaching Michael, he gestured toward a modest guard building. Without unnecessary questions, Michael went inside and sat at the lone table.

The guard opened the folder, pulled out a thin sheet of paper, and handed it to him along with a silvery pen.

"Check and sign to confirm

Name: Michael

Purpose of visit: to seek the truth

Duration: unlimited

I acknowledge the seriousness of what's happening and promise not to do anything foolish.

The last line looked odd and somewhat comical, but Michael pretended not to be fazed. He signed it.

"Great. Follow me," the man said, snapping the folder shut.

They left the building and walked along a narrow road leading toward a primary complex. Upon reaching a massive door, the escort held a key card to a panel. The lock clicked, and the door opened, revealing another security post.

The man in uniform ordered his colleague to escort Michael to the first office. The new guard silently nodded, indicating for Michael to follow. Michael sensed the tension in the air but walked forward with resolve.

They walked for a long time, though his sense of time—and space—gradually slipped away. The entire journey through that corridor, long and seemingly endless, felt like it dissolved into the infinity of this strange building. Its architecture outside and its layout within were both distinctly unusual—everything here felt foreign, as though it wasn't built for people. White walls bathed in an unnatural cold light bore no markings or signs. It felt like the building breathed with its own quiet, mysterious rhythm.

The room they were heading to had been visible from the corridor's start—positioned at the far end, right in the center of a broad space resembling an empty arena. At first, it was just a distant blur, but its outlines grew sharper with each step. Michael soon noticed at least three corridors converging on it from different angles. It reminded him of a child's drawing of the sun with rays radiating out—confidently drawn yet slightly absurd, as if intentionally simplistic.

When they drew nearer, Michael realized there were five corridors, all identical to the one the guard led him down. Everything seemed symmetrical, as though the environment itself imposed a certain harmony. They stopped at the door, halting just half a meter from it. That short distance felt like an insurmountable boundary.

The guard froze, turning into a silent statue, his face expressionless. The only thing betraying his involvement was the faint crackling in his earpiece, which Michael began to notice after a few minutes—a dull, brief static that sounded like a secret code known only to those in the know. The guard nodded to someone unseen, stepped forward, and opened the door soundlessly.

Inside was an immense room—something like a hangar or a conference hall—flooded with artificial light. The space was organized so meticulously it gave the impression that every object here had a specific purpose. Dozens of tables with computers stood in neat rows as if under the command of an invisible conductor. In the corner, beneath a massive wall lined with monitors, several people in pristine white coats moved with precise, methodical motions. They appeared absorbed into this technological domain, part of its mechanism.

At the center of the room stood a curious device resembling a colossal old clock, complete with a vast dial and numerous moving components. They ticked with a profound mechanical rhythm, strangely harmonizing with the place's quiet. Three scientists nearby paid no attention to anything else, immersed in a lively discussion, their gestures underscoring their words.

A bit further on, around an oval table, sat five individuals—three men and two women. Their stern suits, measured posture, and deeply lined faces marked them as people of authority. Every eye was fixed on Michael, examining him like a rare specimen. One man, the tallest, raised his hand, inviting Michael to come closer.

He stepped forward slowly, sitting on the soft chair offered a few meters from the table. A sense of being on trial intensified. The entire scene felt like a legal hearing in which he was simultaneously witness, defendant, and judge. Background sounds—the rustling of paper, muffled chatter among the scientists, and the occasional clicking of keys—merged into a tense backdrop, magnifying the pressure.

"How shall I address you?" Michael asked, breaking the silence. His voice was firm, but he felt a knot of tension inside, pulling him downward. He didn't intend to address them with any unique title yet saw no way to cut through the silence.

"However you wish," said the man calmly, his deep voice resolute. "We realize you have many questions, and we can answer most of them. We're listening."

Michael felt every gaze at the table, pinning him down as if scanning each of his movements. Rising, carefully weighing his words, he removed his watch and extended it to the table.

"This," he said, feeling an odd relief, "is what you've been searching for all this time. At least, if I understand correctly, it's part of the code you need."

The man at the table furrowed his brow and inclined his head slightly. "Keep it," he said after a pause. It's a valuable gift for you—one that Olivia once made."

Michael looked at the watch, turning it in his hand. Under the dim light, an engraving glimmered on the back plate: "Never miss a single minute. Love, Liv." It struck a painful chord within him as if the name etched into metal held memories he couldn't yet reach.

"You've misunderstood," the man went on, his voice tinged with weariness. "You assume that, over the years, we've failed to grasp simple truths. These combinations mean nothing to us. In the wrong hands, they could do a great deal of harm to many people… and their souls."

Michael frowned, anxiously twisting the watch's band in his fingers. "What do these ciphers mean?" he asked, settling back into the chair and fastening the watch around his wrist.

The man leaned forward slightly, folding his arms on the table.

"One of our old experiments," he began. "If you use three sets of numbers matching fundamental physical constants on your side and combine them with one simple mechanism, you can find places where certain forces don't apply. That's where the barriers between both sides of a single reality fade. We call this the zero point of light's demise and darkness's birth. In that place, you can travel between sides… without special abilities."

"Transfer objects and matter?" Michael clarified.

"That's just one of a hundred properties of that point," the man replied, slightly shaking his head.

Michael studied the faces of those seated at the table, trying to detect any sign of emotion. He realized they were adept at hiding what they felt. The question echoing in his head slipped out unexpectedly, even to himself:

"You didn't kill those people, did you?"

The man's face darkened, but he answered without hesitation:

"Unfortunately, we're responsible for many deaths. But it was never our goal. Our laboratory was created for other purposes. Yet, as I said, we've played a part in many deaths."

"You tried to help…" Michael muttered almost in a whisper, lowering his gaze. "The people in this town—are they the ones in a coma on the other side?"

The oldest of the women at the table leaned forward slightly. Her face was deeply lined, yet her eyes reflected a strange combination of sadness and resolve.

"Yes and no," she began, her voice softer than the others. "Most of the inhabitants on our side are the deceased. For some reason, they're bound to this site and can't leave it. Over time, they've learned to exist here. As you've noticed, time flows differently. Some are near death on your side. They're like tourists, appearing here only briefly, and then their light fades. Some have come here because their bodies on your side aren't functioning properly. Temporarily or permanently, they can't live fully."

"Those who are in a coma," Michael said pensively.

"Yes, exactly," the woman confirmed. "Those who are in a coma. We do everything we can to find ways to awaken them and somehow affect the body on the other side while we're here. Unfortunately, we've mostly failed. Only a few patients left this side and wake up on yours. The method to reach each patient is individual."

"And the children who were on the list with other patients from your lab—are the children in a coma on the other side?" Michael asked his tone a mix of distrust and concern.

For a moment, the woman in the formal suit dropped her gaze as though choosing words carefully to soften the truth.

"Yes," she replied. "They were in a coma, and we tried in every way to help them. But sadly, only a handful made it back. We keep studying this, yet the laws of this world constrain us, and we can't bypass them."

Her voice was measured but filled with bitterness, as though each failure weighed on her.

"For now," interjected another older man, his tone more resolute, almost defiant.

Michael frowned, his gaze roaming the faces around the table.

"Then why not simply put these people to sleep on this side so they can wake on the other?" he asked, sounding naively logical, yet to him, it seemed convincing.

The man who had spoken earlier shook his head.

"That brings us to another group of people living on this side," the man began. "Dying here results in absolute death on both sides. And death in a coma on your side causes death here as well—but with a significant time delay."

He paused as though allowing Michael to digest what he'd heard.

"There are anomalies like you," he continued, altering his tone slightly. "If you die on this side while you're in a coma on the other, you'll most likely wake up. But that, too, depends on many factors. Some like you never regain consciousness on your side."

His words felt like a riddle hinting at something more significant. Michael instinctively touched his watch as if trying to draw an answer from its impassive face.

"There have been a few who managed to die on this side and, for some reason, wake up repeatedly on your side," the man added. "Among them are anomalies. Most people need to slip into a coma or a deep lethargic sleep, but there are those like you— ones who can go to sleep on one side and wake up on the other at will. Over time, they won't even need to fall asleep."

Michael felt a chill flash across his skin.

"But your kind—people like you—are a rare anomaly," another scientist interjected. "In almost every case, dying here also means dying on the other side. We can't kill every patient on the off chance that they're one of the rare ones who'll wake up over there."

Michael noticed the scientist's expression darken as he continued: "Unfortunately, Many of our patients are children. If our methods don't succeed, they leave and try to find a way out of this side on their own. Others remain, losing hope. The townspeople do what they can to give them purpose—though it doesn't always work."

The weight of those words pressed down on him, and Michael felt his heart pound faster.

"But we haven't given up hope of discovering how to wake them," said another woman, her voice softer than the rest but resolute. She met Michael's gaze, her eyes holding both compassion and determination. "When children show up on this side, they're often helpless and confused. Sometimes, they're lucky: others here help them adapt or even manage to send them back. But that's rare."

Michael tensed involuntarily, his thoughts tangling with questions, many unanswered. One thing, however, was clear: this world, as strange and severe as it was, kept struggling for life despite its limits and rules.

"Do people on this side sense anomalies like me?" Michael asked, leaning forward. His voice was firm, but he felt a slight tremor within.

The first scientist, seated closest, gave a small nod. "Yes, they do," he confirmed. "Most inhabitants here know exactly who you are. But..."

He fell silent for a moment as if searching for the right words. "Too often, trouble follows those like you to this side. So, people here prefer not to speak openly. They don't usually show their hand to a stranger—especially an anomaly. But you've probably noticed some do look at you differently."

Michael recalled the woman at the gate and how she held her breath upon meeting his eyes. It was as if she recognized something he couldn't yet grasp.

"There's even a cult," the scientist went on, lowering his voice almost to a whisper. "These people try to uncover the secrets of our world and bring their benefits to theirs. They believe they know how to handle the crossings and exploit the properties of light's death point. But if they succeed, the consequences will be dire. Very dire."

Michael felt his breath catch. The scientist's words sounded like a warning underpinned by fear.

"Who's Roy?" he suddenly asked, with a confidence that even he didn't understand.

A tense silence fell across the table. For a moment, even the mechanical ticking from the device in the room's center seemed too slow. The scientist cast his gaze aside before mustering himself to continue: "Roy isn't exactly a 'who.' He's another sort of anomaly—he has no body on your side, yet he can cross between sides," he said slowly. He's gathered a following of many people. On both sides of this world."

A tightness surged inside Michael. The scientist's words hung in the air, letting Michael's imagination fill in the details.

"These followers," the scientist continued, "often don't realize what they're doing. Many just follow him and believe in what he says—his promises. But they forget Roy has his agenda, which rarely aligns with the interests of either this world or yours."

Michael paused in thought. That name— "Roy"— seemed to stir something faint within him, like an echo of a memory he couldn't grasp.

"So, he was born on this side?" Michael asked.

"He wasn't born on this side," the man explained calmly. "He was born on yours but ended up here through a series of events we can't explain. Nothing anchors him to your side, yet he can still move between worlds. We suspect his crossings are time-limited, but we have no proof."

"How long has he been alive?" Michael asked, squinting.

"As far as we know, over two hundred years and thirty-four days, according to the time flow on your side," came the calm reply, laden with an unspoken heaviness. "He was the first traveler between the two sides that we ever documented."

"What's his goal?" Michael frowned, trying to comprehend.

"He wants to merge our worlds, forcing them together," his interlocutor said, pausing as if awaiting a reaction.

"But that goes against the essence of existence. Such a union would be the end of everything."

Michael froze. The words sounded impossible, yet some of him sensed they held some truth.

"Why are you telling me this?" His voice trembled slightly. "Why am I not detained or experimented on?"

His counterpart leaned in a little as though attempting direct eye contact.

"We believe in your abilities, Michael."

"And how do you know my intentions?" Michael asked sharply.

"We don't know your intentions," came the surprisingly gentle reply. "But we were able to study you fairly well from our previous meetings."

"Previous meetings?" Michael repeated without appearing too fazed. It didn't exactly shock him—he'd considered it—but the thought of this not being their first conversation still unsettled him.

As if he could read Michael's mind, the man said, "Memory loss is one of this world's defense mechanisms. Only rare anomalies like you can recall your visits. Even then, there are limits. Radiation from certain artifacts—like that crypt in the cemetery—recovered some of your memories."

Michael's scowl deepened. The word *crypt* echoed in his mind like the remnants of a long-forgotten dream.

"We believe Roy bet on this aspect of the crossing. He likely knew you wouldn't remember anything that could compromise him. You've learned and understood much in your visits to our world. For Roy, you might've been a valuable source. But once you started sensing and realizing more, you threatened him and his mission."

Michael fell silent, his gaze drifting for a few seconds to where several older men in gray coats pored over scattered papers and folders. Their motions seemed chaotic and orderly, as though each knew his role in this strange mechanism.

"Do you know where he is right now? How to stop him?" Michael asked, his voice louder than he'd expected, though he strove to appear composed.

The scientist maintained eye contact, not dodging the question. Weariness etched his features, yet his voice held unwavering conviction. "We don't know where he might be nor how to capture or stop him. We've never set out to hunt or destroy him. We can't harm any being—even if our survival depended on it."

Michael's fists clenched, tension rising, but he forced himself to breathe calmly. "But could you lock him up? In some form of prison or an equivalent? Isn't that possible?"

The scientist shook his head as though the suggestion was difficult and conflicted with their essence. "In his case, we can't detain him without causing harm."

"You tried to capture me by force. If I recall correctly, you sent armed men after me—at the lighthouse and later at the psychic's house. Isn't that so?" Michael straightened, his voice growing firmer.

A female scientist, standing somewhat aside, stepped forward. Her face remained calm, but her gaze was piercing.

"We weren't sure it was you; we just sensed a presence at some point. It can happen in various ways," she said in a measured tone. "We believed we'd caught Roy earlier. But it turned out to be part of his plan. He used us to get to your friend—Olivia."

"Olivia?" Michael leaned forward slightly, a knot of tension in his chest.

"Yes. By killing her in this world, he pulled her to his side once she woke up in yours…" The scientist's voice faltered. "She didn't remember her previous awakenings so that she couldn't resist. Now her memory has returned, but… she can't return."

"And soon it won't matter anymore," the scientist added quietly, looking somewhere beyond Michael's shoulder.

281

"She'll disappear?" he asked, barely managing to steady his voice.

"Her light will fade entirely," answered an older scientist, lowering his voice as if he feared the words themselves. "For now, she'll remain on this side for the rest of her days, but she won't lose her memories—they'll fully return. You still have time to speak with her."

Michael said nothing, processing the implications. The words "Her light will fade entirely" echoed in his mind.

"How can I remember everything?" he finally asked.

The scientist shook his head, the air of someone long accustomed to facing such questions.

"That's beyond our power. Only time and the forces of this side can help you. We don't control that process."

"Can I leave?" Michael asked, sounding calmer now.

"Yes, of course. At any point, if you have no more questions."

Michael nodded, gave his thanks, and rose from the chair, heading for the door. He was nearly there when it swung open, revealing a short, sturdy guard. With a slight chin tilt, the guard indicated Michael should follow.

The corridor to which he led Michael was as long and featureless as the last, but this time, offices with large windows lined the walls. Inside them, work bustled—people moving animatedly, arguing, trying to prove something to one another.

In one of the offices, its maroon curtain partially drawn, Michael glimpsed a little girl. She sat on a low sofa, hugging a huge plush toy nearly half her own size. She was speaking sadly to the toy; nearby, in a small armchair, a young woman with a tablet was tapping at the screen as though recording the girl's story. The room looked oddly staged, almost artificial—like a low-budget drama set.

"Please follow me," the guard's voice called out. He moved closer and motioned for Michael to continue. "I'm told to get you out as quickly as possible."

Michael nodded, offering no resistance. Within a minute, they were exiting the building. Passing a small security post, the guard escorted him to the first barrier and then bid farewell, ordering the gate to close.

Michael continued down the road, pausing briefly at the next set of gates and surveying the surroundings. A landscape stretched out before him, its distant houses barely visible. There was nothing for him here, so he pressed on.

Reaching an intersection, Michael noticed an old bus parked at the stop, its doors already closing. He shouted and ran. The bus started pulling away, but the driver slowly reopened the door.

Michael nodded, tossed a few bills to the driver, and found a seat. This time, he sat in an aisle seat, not bothering to look out the window. Lowering his forehead against the seat in front, he removed his watch.

Don't miss a single minute. Love, Liv.

"What did we manage to forget?" Michael whispered, barely audible even to himself.

Suddenly, the bus braked sharply, pitching him forward. The watch slipped from his hands and fell to the floor.

It was so abrupt, too abrupt for a city where everything usually moved in a lazy calm.

Michael hastily picked up the watch, put it back on, and straightened his sleeve.

"We can't go any farther," the driver declared curtly.

Michael looked ahead. A strange, almost surreal sight spread out before him.

In the middle of the road stood an old car engulfed in bright red flames tinged with bluish hues. The fiery tongues danced through the cold night air, splitting the silence with crackling and hissing sounds. Thick shadows spread on the asphalt around the vehicle, their outlines quivering like mirages under the flickering light. Michael was standing beside the bus driver, silently watching as the fire slowly but steadily consumed the car. Heat distorted the air around it like reality was giving way under its onslaught.

Something about the scene felt important—familiar. He couldn't explain what exactly, but a sense of alarm pulsed in his temples. Michael strained his eyes, trying to see through the smoke. Suddenly, realization struck him like lightning. He knew the car. It belonged to the older taxi driver he'd encountered more than once at critical moments, always appearing in the right place at the right time.

He stared intently at the driver's seat, but it was empty. The flames were already licking the steering wheel, yet no sign of anyone inside existed. Instinctively, Michael began scanning the surroundings. On the roadside, something dark and motionless caught his attention. His heart clenched, and he felt a surge of anxiety rising within him.

The bus door opened unexpectedly with a soft click as if the driver had guessed his thoughts. Without hesitation, Michael sprinted toward the figure lying by the roadside. The wind carried the stench of burning metal, but he barely noticed. Approaching, he carefully turned the person onto their back. It was him—the old taxi driver. His face looked pale, almost waxen, but life still lingered in the body. Michael bent in closer and heard weak, uneven breathing.

A deep wound gaped on the taxi driver's temple, from which a thick burgundy flow seeped slowly. It trickled around the edge of his face, running down onto the collar of his antique shirt. As Michael straightened up slightly, something warm and wet landed on his hand. He glanced down—a bright droplet fell onto the older man's shirt, adding a stark color to the gray night.

Suddenly, a stabbing pain shot through Michael's neck, like the thrust of a knife. He staggered, clutching his throat, but his hand met something sticky. Blood gushed from a torn artery. His throat filled with the hot fluid. Unwittingly, he dropped the man's body as his consciousness spiraled into darkness.

The last thing he saw before everything went black was a silhouette—human yet strangely blurred, as if dissolving into the night air. The figure retreated, merging with the darkness. Roy.

He jerked upright, gasping for air, pressing both hands to his neck. Barely aware of his surroundings, he reeled like someone who'd just burst from icy water. Nearby, a torch rolled across the floor with a clatter, scorching the air with its heat before stopping against a large chunk of stone. Its glow lit the walls, where coarse plaster peeled away, and the dancing shadows mocked his disoriented state.

He stood still until the trembling in his hands subsided, and his breathing steadied somewhat. After several long minutes, Michael looked around and realized where he was. This underground room beneath the lighthouse was familiar to him. Bare walls, the stale odor, a damp floor reflecting the dim flicker of the torch as though the flame was drowning—everything reminded him how long this spot had stood lifeless.

Michael sank heavily to the floor, leaning against the wall. Finally, the tension receded, and weariness swept over him in a wave. He stared at the waning torch flame.

"That was... seriously unexpected," he muttered, his voice trembling but laced with a growing resolve. "Never mind. I'll figure out how to pay you back in full."

He ran a hand over his face, leaving streaks of dust and sweat on his skin. His thoughts were tangled, but gradually, a semblance of a plan emerged from the chaos.

"If he planned on wiping my memory again, I may still have a chance—however slight—to get close. But if he wanted to finish me off once and for all... Meeting him now might be a bad idea when I know nothing about him." Michael exhaled and rubbed his neck, where he still felt the phantom ache of that bloody wound.

He lowered his head, reflecting on what had happened. The puzzle slowly formed in his mind, though many pieces remained missing.

"How did he even find me?" he muttered, glancing toward the dying torch. "Why so precisely? And what was that stunt with the taxi driver? He didn't pop up right away on this side, meaning he couldn't sense my location, or at least not right away. Last time, he was simply informed by phone."

Michael straightened up, his eyes flashing as if a new spark had been lit inside him.

"All right, first I need to figure out who I'm dealing with," he continued, his voice gaining a firmer edge. "The scientists mentioned they nearly knew the time he last showed up. So maybe there's a way to find clues about people who were in a coma or near death around here back then. Of course, that might not show up in electronic records." He sighed. "I'm guessing he's probably local. Which means I can check old documents. Population records, archives, historical references—anything."

Michael rested his head against the wall and shut his eyes.

He thought that walking about the city so freely probably wasn't the best idea, either. Who knew when they'd find the two recent corpses in the crypt—and might the police quickly link him to them? He needed to set his objectives clearly.

First, he had to seek out information about Roy. So far, the only clue was the symbol of Veles, a mark scratched onto a coffin and various notebooks. So, local folklore might be the next step. But as far as he knew, Veles was part of the Eastern Slavic tradition, which shouldn't have reached here in those days. He'd have to figure out how to check.

"Damn..." Michael exhaled through clenched teeth. "That twisted bastard has followers, maybe more than a few. I have no idea who I can trust," he muttered angrily.

"Maybe I should go back to the hotel. Somehow, it makes me feel calm and safe." An idea—maybe a dumb one—flitted through his mind, but no better plan had presented itself yet.

"Getting out of my tomb can only happen through the exit in the rocks. I need to see if it's high or low tide and whether I can open the door. Hard to fathom how it's withstood water pressure all this time," he continued thinking.

He approached the hefty door hidden in the rock wall, carefully sliding aside a small stone that concealed the mechanism. Resting his hand on the cold metal handle, he felt it shift slightly under his grip. Michael slowly pressed down, preparing to let go at any instant if the water pressure began forcing the door inward.

To his relief, there was no resistance. The door gave with a low creak. A tunnel opened before him, lit by the flicker of his torch. The air smelled damp, and a thin ribbon of silver water trickled along the ground, refracting the flame's glow.

"So it's not fully dry here, but the tunnel isn't flooded. Likely low tide," he remarked.

He didn't have time to confirm his assumptions. With resolve, Michael stepped into the tunnel, shutting the door behind him hard enough to send a dull echo through the cave.

A few minutes later, he emerged outside, drawing in a deep breath of cold, damp air. The nocturnal scene was framed by looming cliffs, lit only by moonlight. Michael lifted his gaze, trying to spot a familiar landmark. The clearing with the lighthouse's foundation rose higher up the slope, marking his way.

He planned his route in his head, lining it up with the lighthouse's position and recalling where he'd left his car. Ten minutes of weaving between prickly branches and rustling dead leaves brought it into view.

Walking over to the vehicle, he instinctively patted his pockets. To his surprise, the keys were still there.

He opened the unlocked door quickly, sliding into the driver's seat. He caught his breath and felt an unexpected pressure against his back. Twisting his shoulders, he froze: his backpack had been slung behind him all this time.

"What the hell... I'd forgotten I even had it," he thought. Taking the pack off, he tossed it onto the passenger seat and rifled through it. He found the tablet inside, the screen shattered by cracks and bits of the casing creaking under his fingers.

"Damn — definitely not going to get anything out of that," he muttered.

He recalled the path he'd recently traveled and felt sure he could retrace it without the GPS.

"Easy enough — almost all straight roads," sounded in his mind.

He started the engine and guided the car onto the narrow road leading back to the city. Night's shadows advanced behind him, cloaking the street in thick darkness. Flickers from the headlights deepened his sense of disconnection. The car moved at a slow pace, reflecting his mood — troubled yet focused. It was as though he wanted to postpone facing something unknown but inevitable.

Thoughts came in waves—his meager information, the tormenting uncertainty—frightened him. He clung to the belief that the hotel would be a safe spot. "You'll be safe there," Olivia said in his head.

He saw no reason to doubt her advice.

The car's headlights cut the dark, sweeping over houses lining the road and sparse trees that seemed less like vegetation and more like silent sentinels. Their shadows formed a discontinuous theater, shifting in real-time with every meter he advanced. Topped with yellow tungsten bulbs, old streetlamps served as relics of a past era, reminding him of when these streets bustled with activity. Their light fell onto the occasional square of cobblestone poking through the asphalt, lending an ancient tinge to the nighttime scene.

These images might have been ripped from the pages of old novels. Oil-lamp streetlights cast a soft, wavering glow. In those days, locals would come out morning and evening to ignite or douse them, giving the damp, rainy climate a cozy sense of comfort.

But now, the weather was oddly calm. It was almost perfect for this region—no rain, no thick fog, only a faint breeze seeping through the car's cracked window and mingling with the warm air from the heater. That slight wind wasn't enough to drown out the car's low, steady rumbling, as though it was part of the night's show.

Arriving at the hotel, he sat in the car for a few seconds, surveying the nearly empty street. He decided not to park in the small lot out front.

"You never know who might be aware of this 'unexpected acquisition' of mine," he thought, killing the engine.

Leaving the vehicle a few blocks up the street, he walked briskly back to the hotel. The late-night hush wrapped around him, broken only by the wind's sigh and the occasional twig crackle.

Upon reaching the hotel, he found the main door locked. It didn't surprise him—it was late, and the city had long been still. He glimpsed a figure rocking in a chair by the fireplace through the murky glass. The dim reflections of the flames cast erratic silhouettes on the walls. Michael hesitated, then knocked on the door. The faint taps didn't draw attention. He knocked louder.

The figure in the chair suddenly froze, going motionless so abruptly it made him uneasy. After a moment, it resumed its slow rocking as though nothing had happened. Michael was about to knock again, but a startling appearance from behind the door interrupted him—a lone older man, silent, watching him intently. He stood like that for a few seconds, then opened the door without a word.

"I'm staying in a room on—" Michael began, but the old man cut him off with a brusque aside:

"Make sure you lock up after you."

Michael nodded, stepped inside, and secured the door with a small, well-worn lock. Dim light reigned in the lobby. Only the fire in the hearth provided any illumination, licking lazily at the logs with a gentle crackle. Soft warmth emanated, lulling. He crossed the room quietly, trying not to make any noise. The ambiance felt suspended as if the very air was steeped in time.

Approaching the armchair, he realized the occupant was the same elderly lady who'd once told him about a painting. She sat facing a chessboard, the pieces set in a configuration he found vaguely familiar. Her slight movements seemed to merge with the hush of the night. Michael stepped closer and, without diverting his gaze, observed the board.

"Do you play chess?" came a voice unexpectedly, causing him to flinch.

He suddenly realized he'd spent several seconds transfixed by the interplay of light and shadow on the chessboard's black-and-white squares. Every piece sat in its proper place except for one—a white pawn advanced to E4.

"Unfortunately, I'm terrible at this," he confessed, embarrassed but smiling. "I got carried away by the moment: such a pleasant atmosphere and that chessboard, which seems perfectly in place."

He paused as if gathering his courage, then added, "May I trouble you with a few questions? I'm really not in the mood to sleep. I was thinking, maybe I could chat with a charming lady?"

She didn't smile broadly, but something warm flickered in her expression. "Why not? How could I refuse such a gentleman?" she replied, meeting his gaze with a slight wink.

They smiled simultaneously as though it was more than a mere exchange of words—a moment of silent understanding.

Michael settled into a chair, leaning forward slightly to catch the tone of their conversation. The room seemed to fill with quiet, marked only by the occasional crackling of the logs in the fireplace. The flames danced in an odd rhythm, casting warm reflections on the walls, where paintings of various sizes hung. Michael hesitated, lost for words, instead watching the fire lick at the edges of the logs. It was mesmerizing, like an old silent film, and his thoughts drifted beyond the comfort of this space.

"Very soothing," remarked the woman, shifting her glance from Michael to the flames. "I've always loved to watch fire. It holds everything within it. Like life, it flares up, reaches a peak, captivates you, and then gradually dies down to ashes. Every movement of the flame is unique, just like life."

Her voice was soft, almost tinged with sorrow, yet her eyes gazed admiringly into the fire. It was as though she saw something in it beyond warmth. Michael felt the moment was worthy of a painting—every detail perfectly arranged: the flickering glow of the fire, her thoughtful gaze, the paintings on the walls.

"I really liked your painting on the landing," he said, seizing a topic that might steer the conversation. "The one with the pub on the cliff. It's just stunning."

The woman gave a faint smile, a fleeting trace of pride.

"That's not my only piece. Every painting here is mine. I've been painting as long as I can remember."

Michael looked around in surprise. He'd barely noticed the hotel décor before, but now the walls came alive, like pages from an old book—large and small paintings filled nearly every free spot. One was perched on the coffee table, another near the fireplace. Their subjects were as varied as if they reflected the emotions and moments the artist had lived through.

"That's amazing. I'm ashamed I never noticed how many paintings are here. Why are they all in one place? Do you have a special admirer living here?"

For a moment, she glanced away, then let out a sad little laugh. "You could say that. This hotel belonged to my husband's parents. Apparently, they secretly bought my paintings wherever I sold them and displayed them here. I learned about it only after they died, and we moved in."

She hesitated, choosing her words, then continued, "We parted on bad terms when we left. They were against our marriage. My husband and I wanted to be independent, even though we barely had enough money for rent. I painted and sold what I could, but nobody wanted my work. We never asked them for help. But it turned out they couldn't just stand aside. Through acquaintances, they kept tabs on us and started buying my paintings. It supported me to keep going—I tried harder and improved, and eventually, studios started buying them too."

There was regret in her voice. "I never thanked them."

Michael leaned forward slightly as if to comfort her. "So these paintings are your early works? I can't imagine how incredible your later pieces must be if even these are so impressive."

His words drew a faint smile from her, though the hint of sadness remained. Once more, she glanced at the flames as though seeing reflected memories there that both burned and consoled.

"I see you often painted that place," Michael said, gently turning a small picture on the table to show her what he meant—a canvas depicting the same pub on a cliff he already knew.

"I spent a lot of time watching it," she began, momentarily lost in her recollections. "My parents, as well as theirs before them, went there often. It probably became a pub later—at least, I like to think so."

She broke off as if deciding whether to continue. "But that story… it'd take more than one night to tell. Are you truly interested?"

"Absolutely. Why not?" Michael encouraged her, trying to sound genuinely interested so she would continue.

"They're mostly rumors," she said quietly, as if afraid her words might bring the tale to life within those walls. "I never got the whole truth. After my parents vanished, there was no one to ask, and no point, really."

She paused for a second, then, leaning in slightly, began her tale: "Long ago, centuries back, there was a cult in our area calling itself 'Na Dorsair Anam,' which translates to 'Guardians of Souls.' According to legend, it was founded by scientists of Slavic origin who emigrated from Eastern Europe. Their main pursuit was immortality—like many sects of that time."

She paused as though weighing her words, then continued, "They believed the soul was an energy source that could be preserved. To them, the body was a temporary vessel, and the brain was the seat of divine consciousness. They conducted experiments—some scientific, some pseudo-scientific, some outright occult. Their idea was to find a way to transfer souls or store them for a later return to the world."

Michael narrowed his eyes, listening intently, determined to miss none of it.

"They supposedly developed methods to slow the decomposition of brain tissue using alchemy and strange rituals. Over time, they amassed many followers—not just scientists but monks and preachers as well. And though their beliefs were rooted in the old Slavic pagan pantheon, they adapted it to local traditions."

"Veles," Michael said softly, recalling. "The god of the boundary between worlds, wealth, magic. A guide between the realms of the living and the dead."

She nodded. "Yes, exactly. In Celtic mythology, there's a deity with some similar traits—like Dagda, the creator and keeper of life and magic. Maybe that's why the cult was able to blend in with local beliefs."

She paused, gazing once more into the fireplace. "But as far as anyone knows, they never did anything especially horrific—at least, nothing was documented. In fact, they hardly stood out. Their gatherings were secret; their experiments were hidden. No one really knew what they were doing."

Her voice dropped to almost a whisper. "My parents were part of that cult too—or what remained of it. Over the decades, it lost its power and slowly vanished. Their generation was likely the last. And, like the cult, my parents disappeared. One day, they just never picked me up from school."

She fell silent, her thoughts drifting, and again, she looked at the painting on the table.

"But the grapes that grew there were amazing," she said with a soft smile, her face lighting up with a warm memory. "All tangled with the sweetest, most wonderful blueberries."

Michael fixed his gaze on one of the paintings hanging on the wall as though noticing its details for the first time.

"I've just realized how meticulously you depicted the plants in this landscape," he said, leaning back to take in the entire painting.

"I love painting plants. They're always beautiful," she replied with a gentle smile, remaining seated. Her eyes drifted leisurely about the room, lingering on the paintings adorning the walls. "Over there"—she motioned toward one of the pieces a short distance away—"Calluna vulgaris and Gentiana. Their blooms are incredible—vivid, intense, like fire. All those plants come from that place. Most of my work is about that hill by the cliff."

She paused briefly, then turned to a small canvas on a table near her.

"And that, it's quite a rare plant," she said, indicating the flower pictured there. "It doesn't strike you with vibrant colors, but it captivated me. I painted it again and again. That's Lomatogonium."

Her tone softened as if lost in thought.

"Poets attribute mystical properties to it," she said. "They claim it protects the mind, boosts magical energy... All of that sounds odd yet beautiful, of course. That is probably not true. But the flower bewitched me for a very long time."

Michael nodded, studying the small canvas. *What an interesting place*, he thought, once again looking at the paintings that filled the walls.

"Does that pub still have owners? Maybe grandchildren or great-grandchildren?"

"I don't know," she said, shrugging slightly, her hands resting calmly on the chair's arms. "I never knew who ran the place."

"Actually, I always thought there was just one older man there who looked after it—no relatives," she answered, her gaze drifting distractedly around the room. "But I never really gave it much thought. Certainly, it hasn't operated as a pub for ages."

Michael mulled this over, his gaze lingering on the paintings.

"They're wonderful," he said somewhat offhandedly as if the words had slipped out. Realizing he'd sounded abrupt, he added, "Anyway, I need to get some rest. Thank you for the story."

He rose from his chair, inclining his head to show gratitude.

"You can take this painting as a keepsake," she said, motioning gently toward the small canvas on the nearby table.

"Thank you," Michael replied with a smile, then shook his head. "Better it stay here, at least until I sort out my affairs. I'm afraid I'd lose it or damage it somewhere along the way."

"As you wish," she said softly, her gaze drifting to the window.

"Thanks again," he repeated.

Michael turned to leave, but just as he was exiting, he caught her voice, barely above a whisper:

"Good luck, Michael."

Heading up the stairs to his floor, he almost automatically opened the familiar door. Stepping in and shutting it behind him, he felt a sudden, unusual relief. In place of tension came an inexplicable calm, as though the air in this room held an unseen, comforting glow.

He dropped his backpack on the bed and collapsed beside it, stretching his legs and closing his tired eyes. But he couldn't sleep.

A sudden realization jolted his mind like lightning in the night sky, and he opened his eyes. A fleeting memory sparked—words from one of the scientists about people who could transport items between worlds by moving themselves.

"What if…" he murmured, unable to contain excitement.

He rose from the bed, heart pounding a little faster, and went to the hiding place he'd picked on the other side. The precise image materialized in his mind: a small partition behind which he'd stashed his find. Michael slid it aside and froze for a moment. Before him lay a thick folder covered with a thin layer of dust, and on top, a small box neatly wrapped in brown paper.

Carefully, as though afraid to break some fragile secret within, he lifted out both the folder and the box. Returning to the chair, he wasted no time opening the folder. His fingers flipped through the printouts, eyes devouring every paragraph.

Now, every page, every snippet of text, grew clearer in a way it never had before. What once seemed a random flow of data formed a coherent picture. This time, he understood almost all of it.

Only a few pages remained puzzling, but he had strong enough hunches to proceed. One prominent article described an elderly doctor who claimed to have discovered a way to preserve donor organs indefinitely. His conclusions strangely blended science and mysticism.

Then came a recipe that stirred odd feelings in Michael:

- Water from the first underground source

- Heather extract for soul protection

- Gentian and juniper for antiseptic properties

- Honey, for stabilization

- Drops of whiskey for "alchemical transformation"

- Pine resin for a protective coating

- Powdered dried blueberries to enhance the antioxidant effect

Further down on the page was a clipping from an old newspaper about this same doctor's public execution, sentenced for experiments on living people that caused numerous deaths. He was found guilty of monstrous crimes and condemned to die.

Michael paused, staring at the doctor's photograph, which depicted a gaunt face but still with a fierce determination in his eyes as if his beliefs were unshaken even in the face of death.

He spent a few more minutes skimming the remaining sheets before shutting the folder and stuffing it into his backpack. Standing with a heavy push off the bed, he headed for the door. It was perfectly clear that he needed to go to that place—too much pointed him there from the start. As far as he could recall, everything pushed him in that direction. Taking the stairs down, he passed the painting on the wall without glancing at it—maybe the first time he had done so. In the lobby, he paused, turning toward the fireplace, hoping to see the elderly lady, but the chair stood empty, the chessboard frozen in its standstill with the pawn on E4. Pulling up his collar, he left the hotel decisively.

Walking briskly to the car he'd left parked a few blocks away, Michael watched the city slowly awaken. Dawn was breaking, and shafts of orangey light chased away the gray hue on the old building facades. A light wind tousled the trees, dislodging the few leaves that clung to them. He opened the car door in one quick motion and dropped into the driver's seat. The engine started without a hitch, and five minutes later, its weary groan carried him onto a wide road shrouded in early dawn mist.

The drive turned out to be shorter than expected. The route was familiar from his "previous life." A narrow, winding strip of asphalt twisted between old groves and the occasional field. Along the roadside stood dark trees like silent sentinels. Many of them had shed their leaves, their branches thick with moss, looking sickly yet majestic. The green tunnels formed by intertwined treetops begrudgingly let the headlights through, barely moving in the faint breeze. The world felt motionless, stuck in its own damp, clammy hush.

After a while, the road got worse—narrow and battered, its old potholes filled with rainwater. The taxi driver had once said this was the quickest route, and Michael trusted his word. He pressed on, hardly giving it thought, as though steered by some unspoken force. When the hill with the pub emerged in the distance, he eased off the gas. Slowing now, he realized he'd been driving purely on emotion, giving himself no time to think or plan.

"Well, might as well keep it that way," he muttered aloud, a slight smirk curling his lips.

Michael parked the car carefully beside the building. Dawn was just beginning, and the pale morning light uncovered the dead silence of that place. The pub's windows and doors were boarded up, covered with dust and grime, telling him it had been abandoned for some time—like a forgotten sentry left to guard emptiness.

He exited the car, opened the trunk, and surveyed its contents. There was little inside, but his hands instinctively found what he needed: a small flashlight and a hunting knife. Though they didn't inspire much confidence, they brought a degree of reassurance.

Standing before the pub's massive door, he hesitated a few seconds, waiting for a sign or inspiration. However, an inner voice suddenly told him this wasn't the right place to start. Turning around, he headed toward a small house about a hundred meters away.

At first glance, the house looked ordinary, almost inconspicuous. But as Michael drew closer, he noticed how badly it had deteriorated. The roof had collapsed long ago, open holes revealing patches of sky. Walls overgrown with horsetail and juniper gave it a strange, nearly unnatural look, as though the house wanted to blend into the earth and vanish from human eyes.

Flowers thrived around the property. The untended garden had run wild, taking over every inch of ground. Among the splotches of color, he spotted clusters of Gentiana—lilac flowers, gentle yet bright, sprawling over the ground like a threadbare carpet. Once, they might have been laid out in neat beds, but the years had allowed nature to take over. Like everything around, the Gentiana had become feral yet vibrantly alive.

Skirting the ramshackle structure, he soon located an overgrown entryway a few meters behind the house. It was disguised as a small shed, now rotted away; its door had long since fallen off, resting half a meter above a tangle of ferns, revealing another small door in the ground.

Michael tested the shed's integrity, pushing it lightly to ensure it wouldn't collapse on him when he went down. It hadn't seemed reliable at first glance, yet it didn't buckle; evidently, over the years, the plants had not only covered it from the outside but grown inside, reinforcing it. Clearing a path through the doorway, he stepped into the shed and worked on opening the second door.

The ladder was nearly flat and slightly angled to the ground, so this door was in better condition than the first. It resisted his efforts. He fiddled with it for ten minutes, prying around with the hunting knife from every side. It was definitely locked from within. Eventually, he broke the hinges, cracked enough of the door to fit an arm inside, and removed a thick board blocking it. Now, nothing prevented him from opening it; bracing his feet, he yanked it toward him. With an awful creak, it gave way.

Michael pulled a flashlight from his pocket, scanning for traps, and shone it forward chaotically. Everything looked normal. A short concrete staircase led down perhaps five or seven meters. A thick layer of dust coated the steps and walls, consistent with the structure's age. He descended slowly, overseeing each step while peering into the distance. The dust kicked up by the open door swirled in the air, hampering both his breathing and visibility.

At the bottom, he came upon yet another door—this one metal, looking as though it had been taken from a submarine. Next to it stood a small cabinet with a warning about high voltage. Michael opened it to find a large, old-fashioned switch in the off position.

He flipped the switch and waited. At first, nothing happened. As soon as he stepped back, though, metal groaned, and a faint hum sounded. A lamp overhead began slowly to glow a grimy yellow, and at that moment, a light above the metal door turned faintly green. The door gave a click as though inviting him in.

Michael pressed the cool metal handle and pulled. The hinges squeaked against the dead silence, but the door yielded without struggle, letting him enter the next room. What greeted him was utterly unexpected.

A chamber stretched nearly thirty meters long and almost as wide, lined with about a dozen computer desks holding ancient CRT monitors—vestiges of another era. Other desks were cluttered with massive old printers and bulky office gear. The weak overhead lighting fell across these forgotten machines, heightening the sense of abandonment.

A sizeable semicircular table of heavy redwood stood at the center of the room. It bore a symbol Michael recognized, sending a chill through his chest. Around the table were dozens of chairs as if waiting for a secret council. The walls displayed huge topographic maps, dust-covered, with more modern (though clearly outdated) monitors fixed next to them.

Moving closer, Michael noticed some large sheets of paper on the semicircular table. These turned out to be local maps with detailed notations about mineral deposits. Rows of numbers and text flickered before his eyes, but what caught his attention more was at the far wall.

There stood a tall shelving unit crowded with glass cylinders. Despite their murky fluid, Michael could see human brains in some. The shelf appeared old and rotted; its lower section had cracked, spilling dozens of cylinders onto the floor. The shattered vessels had left black mold patches growing there, a stark reminder of time's passage.

The contents of the remaining cylinders had also decayed with time. The fluid in most had evaporated, leaving behind dried organic matter. Some cylinders had cracked, their cloudy fluid leaking out, staining the shelf with dark splotches. Only a few containers seemed intact. The liquid remained clear inside them, and the organs were disturbingly well-preserved. Each cylinder had a small gray folder with a white spine, some labeled with names, but more often, "Experiment No. ..."

Michael pulled one folder out, flipped through, and recognized detailed records of an experiment: a brain immersed in a special preservative fluid, complete with chemical formulas mixing science, rare herbs, and mention of unknown elements. The exact timelines for adding components showed the author's meticulous nature. Scanning a few more folders, he saw the same thing repeated—endless attempts to preserve organs.

Replacing the folders, Michael stepped away from the shelf, a growing sense of horror welling within him. Near the shelf was a small brown door with a round metal knob. Feeling a sudden urge, he opened it and entered another room.

This space felt different—like a lounge or an old smoking room. A few large, dark-brown sofas of archaic design were arranged in a semicircle. In the center stood a low coffee table with a glass top littered with ashtrays, old papers, and faded yellow newspapers. On the wall hung a large monitor, and beneath it, nearer a corner, stood a metal cabinet with numerous drawers, like a library card catalog.

Michael approached and opened the top drawer. Inside were cards with photos and brief descriptions: name, age, gender, occupation, etc. The pages had yellowed but were still readable. Michael leafed through them, searching for something vital until his eye landed on a second drawer labeled "R—S." He opened it and started flipping through. Moments later, he found the file he'd been seeking.

Faded text on the paper bore a photograph affixed—actually a photo of a pencil sketch—a gaunt man of about thirty, short-haired. The face was unforgettable: Roy—actually, Roy Morov Velin. Under the photo, read a concise summary: birthplace—Cluj-Napoca (Transylvania, Austrian Empire); year of birth—1754; date of death—none—occupation: founder.

Lower down was a note: "A scientist, alchemist, and mystic, known for his work bridging science and ancient beliefs. He was accused of heresy and banished from his hometown for clandestine experiments rumored to have caused multiple deaths. His worldview blended knowledge of nature, magic, and forgotten pagan rites."

Michael crushed the page in his fist and flung it against the wall. His breathing grew labored, and the weight of this revelation pressed heavily on his mind. But there was still one more door. He strode over to it, opening it in one swift motion.

Immediately, a dense, choking odor rushed out—a mixture of moldy dampness, rusted iron, and decay, forcing Michael to recoil. Metal tang interlaced with chemical fumes, prompting him to cover his face with his sleeve. The space that met his eyes looked like an operating room, akin to a butcher's workshop. Brownish-red stains marked the floor and the large table, evidence of gruesome experiments. Michael slammed the door shut, unable to stare any longer. Everything was already too clear.

Crossing the room, his eyes again flicked to the coffee table. Anatomical diagrams and some printouts with photos of various plants and flowers were spread across the glass surface, but nothing stood out. Glancing around, he spotted another door in the far corner, locked. It is an ordinary interior door, not exceptionally sturdy.

Without hesitation, Michael threw his shoulder against it. With a dull crack, the frame splintered, and the door fell inward, swinging on its hinges until it stopped. Before him lay a central office. Its imposing, nearly threatening décor left a strong impression.

In the middle stood a giant carved wooden desk, its many layers of lacquer worn and dulled over time. Two matching chairs sat before it, and across from them was a big armchair, almost like a throne. Bookcases lined the walls, crammed with volumes. A dark red rug on the floor was so thick with dust that it muffled Michael's steps. Dim light from an antique chandelier added a sinister vibe.

On the desk was almost nothing—just a few thick blank sheets of paper and a silver pen in a holder.

Circling around, Michael tugged on a desk drawer, which he found locked. The old, frail mechanism gave way with a strong pull. Inside lay only an ancient revolver with six bullets in its chamber. Michael took it, tucking it into his belt.

Beneath the drawer was a small, locked compartment that was easy to force open. Inside it were documents in folders. Michael sat on the floor, sifting through them. Most contained text, diagrams, and notes, but one folder caught his eye—a file on himself.

Opening it, he saw reports of surveillance. It recorded attempts at recruitment, his refusals, and subsequent actions. From these documents, he gathered that for the first time, "on the other side," he was forced into the situation. The first time, he fell into a coma and met an agent who tried to persuade him to cooperate, but the attempt failed due to partial memory retention.

The report described four failed tries to wipe his memories before they succeeded on the fifth, believing it lost forever. It also referenced his connection to Olivia: *Michael thought we were together from the start*. Eventually, circumstances drew them together, though the details weren't precise. The records mentioned a need to separate them and implant a new reality for each, possibly what had driven Roy to kill Olivia and a random witness. In the end, there was a hypothesis that Michael possessed specific talents that could help study crossing between sides.

The final entries were dated ten years earlier. So, at least a decade ago, they'd been destroying his life. Michael suspected Roy continued his schemes beyond that, especially given how many times his memory had been manipulated and how many times he'd died on that side, only to begin again here.

The burden of his past, of such blatant injustice, weighed heavily on him. He closed the folder, tossed it onto the floor, and rose to his feet.

He stepped out into the large room and headed toward the shelf lined with glass cylinders. On the topmost shelf, in the middle, stood a cylinder labeled with a wooden tag on which the words "R M Velin" were engraved in gold letters. Michael's hand instinctively went for the pistol at his waist, and he froze, the barrel aimed at the cylinder. Inside the transparent, viscous liquid floated a brain like an oversized jellyfish in cramped quarters.

This might not work, flickered through his mind. *If I destroy his body—or what's left of it—it won't guarantee he dies on the other side. And if he dies, how much time will pass there before he's gone forever? Maybe it'll only prevent him from coming back here.*

The very fact that Roy could keep coming back without a physical body—just a brain preserved in an old bunker—confirmed Michael's suspicion. He lowered the gun, stepping away toward the table in the middle of the room. Turning a chair around, he sat down, staring at the shelf. Time passed slowly. The countless minutes he spent thinking led nowhere.

Finally, he turned toward the table, leaning his elbows on its surface. Among the printouts lay a newspaper article page in which Mikela explained the existence of two sides of one reality. She proposed hypotheses, including one about different flows of time. Michael had guessed as much. The article maintained that having a physical body on "that side" was impossible. That world, termed the "spirit world," was supposedly unreal. People stayed there briefly as souls or projections while interacting with objects, which was deemed an illusion.

But to Michael, both worlds felt undeniably real, with genuine sensations. *No, it's definitely not just some projection of another reality. He thought I felt everything—water in the shower, paper in a folder.* Suddenly, his train of thought broke off. He froze. The pages in that thick folder had ended up on this side…

It dawned on him that if they turned up here and only I knew about them, then it was probably me who brought them. If I can bring objects here, maybe I can also bring them back.

His gaze slid over to the shelf, holding those grotesque glass cylinders under the dim lamp. "Might as well try," he whispered.

First, just in case, he needed to safeguard his body on this side. Even though nobody seemed to have entered these rooms in ages, anything could change at any moment. Rising from the chair, Michael headed for the exit.

Outside, he was hit by a powerful gust of wind that resisted as he tried to open the doors. A storm had come. Rain battered his face with razor-like speed, forcing him to squint. The wind bent the trees, heightening the sense of chaos. The weather had shifted.

Michael made his way to the boarded-up old pub. Circling around to the back door—once used by the staff—he found it haphazardly boarded up, though one gap allowed him to pry loose aboard. Using it as a battering ram, he struck around the lock. After a few well-aimed hits, the lock gave. Grabbing another board, he tore it away, clearing the doorway. He slipped inside and pulled the debris behind him, shutting the door.

Instantly, the stale stench of neglect and alcohol enveloped him. Mold coated the walls of this place, which had been abandoned for years. Moving through a short hallway, he yanked down several old curtains. Emerging into the main hall, he went behind the bar and spread the fabric on the floor there. He settled on the makeshift bedding, hiding behind the bar, gun in hand, covered by a piece of the curtain.

Michael steadied himself, slowing his pulse with measured breaths. This time, it took only a few minutes for his body to drift into a light oblivion.

A fitful breeze blew cold raindrops onto him, their weight building until they dribbled down his face and neck, slipping beneath a still-not-fully-soaked shirt. He opened his eyes to find himself on that old, painfully familiar wooden pier—the same recognizable smell of damp, partially rotted boards mixed with fish and decaying seaweed.

He lay sideways on a pier bench. Nobody was around. Dawn had just begun, and the sun was scarcely rising, but the ominous gray clouds on the horizon delayed it. He rose from the cold bench, unsteady, and headed toward the square. Roy had surprised him last time—he couldn't let that happen again. This might be his final chance.

Must act fast, Michael thought. Somehow, Roy had tracked him down. Probably, he'd been watching the lab, or one of his people had informed him Michael was leaving the building. But that no longer mattered. Michael planned to reach the cliff-top pub and get beneath it. On this side, presumably, the pub was open, and the bar patrons likely served as an underground bunker guard. Last time, the bartender had given him a ride—he'd probably tipped Roy off to his presence. But maybe Roy believed Michael was dead and wouldn't expect him now.

He recalled the taxi driver's words: *From the fork, go almost straight along the cliff.* But the route was dangerous, especially in this weather... which was always strange.

Before reaching the square, Michael turned down a side street, searching for transport. He spotted a small car driven by a significantly older woman. Waving his arms, he tried to flag her down. After a short hesitation, she braked. A kindly old face in huge black-framed glasses peered through the window.

"Can I help you?" she asked slowly, sounding unsure.

"Could you drop me off on the road out of town, where the trail to the pub starts?"

"I'm not going exactly there, but I can let you out near it," the old woman replied.

Michael nodded, trying to open the front door, only to see a small dog, as old as its owner, curled up on the passenger seat. The creature stared at him disapprovingly. Quickly, he switched to the back seat and got in.

The ride lasted barely ten minutes. They said nothing the whole time. As they stopped, the older woman pointed toward a scarcely visible path disappearing into the horizon.

Michael thanked her and climbed out of the car. Pulling up his collar, he walked away without looking back, heading for that trail.

Stepping onto the path, he realized why the taxi driver had spoken with dread. The path was almost invisible—at times, it vanished entirely, and Michael walked more instinctually than any sign of a trail. The footway was close to the cliff's edge, or perhaps the cliff began right where the path ended. Finally, he reached the flatter ground. Pushing aside the wet grass that clung to his legs, he spotted the single-story pub in the distance.

He quickened his pace, now half-crouching. Skirting the bar, he nearly hurled himself into the wild growth of grapes and blueberries. Only a few meters remained between the shrubbery and a small shed that led into the underground hideout on the other side. He sprinted toward the shed without stopping to think, though caution might have been wise. Luck was with him: nobody stood by the entrance or on the steps after the first door.

He paused a few seconds to catch his breath, then continued down the stairs. On the landing below, he found a different door. Actually, it wasn't a door—a light curtain blocked entry into the room. Cautiously, he pulled it aside and peeked in.

The room was dark. A weak overhead light didn't suffice for such a space. Even in the gloom, he could tell it was used as a cellar for storing barrels—likely whiskey or wine. There were many. Michael hugged the wall, heading for a far corner where, on the other side, he remembered a shelf.

Let this work, he thought. But before halfway through, he heard heavy footsteps behind him. He dropped behind one of the barrels, turning toward the sound. Two tall men came in seconds later, grunting as they lugged a large barrel inside. They carefully set it in an empty spot, caught their breath, glanced around, and left.

Michael waited a bit longer, then continued. Suddenly, he heard the lock engage from the outside. Apparently, those guys hadn't forgotten to secure the door.

"Well, it can't all be easy," Michael muttered, almost philosophically.

As he moved closer, he realized the corner was empty. No shelf, no cylinders. He took another step, and a sudden stabbing pain exploded in his head. His vision went white, and he collapsed. Pressing his hands to his eyes, he rubbed them feverishly. Only after some minutes did his sight return. At the same time, he felt a metallic taste in his mouth and a warm, thick fluid dribbling from his ears and down his neck.

He ran his hand beneath his ears, which appeared stained in a dark red hue. Thin streaks of blood trickled from his ears and nose, clotting at once on his skin. Michael squeezed his eyes shut, then opened them to see, right before him, that same wooden shelf filled with those dreadful cylinders. For another minute or so, he sat, utterly spent. His arms and legs felt like jelly, barely responding to him.

Mustering his strength, he stood and dragged himself over to the shelf. Leaning on one of the ledges, he gazed at the cylinder labeled "R M Velin." *Well, I can permanently destroy it later,* he thought. He picked up the cylinder and headed for the exit. After a few steps, he set it down and returned to the shelf. Seizing its frame, he yanked it sharply, toppling the entire structure. A loud crash rang out as dozens of cylinders shattered on the concrete floor, echoing painfully in his ears. *Now* he could go.

Grabbing the cylinder again, Michael made for the exit. Nearby, he spotted a black trash bag, which he quickly emptied and slid the cylinder inside. Climbing the steps, he tugged on the doors several times. As expected, it was locked from the outside. But, since it opened outward, forcing the flimsy wooden door wasn't difficult. He tried to make as little noise as possible. When it finally gave, he waited a second before stepping out, checking that no one was coming. Then he emerged, crouched, and ran through the grape and blueberry bushes behind the pub, hiding among tall shrubs.

He moved along the path more slowly now, formulating his next steps. From everything he had learned recently, it seemed crucial to make Roy confront his own remains. But he needed a secure place to stage this meeting.

The best way to lure him out is to expose myself by visiting the lab. They're likely monitoring it, and I'll be ready for an attack this time. The scientists might help detain him, although they'll surely refuse to do him any harm. Even a long captivity would be enough. So that's settled — the bus stop, Michael thought.

With these thoughts, he stepped onto the paved road and headed toward the bus stop. Near it, he noticed a small hardware shop. Carrying the trash bag around was inconvenient, so he went inside. Several backpacks were hanging right by the entrance. Without much thought, Michael grabbed one, approached the clerk, and handed over some money. The clerk gave a silent nod, and Michael returned to the bus stop, stuffing the trash bag with the cylinder into the newly purchased backpack along the way.

He didn't have to wait long for the bus. After about twenty minutes, an old bus driven by a young woman arrived. The door opened, Michael boarded, dropped some coins for fare, and sat in the rows right behind the driver.

The ride wasn't long. He barely thought of anything during it, simply gazing at the soggy gray landscape outside the bus window.

Michael hopped out onto the wet gray asphalt when the doors finally opened. After several looks around, he quickly descended a well-kept road toward the lab. The doors opened almost immediately at the first gate, letting him through, and the second gate did the same. As soon as he reached the gates, they swung open, the guards behind them stepping aside in unison. One guard requested him to wait for an escort and indicated a spot a few meters from the gates. Michael complied. A few minutes later, another guard arrived and gestured for him to follow toward the main building.

They entered and proceeded down a long, bright corridor to the central room where he'd been received last time. Just as before, they halted outside for about a minute. Suddenly, the guard's mono earpiece crackled; he opened the door to the room. Inside, work was bustling: several dozen white-coated personnel were busy with tasks or deep in discussion. At the large table, this time, sat only one scientist. He invited Michael to sit in one of the chairs a few meters from the table. Michael obliged.

"What brings you this time?" the scientist began.

"I think I have a chance to catch your possible main enemy. He won't be able to slip away because I likely have something to interest him. But since I'm no fighter and not armed, I would like you to spare some of your operatives to apprehend Roy.

"You do realize we cannot harm living beings?"

"I'm not asking you to harm him. If it comes to that, I'll figure out a way. All I need is an armed group for intimidation."

"In that case, we can help you under one condition. Our staff should not be put at risk, if possible."

"Of course. There's a lighthouse near here, which you probably know about."

"Certainly," the scientist replied curtly.

"I need a few of your soldiers to station themselves in and around the lighthouse. At the right moment, they can surprise the target by suddenly appearing. And afterward, they can escort him back here for detainment, at least for a while, until I figure out what's next."

"That can be arranged," the scientist said, stretching his words. "I'll have them set up an ambush near the lighthouse." He leaned slightly toward the table, and nothing happened for a few seconds. He didn't change expression, focusing intently on a spot before him.

"It's done. They'll be waiting for you at the lighthouse, well hidden."

"Great. Then we have a little time. He's probably already been told I've 'come back from the dead' again, and he'll be heading this way. Might I ask you a few more questions?"

The scientist nodded, and Michael thought for a moment before continuing:

"As I've gathered, I've been here many times—this city in particular. Why doesn't anyone recognize me except you? You mentioned everyone here knows who or what I am. And how could I at least partially restore my memory?"

"You interacted with very few people during your presence on this side. Most of the time, you remained inside the lab, working security and later conducting research. You helped us in several areas of rehabilitation and uncovering our patients' true nature. Thanks to you, some of them managed to return home to their side. But your greatest contribution was developing knowledge of the zero point—where light dies, and darkness is born—along with Olivia. You both made major advances, particularly with children. But at some point, we lost you again, and on subsequent visits, you faced partial opposition here, having been recruited to certain other interests. As we said before, we can't currently restore your memory. We're still working on it, but our only success was with your acquaintance, Olivia. And after she left our side and came back, she lost that knowledge. She worked with our patients for a long time, helping them regain their memories."

"Where is she now?" Michael asked, surprising even himself.

"She's in the children's center attached to the lab. She's recalling a lot, continuing to do so until her light fades."

"How much time does she have left?" Michael asked, his voice tinged with sadness.

"We're not sure. Could be hours, could be years."

"Can I see her?"

"Yes, of course. She'll be free in a few hours, and you can meet with her then."

"Then let's postpone that. First, we need to capture the criminal."

"She'll wait for you. She's quite strong."

"I think enough time has passed; I should head to the ambush site. Thank you for your help and for answering my questions."

"I hope it goes well for you," the scientist said politely, nodding once and lifting his hand in a goodbye gesture.

Michael stood from the chair and turned to the door with a slight wave of his own. As he moved within a meter of it, the door swung open, and the same guard waited outside. The guard gestured in another direction, indicating it would be the quicker route for Michael's mission. Without speaking, Michael followed him. Once they exited the building, they headed back to the checkpoint, where the gates were opened in advance. The guard stopped at the first perimeter, and Michael continued to the next. The moment he reached the second gate, it opened nearly on its own, letting him out.

Taking a quick look around, he strode across the lawn in the lighthouse's direction. He could see its tower even from here, though tall trees tried to conceal it. It was practically next door, and Michael arrived in less than ten minutes, never once looking back. Only as he approached the lighthouse did he glance around. Seeing no one, he moved closer, placing both hands on the old stonework. Closing his eyes, he tried to steady his breathing and racing heart. But before he could fully calm himself, footsteps sounded in the bushes from the direction he'd come five minutes earlier.

Michael spun around to see Roy approaching, pistol in hand.

"I was sure that time would've been your last disappearance," Roy growled hoarsely and angrily. "Guess I'll have to kill you yet again."

"And how many times have you done that?"

"Not enough."

"Give it up, Roy. You won't get out of this alive. Surrender, and I'll spare you."

Roy smirked, but at that moment, three guards with automatic rifles emerged from behind the thick greenery. Two more appeared on the lighthouse's first tier, and a couple came around from the opposite side.

"Interesting," Roy said with a sneer. "You have no idea who you're dealing with. This isn't over."

He raised his pistol, alarming the guards, but after a second, he bent his elbow, putting the gun to his temple, and pulled the trigger. The lifeless body collapsed onto the damp ground. Without a word, the guards lowered their weapons and disappeared back into the undergrowth. Their task was complete.

"Well, I guess that was the end," Michael said quietly, as if to himself.

He stood there, bemused, surveying the unexpected scene for a moment. Then he slipped off his backpack, opened it, and retrieved the glass cylinder in a black plastic bag. Removing the bag, he found another surprise: in the cylinder, it was as though everything inside had begun dissolving in acid. A white foam swallowed the contents within seconds, leaving only transparent water.

He looked around but saw no sign of Roy's body—only an old pistol resting on the flattened grass and his own wristwatch. Approaching, Michael picked up the watch. With a reflexive motion, he wound it, then strapped it onto his wrist. He lifted the cylinder of clear fluid, placed it into the backpack, and hurled the pack onto the lighthouse's first tier.

That's done, but I still need to find and deal with his followers. Later, though. First, I have to see Olivia, Michael thought, heading toward the lab.

Before long, he was nearing the facility again, though he chose another approach this time. According to the old scientist, Olivia was in the children's area of the compound. He was nearly sure it was the small round building with greenhouses, which he'd seen a short distance from the main complex. Approaching the first security fence, the guards let him through without question. That building sat behind only one line of fencing, so the next step was simply entering it.

He found the little entrance door unlocked and stepped inside to a casual nod from a guard and a few scientists. The interior of the building was bright and warm: dozens of aquariums teemed with colorful fish, and vibrant flowers and other flora graced practically every free spot. It was indeed a wonderful place, radiating joy and calm.

Walking further in, Michael spotted through a large window the room where Olivia was tidying up children's toys. He tapped on the glass to catch her attention, gesturing for her to come out. Olivia glanced at the noise and beamed at him with a gentle smile. They gazed at each other, barely moving, exchanging only faint smiles.

Michael felt a pang in his chest—looking at Olivia almost hurt, as though someone had turned up the brightness on everything, making the white light painfully intense. A sudden dread clutched him, and he stared intently at her, refusing to blink. He noticed a single shining tear rolling down her cheek, and at that moment, the light vanished—and with it, Olivia.

"Liv," he whispered, sliding down the glass to his knees.

He stayed there, motionless, barely moving. Nobody passing by disturbed him. Memories flooded his mind—now he remembered it all, every single awakening. Olivia's sacrifice had rekindled his forgotten recollections. He couldn't hold back a few cold tears trickling down his cheeks.

Summoning his composure, he stood and approached the security desk. Asking for a paper and pen, he removed his watch and, flipping it over, unscrewed the back plate. In tiny writing, dozens of lines of numbers and letters were on the inside. Carefully, he copied them onto the paper, handing it to the guard.

"Give this to the Keepers," he said. "And let them know we'll meet again." Then he replaced the watch's back, winding its old mechanical mechanism—a brand written in Cyrillic—and paused briefly. Nodding vaguely to the guards, he passed through the door and instantly faded into nothingness.

He opened his eyes to find himself behind the old bar counter, which had once seen countless raucous, probably festive times but was now sealed away by neglect and apathy. He took a notebook out of his backpack, quickly sketching in pen that familiar barefoot stranger in the white dress by the pier—the journalist. Snapping the notebook shut, he returned it to his jacket pocket and stood up. Clutching his worn backpack in one hand, he grabbed a bottle of whiskey sitting on a shelf with the other. Twisting off the cap with his thumb (not using the other hand), he took a deep swallow, then set the bottle on the first table near the bar. He took a few steps but turned back, picking the bottle up and placing a banknote under it as payment. Then he slipped outside, doing his best to replace the boards.

Dropping into the driver's seat of his car, he sped off without warming the engine. The trip was brief; his mind was nearly blank. Perhaps, for the first time, all the old riddles had been solved—except one. And that was precisely what he intended to remedy now.

He pulled up at the local newspaper office. Entering, he stumbled upon chaotic employees rushing around, carting bundles of printouts. In this reality, the newspaper's office started immediately without a lobby or corridors—just one large open workspace. Walking up to the nearest desk, where he assumed the secretary sat, he introduced himself.

"How can I help?" she greeted him, smiling.

"I have an odd request—I'm looking for someone, likely an employee here." He pulled out his notebook, carefully flipping to the page with his sketch.

"You've drawn her well," she said. "That's Catherine. But she's not in right now; she's at lunch, probably in the café across the square. She likes to sit there."

"Thank you. I think I'll join her."

He left the newspaper office. He left his car in the parking lot by the building, only retrieving the backpack from the front seat. Then he headed to the café, cutting diagonally across the square. The café was bustling at this hour: every table was taken, and many customers were ordering to-go and waiting in line. He saw her straightaway—she was sitting at the same table where Michael usually sat in the other world.

Michael slid the backpack onto one shoulder and, walking toward her, pulled out an old, small box adorned with glitter and butterfly drawings. The journalist was there, poring over dozens of printouts scattered across the table, with only a single cup of coffee and an empty saucer to keep them in place. Startling her slightly, he placed the little box on top of the printouts. She picked up the box, about to say it wasn't hers, but stopped short.

A few seconds later, she took the box in both hands and gently opened it, pulling out one of the brightly colored crayons.

"Thank you," she said softly.

Thus ends the first book

Made in United States
Cleveland, OH
12 July 2025

18451027R00184